ASHLEY CHAPPELL

OF WAR AND TATERS

Of War and Taters

Ashley Chappell

PROSPECTIVE PRESS
Winston-Salem

P ROSPECTIVE P RESS LLC

1959 Peace Haven Rd, #246, Winston-Salem, NC 27106 U.S.A.
www.prospectivepress.com

Published in the United States of America by PROSPECTIVE PRESS LLC

TRADEMARK

OF WAR AND TATERS

ISBN 978-1-943419-79-1

First PROSPECTIVE PRESS trade paperback edition

Printed in the United States of America
First printing, April 2019

The text of this book is typeset in Lora
Accent text is typeset in Rockwell

Of War and Taters

Chapter One

"Maybe we could find a home for him somewhere." Stanley regretted allowing the words to form before they were even out of his mouth. Isabelle ignored him pointedly enough to convey to him, by the sheer force of her silence, that this was strictly out of the question. She was a champion-level ignorer. Instead, she continued to cuddle the ragged dog that had scampered into their yard and pretended Stanley wasn't there.

There are universal rules in the dog kingdom requiring that strays over a certain size looked like a sort of Labrador soup, while those under a certain size were bound to look like a terrier cocktail. This dog was of the latter variety. It came complete with scruffy fur, uneven floppy ears, a fuzzy mustache, and even a patch of what might have been ancient bubble gum preserved in its wiry coat under the layers of muck and grime. There is another tendency of this variety of stray which was especially irksome to Stanley at this particular moment. It was the apparent form of telepathy that enabled these dogs to wander innocently into the one yard on the block where they would find a person who would open up her icy heart to their filthy floppy ears, and instantly lavish more physical attention and snacks on them than she had her husband in...well, ever.

"He just needs a bath." She directed her stern, this-is-how-it-is-so-deal-with-it voice at Stanley, then turned a very un-Isabelle sort of baby voice toward the dog. "Isn't that wight, Mr. Cuddle Face? Yes it is, mm-hmm, yes it is."

"Sure, a bath," he replied skeptically. "But I doubt we have enough gasoline to get him clean." Isabelle flashed Stanley another one of her patented silences. He looked at his watch. "All right, I have to go before I'm late. What are you going to do with it?"

"Well," started Isabelle, still addressing the dog directly, "we're going to have a B-A-T-H first, then we're going to get ums a little leashie and go for a walkie."

Even the dog looked vaguely embarrassed, Stanley noticed. "You're really planning to keep that filthy mutt?"

"That filthy mutt, as you call him, happens to be Mr. Cuddle Face. And why shouldn't I keep him? I can't believe you would have me leave him out on the cold streets to starve to death!" Mr. Cuddle Face added his two cents by panting heavily in the hot sun and belching rather loudly for a dog his size. "See? He's already got an upset stomach, Stanley."

"It's probably just indigestion from the last roadkill he ate." He anticipated the throw and ducked under the flip flop hurled at him. "Okay, okay! But I still have to get to work. You and Mr. Cuddle Face," he said slowly and painfully, "will have to have your fun without me."

Isabelle's bored look was a pretty good indication that Stanley hadn't been invited anyway. He sulked his way back into the kitchen to swallow the last of his lukewarm coffee before sliding the final accoutrement onto the uniform that marked his office. He was very ready to venture out into a world where it actually mattered that he was wearing a shiny badge that read Sheriff.

Actually, it read 'Sherriff,' but Stanley was not a man to allow poor spelling to interfere with his pride and authority.

Only wives could do that.

• • •

It was one of those picture perfect late spring mornings that began with a bright and cloudless sky under a gentle flesh-warming sun. It was the type of beautiful morning where you knew that by noon it would turn into a flesh-melting sun until the clouds rolled in for lunch, for which you'd be grateful until the torrential rain began in the afternoon.

Such is the price of a picture perfect morning.

All of the citizens of Merit were waking up at various intervals, dotting the fresh breeze with intermittent yells for the dog to come in, cursing the paper boy's aim, and the occasional honking horn as commuters mingled with the farm machinery on the town's only throughway. Still, not one of them failed to appreciate for a moment that yes, this truly was a glorious morning.

It would be nice to think that even the current residents of the only jail cell in the Merit Sheriff's Office were also able to enjoy the wonders of nature this morning, but they didn't wake up with any romantic notions like this in mind. In fact, they hadn't even been to sleep at all. They had been too busy working out the details of their latest peace treaty, and all eight of them were wearily gathered around a map drawn on the stone wall with a piece of purple chalk. It was a complete map of the town...or rather, something that began as what they thought of as a complete map of the town, until one or more of them had remembered various side streets, alleys, and other points of interest that had been artfully squeezed into the original.

"All right," began Tyler. Together, the eight children comprised the Upper and Lower Jelly River Gangs, and Tyler was the leader of the Uppers. "Is there anywhere else ANYONE can think of that we've missed? We're in agreement that all streets are covered, right? Good. Now think hard. It's important that this treaty covers all possible territory to avoid further fights. And grounding."

"Tyler, has anyone claimed the dumpsters behind the science lab at school?" Jordan, the queen of dumpster divers, had a vested interest in those. She'd found the coolest parts of her "items of interest" collection there.

"Dibs!" Screamed Brewer, the leader of the Lowers. "I mean, I claim that territory for the Lower Jelly River Gang," he continued more regally.

"Aw, what gives you the right?"

"Settle down, Beazer," said Tyler. "But yeah, what gives? You've already got the dumpsters behind Mad Mother Hinkle's grocery, and under the bleachers at the football field. No, I challenge that claim. It should go to the Upper Jelly River Gang."

"The H-E Double Hockey Sticks it should!" A couple of the more sensible gang members clapped their hands to their mouths at Crow's profanity. "You guys got the marsh, Mr. Durbin's goat farm, the orchard, AND the Stop-and-Go, and all we're getting is trash!"

"Crow's right. I'm sticking to my claim for the Lowers, Tyler. You wanna say somethin' about it?"

Tyler wished he'd made a motion for a nap earlier. They were so sleepy that it was getting hard to think, but this was probably the most important peace treaty of their lives. Way more important than the one they'd made last week, at least. That one didn't work anyhow, considering they'd left out all the really neat stuff that wasn't right on a road. That, in fact, was what had gotten them into trouble in the first place. The Uppers never wandered into Lowers territory and vice versa, but there was so much to see that hadn't been officially claimed yet, and the natural response to running across one another on unclaimed ground was to scrap half-heartedly while they both tried to stake a claim. Frankly, he wished he'd thought to call dibs on the lab dumpsters before Brewer did, but it was going to be up to him to lead by example; he was the oldest by nearly three weeks, after all. If it was give up the dumpsters or risk getting into another fight, so be it. The Lowers could have them.

He stood tall and looked Brewer in the eye. "All right, I'll make you a deal. We'll give you the dumpsters behind the lab, but ONLY if you give us the bleachers at the football field at every other home game." This just proves that ten-year olds really knew where to find the good stuff.

The air was tense. There was a sharp intake of breath as the other gang members all edged away from their two leaders. If there was going to be a fight they wanted to be far enough away to affect at least a passable illusion of innocence.

Brewer returned Tyler's stare and leaned in closer. Expecting the worst, Jordan closed her eyes and Spike pounded a pudgy fist in his hand, preparing for a fight. Then Brewer extended his hand to Tyler.

"Deal."

There was a mutual cheer between the gangs as their leaders ratified their latest treaty. At the beginning of their incarceration after school yesterday they had agreed to call this one "The Treaty to End All Treaties." Spike had suggested calling it TEAT for short, but was quickly vetoed by Jordan and Carrie through red faces and giggles.

"Well now, it sounds like some little angels are up and about and ready to get to school!" The cheers turned instantly to groans as Tyler's mom popped into the hall outside their cell. The two gangs had run into each other during recess yesterday in an unclaimed spot of the school yard under the willows and, as per their custom, fought it out. After this latest fight their parents had called a meeting with Sheriff Stanley and the principal, and all had agreed that a night in jail might teach them a proper lesson. Tyler's mom especially loved the idea, and had volunteered to remain and chaperone, not to mention let the occasional poor tyke out for a bathroom break. She'd fallen asleep after her third cup of hot cocoa around 1:00 AM, leaving the children to complete their plans in private. Now she was back and as big and perky as ever.

"Mo-o-om, please!" Tyler's moment of strategic triumph had just had a wet diaper thrown on it. Up until this point the two gangs had enjoyed thinking of themselves as a secret war council, and even had to pull out Carrie's pocket dictionary a few times to stay in character. The appearance of Tyler's mom brought them back into a harsh, yet dull, elementary school reality. "Besides, I thought we got suspended for three days for the fight yesterday. Doesn't that mean we don't have to go to school today?"

"No, no, dear. Principal Edwards told us that if all of you could make it through a night without killing each other that you could come right back to school today. You're on parole, so to speak."

The gang members flashed their conciliatory leaders a look of irritation.

"Is it too late? To kill someone, I mean?"

"Oh, now Spike, you're just being silly. If you keep that up your parents may just decide to leave you here."

"I'm sorry, Mrs. Tyler's Mom," Spike mumbled as he dug into the floor with his shoe. He wanted to get home before "The Mighty Rocket Avengers" came on that afternoon.

"Anyway," Mrs. Tyler's Mom began, "one of your little friends from school got here this morning and he wants to talk to you before your parents start coming to take you home. I'll send him on back."

As she walked away the gangs looked dubiously at one another. They were pretty sure that all of their friends were standing right there in the room with them. They pressed their faces closer to the bars to see the intruder as he came down the hallway.

From the guilty corners of every childhood there was the memory of that one kid with a weird hobby who never quite fit in, always smelled slightly sticky, and was bullied mercilessly throughout adolescence. The newcomer happened to be the one who filled that role in Merit. He was technically two grades behind the Uppers and the Lowers, but was already in several of their classes because of his extremely high test scores. The rumor was that next year he was going to actually be in fifth grade with them.

"Erwin?" Carrie sneered. "What do *you* want?"

"Yeah, why're you here? Shouldn't you be at home with your mommy?" Crow added.

Erwin strode confidently into the place Tyler's mom had vacated. There was still considerable room left over. "Somehow I just don't feel too hurt by insults hurled at me by losers behind bars. Nice try, though." He pulled his glasses from his face and wiped them with his shirt in the unbothered manner that he'd seen in the movies. It might have looked much more debonair if Erwin hadn't managed to transfer the jelly stain from his shirt to his glasses in the process. He slid them back onto his face and peered at them through the raspberry flavored smudge.

"Okay, so back to the first question," Tyler prompted. "What do you want?"

"I just thought you might like to tell your side of the story to someone who'd listen. Someone like me."

"Why? So you can print it in that so-called paper you stick in all the lockers every week?"

"As a matter of fact, yes." He gave up, took his smudged glasses off again, and found a cleaner part of his shirt to use. "This is just the kind of thing people want to read. A story of rivalry, jealousy, violence…it's the perfect feud!"

There was a rare moment of quiet from both the Upper and Lower Jelly River Gangs.

"What's a ralvary?" Asked Crowe.

"What's a fude?" Asked Beazer.

Bub, the ever quiet and thoughtful Upper, spoke up. "A rivalry means that we're against each other, and a feud means kinda the same thing, but worse. He means that we really hate each other and wanna hurt each other."

"Well that's just dumb," added Tyler. "We don't hate each other." He accidentally glanced at Carrie and turned crimson when she smiled at him. He continued regally. "We don't even really wanna hurt each other. We just fight because, well, because we have to."

"Why?" Erwin asked innocently. This favorite question of children was positively abhorrent to them when used against them. Tyler was obviously upset. Brewer came to the rescue.

"Because we have to, that's why! We're Lowers and they're Uppers, so we have to fight. But we don't mean anything by it."

"So," Erwin dug into his back pocket to get his grubby Mach Jackson notebook. Mach was his favorite Rocket Avenger. "What you're saying is you only actually fight because you're in two different gangs? Would you say it's because you're from different environments, as well?"

The gang members looked at each other. They thought that was apparent. Only two of them even lived on the same street. The others lived up to eight whole streets away.

"Well, duh," offered Spike.

"That's good stuff, really good." Erwin didn't quite know what that meant, so he hoped no one asked. It was what the really good journalists on TV always said. "Would you also say that your parents raised you to treat some people differently from others?" He scribbled notes in his book.

More consternation. The Uppers and Lowers also thought this was obvious. Some people they had to call sir or ma'am and mind what they said, but sometimes you could call them by their first name even though you still had to mind them. Just like rotten old Jessica, the babysitter. And everybody knew talking to strangers couldn't be tolerated at all.

Carrie chimed in. "Okay, double duh!"

"Yeah, don't you know anything? I think you should go home now, Erwin. Our parents will be here soon and we'll have to go to school." Tyler wasn't sure why, but he felt uncomfortable about the questions Erwin was asking.

"All right, but it's your loss. If you don't want the world to know your side of the story I can't force you to talk. If you change your mind, you know where to find me." His dramatic exit was ruined by the fact that Jordan was sticking her tongue out and making an L-shape on her forehead with her fingers. It occurred to him that maybe these things only went so well on TV because the other people knew what was expected of them when the suave journalist or detective came to see them. It was just possible that the world would be a better place, he thought, if more people watched as much TV as he did.

• • •

Meanwhile, across town from the Merit jail—although across town in Merit meant a mere twelve streets away—an irate fisherman was standing on his front porch in his socks. Not that it matters to the story, but there was a hole from which his left big toe was waggling along with his frustration.

"Virginia! Did you move my fishin' boots again?"

"You know I won't touch them things. They smell like you've been fishin' in a septic tank."

"I left 'em right here on the porch last night."

"One of them kids probably ran off with 'em and thought they were bein' cute."

"Cute? Those boots cost me seventy-five dollars!"

"Well, call Sheriff Stanley, but you can probably say goodbye to 'em for good. Wouldn't break my heart none, neither."

• • •

"Well, we have been saying that the place needed a little color. Maybe we should just leave it?"

Sheriff Stanley Grace looked at his deputy for any trace of sarcasm and then back at the odd chalk map that had taken over most of the cell wall. At least, the part of the wall that could be reached by hands that didn't stretch much over five feet high. It wasn't bad, as far as the typical graffiti around Merit went, but it certainly brought to light places in his home town that he'd never seen before. Even the Jelly River that skirted half the town looked about twice its actual size.

"Bertie," he asked the deputy, "according to this map there is a 'Forest of Dred' just behind this building. Have you seen anything like that?"

"There's just Old John's Christmas tree farm. I don't know that there's much dreadful about that. His guard dogs aren't even that big."

"What about a bottomless pit over by your aunt's house?"

Bertie scratched both of his chins. "Well, I think she mentioned that the septic tank collapsed on the vacant lot across from her, but I wouldn't really call it *bottomless*. It's probably more of a really deep and really smelly pit than anything. I can't even begin to guess what the Hall of War would be." He pointed to a purple square marked in the middle of the woods not too far from the mine.

Stanley smiled. The world really did seem like a bigger and more amazing place to a child's eyes. "You know, when I was a kid we used to play pirates over at the little creek by Mad Mother's and called it the Sea of Despair. We built rafts and would ram each other trying to take over the other gang's treasure." Usually it was a box of polished rocks, he added to himself.

He realized Bertie was looking at him in mild horror.

"You mean you swam in *that* creek? The one that gets all the runoff from the pig farm?"

"Anyway..." Stanley changed the subject and cleared his throat. "I guess we could leave it for a while. It'll at least give the drunks something to read this weekend." He turned away from the map and Bertie, seeking out the coffee on his desk. He made a face as he swallowed it, then sighed heavily. Coffee seemed to exist in a perpetual state of lukewarm muck for Stanley, no matter when he prepared his cup. There was the first scalding sip before setting it aside for a moment, yet no matter how long or short that moment was, his next drinks were always a series of ever cooling disappointment.

"Bertie, how was your coffee this morning?"

"Perfect. Why? Is something wrong with yours?"

"No, no, it's fine." Finding no sympathy from Bertie, he swallowed the rest of his cup quickly. "So let's get started. What's in the news today?"

Bertie was already unfolding the newspaper. There was a sickness that afflicted some newspaper readers that forced them to read it from cover to cover aloud to anyone who might be in the room. Bertie was one of those people. This had gone on for years, despite the fact that Stanley used to read the paper before he came to the office in the mornings. He finally gave up and cancelled his subscription when he realized that there was no stopping the recap from Bertie as soon as he arrived in the mornings.

"Let's see. There's a Jostlem High School Prom tonight; some actor's funeral is today, and... Dang. Hoo-boy!" Exclaimed Bertie after scanning the first page of the Jostlem Times with a trained eye. "It says here that the Jostlem Police have a woman in custody for beating her boyfriend to death with—and I'm not making this up here, Stanley—a *remote control!* Here it is: 'Police responded late Monday night to neighbors' reports of screams. When they arrived they found the victim, thirty-year old Jostlem resident Matt Wilcox, badly beaten and unconscious. His attacker, twenty-eight-year old Nicole Church, was happily watching her movie uninterrupted until an officer stopped the film, sending her into another violent frenzy. The victim's last words were reportedly, "I just wanted to see the car chase again.' Jeez, you couldn't get me to be a cop in the big city for anything with cuckoos like that running around!"

"Can't say that I blame you. Anything else?"

"Well, you won't believe where they found the batteries from the remote. Eww."

"No, I mean anything a little less gross." Stanley looked thoughtful. "But where did they...? Nevermind. I know I'll regret asking that. Is there anything about the weather for this weekend? I promised Isabelle that I'd take her to the circus."

Bertie paused in his perusing to peer at Stanley over the newspaper. "Really? The circus? I mean, I just didn't really think Isabelle was a circus kind of person," he finished lamely, hoping that Stanley wouldn't ask him what kind of person he really thought she was.

"She's not really, but her father is the biggest sponsor and we're supposed to be joining him in some sort of VIP box. But I think that just means it's closer to the peanuts than the others."

"Ah," summed up Bertie. Isabelle's father, Rupert Youngblood, owned the rubber plant nearby that served Merit as its main source of employment. He was what was termed a "merchant prince" and had raised his daughter to be every bit of a princess that she could manage. It was said in the town—well, whispered mostly—that she had proposed to and eloped with a surprised Stanley when she was nineteen to get back at her father for buying her the wrong color car. Mr. Youngblood had wisely retaliated by not only buying her the right color car as a wedding gift, but also changing his will and leaving everything to Stanley in the event of his death. Now Isabelle was forced to lie in the bed she made, quite literally, or be a penniless divorcée. It was never quite understood by the townspeople how much of this situation was clear to Stanley, but he was generally applauded and pitied for remaining married to a woman who had the personality and charm of a menopausal opossum.

Bertie was flipping through the pages of the newspaper to find the weather for Stanley when a very red-faced Old John puffed his way into the sheriff's office at his customary time with his customary empty coffee cup. Ever since Stanley had started offering complimentary coffee in the mornings, Old John had managed to find a reason to come in daily to make a complaint. The one time Bertie had forgotten to put a pot on had led to a few moments of stammering from Old John, claiming he'd forgotten what he was going to say and backing out slowly, casting nervous glances at the empty pot.

Today, however, he sniffed the java-scented air confidently and lit into his tirade of choice as he headed for the coffee pot.

"Dang blasted kids! In all my thirty years in business I ain't never seen no kids rottener than the rotten kids we get today. Betsy and Margie starts howlin' up a storm last night so I goes out to see what the fuss is about, and what do you think I found out there? Nevermind, I'll tell you what I found. I found a trio of little monsters throwin' tinsel all over the place. They done throwed tinsel all over every tree I got out there! Never you mind that it's Christmas tinsel. They ain't properly Christmas trees until someone comes and chops 'em down and sticks 'em in their living rooms. Then they can put all the Christmas tinsel on them they want, but...where's your sugar at? Thanks. But I don't want no tinsel...what's this? Half and half? Ain't you got any milk? Shame what the world's comin' to, half and half instead of milk. Half and half of what, exactly? Anyhoo," he finished as he headed back to the door, stirring his cup. "I reckon you'll find a trail of silver tinsel leadin' away from my tree farm and on up Cherry Lane that'll lead you right to the little monsters. Rottenest bunch a kids I ever saw."

"Good morning, John. See you tomorrow, John," said Stanley as the door closed behind Old John, muffling the cry from his coffee-singed tongue. "Well, Bertie, where were we?"

"Ah, right, the weather. Oh, too bad. Says here rain with possible thunderstorms most of the day. Actually, it's not too different from your horoscope today. You're a Libra, right? Says here that your life is ripe for chaos this week, so be ready with an oar and an umbrella to weather the storm. Home is where the heart of the trouble is. Well, that's not very uplifting, is it?"

Stanley sighed again. "No Bertie, it's definitely not very uplifting. Just tell me the rest of the news, okay?"

He wouldn't have admitted it, but the prospect of a little chaos raining down in Stanley Grace's life wasn't such a horrifying thing after living the exact same routine day after day for the last several years. It wasn't that he wanted anything bad to happen in Merit. Just something *different* for once wouldn't be so bad. By and large, it was a safe, quiet town. There were the occasional calls in the middle of the night about burglars or murders out in the street, but those would always end up the product of a combination of over-active imaginations and animal fights. Even the drunks they occasionally picked up were the funny, happy sort, never the loud, crying, woe-is-me sort. It was all well and good if, like Bertie, the most excitement you could stand was the kind you'd read about in someone else's newspaper. But not for Stanley. He was still young enough to harbor occasional thoughts of day-dream heroics that involved something a little more dramatic than lost kittens found up neighbors' trees.

Right now he'd be happy if it would just bring him something different for dinner. It was Tuesday, and that meant Isabelle's imitation meatloaf. Actually, she didn't call it that. Isabelle was under the mistaken impression that she was cooking real meatloaf, but Stanley didn't have the heart, or the guts, to correct her.

• • •

Not terribly far across town was a dog that was having second thoughts, or would be, if dogs could have second thoughts. They would have been big ones, too. Just this morning he'd been the king of his domain; he knew where the best trash could be found, he knew he could find cold water at the fountain in the park anytime he was thirsty, and he had the whole world to play in, if he wanted it. All of that withstanding, it was a very good thing dogs had such a short memory, because now Mr. Cuddle Face's only concern in the world was with getting his new blue collar off before someone saw him wearing rhinestones.

"Oh, look at oo, Mr. Cuddle Face! What did ums do?" A new concern was firmly etched into the animal's short term memory as the big loud face showed up again with, he was certain, some new horror for him. As it was, he'd managed to slip his back paw up underneath the collar and was now struggling to both extract his paw and push off his collar at the same time while rotating on his free legs. The result was something that resembled a dog losing a ferret fight.

Isabelle leaned over the pup, pulled his paw from the offending collar, and brought him up nose to nose with her. This was far more terrifying for the average dog than one would imagine. Another positive deficiency here for Mr. Cuddle Face was the fact that he could not see color; if he could he'd have been rather more alarmed by the bright red lipstick puckered up at the end of his snout which matched the curly mass of red hair that kept tickling his ears.

Already today he'd been tossed into a bathtub and scrubbed no less than three times with a tropical bubble bath, despite his howls and hopeless growls. The end product was that he now smelled less like a sewer and more like a trash bin behind a daiquiri bar. It was a marked improvement as far as Isabelle was concerned, but the only response it provoked from the dog was that his tail now smelled far more interesting than it used to when he chased it. After the baths, he had been left on the bathroom floor, a sopping wet mess, while she ran out to find him the perfect leash and collar. On her return, Isabelle also had the unkind idea to use the blow-dryer and a comb to hurry things along in the drying department. That caused no small amount of uncustomary fluffiness to his coat. Then, as if the humiliation hadn't been laid on thickly enough already, he'd been paraded around the street at the end of his shiny new leash and collar. He'd spent the entire time being mostly dragged as he was too busy gnawing at the leash attached to him to pay attention to unfamiliar commands like stay, heel, and don't poo there.

Isabelle carried the cowed creature with her into the kitchen, where she'd begun preparing Stanley's dinner. She couldn't stand meatloaf, but she knew he was expecting to come home and find his traditional Tuesday meatloaf with his favorite dish of green bean casserole next to it. She set Mr. Cuddle Face down in the corner of the kitchen nearest the door, where she'd already placed his food dishes. Fortunately for him, the speed with which she had managed to get personalized dishes with his new name on them was a miracle that was lost to Mr. Cuddle Face. At any rate, he was certainly not grateful for the brown lumps of high-fiber, diet dog food he found therein. He turned his nose up at the dishes and sauntered over to her side at the stove, where he could smell the signs of some certainly non-high-fiber activity going on. He affected his best hungry puppy whine to get her attention.

"No, Mr. Cuddle Face, this is *people* food. You go back over to your bowl and eat your yummy beef and gravy." His look as he walked back to the bowl said that he was not yet willing to concede that the gray gelatinous matter in the bowl was indeed gravy.

"That's a good baby boy, yes you *are!*" Isabelle turned back to the meatloaf that she was heavily salting, as was her habit. A second look at the white canister she'd been shaking liberally over the meatloaf had a picture of a smiling puppy, which she didn't remember seeing on the salt shaker before. She turned it over in her hands and read the words Mr. Scratchy's Flea Powder, For Contented Canines! Another turn revealed a skull and cross bones design indicating that it should under no circumstances be consumed. A small smile danced across her lips.

"Silly me! I must have set it right next to the salt and didn't realize it." She accidentally knocked a little more into the mixture with a minor exclamation of "Oops!" then set the flea powder down and picked up the similar salt canister next to it. "Well, Mr. Cuddle Face, I'll bet if we put enough salt in here he'll never notice it. You won't tell on me, will you sweetums?" Her smile swirled with a mixture of innocent sweetness and slightly homicidal intent as she hummed happily to herself.

Somewhere in the vicinity of her feet Mr. Cuddle Face was busy expressing his feelings about the beef lumps and gravy paste in his bowl by piddling on the kitchen rug.

• • •

There are so many different ideas about what happens after death that it is impossible to name them all, but by and large they tend to fall into three categories. On one very broad hand there is the idea of an individual soul traveling to an afterlife, or re-life, suited to its punishment or reward, depending on that individual's actions in life. On another broad hand is the idea that one became part of a higher power or energy, giving up our individuality entirely. Finally, on a mysteriously produced third hand is the notion that after death the party is simply over. Finito. Lights out.

Montana "Monty" Gregory wasn't sure what he believed exactly. All he did know was that death certainly wasn't what it was cracked up to be. So far it had been terribly disappointing, and even rather embarrassing.

His first inclination that he was dead had come when he awoke four mornings ago to his maid screaming. He opened his eyes and at first wondered when the hell he'd ever put a mirror on his ceiling. Then he wondered why, if he were looking into a mirror, his eyes were still closed and his face was a peculiar shade of purple. As a new specter in the spirit world, the sight of his own dead and nearly naked body was not an entirely uplifting initiation. And, to make it worse, if it hadn't been for the mortally tight tie around his neck he'd have been completely naked. He was vaguely aware of a gentle tugging sensation over his shoulder, but was more concerned with finding a way to reach down and jerk the covers back over his body before anyone else saw him like that. He ignored the tugging and went about flailing like a swimmer in a rough current, trying to get his feet back on the ground. He concentrated as hard as he could and finally touched the ground, panting for breath until he realized that he didn't have to breathe at all anymore. His first grabs at the sheet resulted in his hand passing right through. He discovered to his dismay that the same thing happened with anything he tried to touch.

By the time the ambulance arrived, he'd begun obsessing over making physical contact with the world around him. Sometimes he would feel a hint of heaviness or coldness to the items he tried to grasp and he just knew he was getting closer. Sometimes it was a feeling of resistance, as though his fingers weren't wanting to simply push through. Then—finally!—there was the bell. It was a tiny thing, just a bit of metal fringe on the bottom of his curtain, but he'd pushed as hard as he could and he'd heard it. It was just the barest tinkle, but it felt like an Olympic achievement to him after blundering through walls and objects as though he didn't exist.

The tugging feeling at his shoulder grew more insistent after he watched them cart his body away and label the area with Crime Scene tape.

"Stop it!" He screamed at anyone who might be listening. "Just go away and leave me alone! I've almost got it now!" As he ran away from the direction of the tugging he tripped over some of the tape left behind by the police. He quickly turned around and saw the tape he'd disturbed floating serenely to the ground and proceeded to laugh triumphantly, pounding the air with his fists.

Eventually, sometime on the second day during his experiment with clothes, the tugging sensation had gone away entirely and now he found himself wondering what exactly had been trying to get his attention.

In some ways, Monty had come a long way since he died. He could walk again like a normal person instead of floating, he'd learned how to hold solid things again, and he'd found that if he concentrated hard enough he could still wear his old wardrobe, except for his earrings. Despite the fact that his spirit didn't seem to have pierced ears as he'd had in life, he was as whole a person as he'd ever been. The problem was that even though he could now make people see him, it was only a temporary event in their minds and it seemed to irritate them more than anything before they completely forgot he was even there. The only benefit to this, he'd found, was that people didn't seem to remember him long enough to ask him to pay for anything. He was currently taking advantage of this perk while sitting in his customary seat at his favorite bar.

One thing that had surprised him, however, was the fact that he was not alone. There were occasionally others, more or less like him, but mostly less. He'd always believed that ghosts probably existed on some level in the world, but he'd also never expected to actually see one, let alone be one. Sometimes they were mostly whole, fading in and out of focus, and sometimes they looked like they were losing a constant struggle with holding onto their physical shape and resembled a shifting reflection in a funhouse mirror. At worst, they were a mere suggestion of features in a mist. At first this had scared him, though the irony of being a ghost who was afraid of ghosts grated on his nerves. After he'd gotten used to seeing them drift by in passing or occasionally stopping for an odd chat, he mostly just felt sorry for them.

Their problem, he'd decided, was that they simply weren't trying hard enough. In just a few days he'd become practically human again, whereas a few of the ghosts he met claimed to have been dead for decades or more.

Monty focused on his drink and raised his whiskey glass to his lips. Just like the last dozen or so drinks he'd tried to take, this one also poured straight through his chin, making a mess on his pants.

"Damn," he said with the unaffected tone of one who'd expected it to go wrong.

Apparently, drinking was going to require much more practice. Touching things and picking them up had been simple enough. Even talking and being seen hadn't been too difficult. But for some reason, he hadn't been able to figure out how to make his digestive system work again. Actually, he wasn't quite sure that he still had a digestive system to make work, but he'd be damned if he wasn't going to find a way to have a drink of whiskey after the day he'd had. A person couldn't be expected to go to his own humiliating funeral and not get hopelessly plastered immediately thereafter.

He hadn't tried to eat anything yet, but he didn't seem to need anything to eat anymore, either. Whatever it was that held this pseudo-body of his together apparently didn't require food for fuel. He tried very hard not to think of what it might actually require. And since he didn't need it, he no longer craved it. Not even his favorite peach-basted lamb couscous from Toddy's. Whiskey, on the other hand, was different. Whereas food and water were purely physical needs, whiskey was most definitely a psychological need, and finding oneself short on physicality and heaped upon with psyche was a sure way to amplify those psychological needs, whether they could be met or not.

He glanced up at the television set and groaned deeply. "Oh, no, please no! I've already gone through it once. Don't make me watch it again! Joe, hey, over here! Joe, *please* turn that TV off. I can't stand it!"

Joe, the bartender, waved at his ear as if a large gnat had been hovering around it for the last few seconds. Without thinking, he reached for the television remote to turn it off until another customer intervened.

"Joe, what are you doing, man? Turn it up, will ya? That's the actor that was always here in them weird outfits." Monty cast the drinker a dirty look that the man wouldn't have been able to appreciate even if he could have seen it.

"Nothing wrong with my outfits," he mumbled as he crawled under the bar sullenly and turned his attention to the whiskey on his lavender slacks in an effort to block out the televised news report of his funeral.

"Our very own Dana Perki was there to bring you the full story. Dana?"

"Thank you, Barbara and Jim. Yes, today was truly a sad day for movie-goers everywhere as actor Montana 'Monty' Gregory was buried this afternoon after services at Ginger's Funeral Salon to the Stars. The police investigation into his untimely murder is still ongoing, and police are asking for anyone with information to call the tips hotline."

"They never bothered to ask *me*," Monty grumbled.

"Monty's career was launched in some controversy as he was frequently confused with Mount Anna Greggory, the Swedish adult film star, but he maintained media attention and notoriety throughout his career as a hard partier and womanizer."

"C'mon," contributed the patron, "everybody knew the guy was gay!"

There was a thud and a terrible curse nobody heard as Monty's head hit the bar. Hard.

"However," the reporter continued, "events at his funeral cast the actor in a very different light. Our cameras were there to record the touching eulogy by the man who claims to have been Monty's gay lover."

"Joe, do you have a cat in here or something, man? I just heard this awful howl, I think."

Joe shrugged at the customer as Monty pulled himself grimly back over the bar.

"Oh, you heard *that*, did you? Well, hear this: He was just my therapist! Okay, he was actually my colorist, but he gave great advice. Oh, I should have known he'd pull something like this!" He cast another dirty look at a snicker coming from a muddy specter further down the bar. Sometimes ghosts had no feeling of solidarity. Even when that ghost was wearing a priest's collar. He groaned again as the cameras cut to the eulogy delivered by his weeping colorist, Jan Bricker.

"Monty was a special little star among us for the time he was here, brightening up our lives in his special little ways. He was just so very special." He paused to dramatically wipe tears from his eyes. "I know it was so hard for him to live the lie that he did in order to please his public, but I'll never stop wishing that he could have come out from under the thumb of the brutal media long enough to embrace who he truly was. He could never have come out of the closet while he was in the public eye, but I knew he returned my love. He showed me in so many of his special ways that he cared for me." He turned to the huge black urn at the foot of the stage. It was covered with paisleys in gold leaf.

"I will always love you, Monty," he continued, blowing a kiss to the urn. "It just kills me that you're gone."

"No, it killed me, thank you very much!" Monty growled.

The reporter returned to the scene with a sweet smile. "We were fortunate enough to speak with the late actor's mother only moments after the funeral to hear her reactions to the news that her son was a homosexual."

The scene cut again to a pre-recorded shot of his mother. Monty felt his eyes tear up as he looked at the image filling the screen. His mother was a poverty-hardened Irish woman and always wore her hair in a tight bun. Years of scorn had frozen her lips into a permanent purse, easing the transition from a disapproving stare to an infuriated scowl. It was the same face he remembered fondly from his youth, right down to the lump of chewing tobacco in her cheek.

"What do I think about it?" She repeated the question as she stopped to spit impassively. "I alwus knew me son was a homo. I jes thought he'd 'ave better taste in men!"

This was more than Monty could bear. He'd run from the funeral parlor when he saw how Jan's eulogy was going to go, and hadn't even thought to glance at his mother on the way out.

"No, not you, Mom! Why can't you people see it? He's lying! *I'm not gay*, do you hear me? Somebody listen to me! I'm Not Gay!" Monty was surprised to realize confused heads were turning toward him as he screamed his last words. They weren't exactly friendly looks, but at least no one was running from the room screaming as he'd have thought they would when they realized a ghost was sharing their bottle of whiskey.

"Mr. Gregory?" Joe put down the glass he seemed to be perpetually shining. He was reluctant to do so; it seemed contrary to his image of bartender to not be shining a mug. "What are you doing here? Shouldn't you be off bein' dead somewhere?"

Monty ignored the chuckles from the other end of the bar as someone not-so-quietly whispered "...and gay..." to his neighbor. "I am. I'm *here* being dead. So can you all see me?"

"Yeah, man. You're kinda hard to miss. Are those pants standard angel issue?" More laughter.

"Shut-up! All of you just shut-up! I came in here almost every day when I was alive and I don't see a single person in here who wasn't among the masses clinging to my coattails and sucking up to me. You all wanted to be close to me simply because I was *famous*! Well I've got news for you. I'm through here! I'll never set foot in this bar again now that I've seen what kind of *slime* all of you ingrates really are. It's pathetic, I tell you. You should all be ashamed of yourselves!"

Monty distinctly heard the words "hissy fit" once or twice, but no one bothered to reply. In fact, the only one still really looking at him now was Joe, his favorite bartender of the past several years. Joe had picked up his mug again and was carefully re-polishing it while he eyed the half-empty glass of whiskey in front of Monty.

"Here now, did you pay for that drink?"

· · ·

"Garrett, I'm done telling you, we ain't got no raccoons doin' this! Since when do raccoons use door handles, anyhow?"

"Well then, Wilma, I suppose you're gonna tell me what's sneakin' into our freezer every night and makin' off with your casseroles?" Garrett scratched the back of his neck with the corn cob before he put it into the trap and pulled the spring. There were three others like it forming a circle around the spare freezer in their shed.

"It's gotta be some poor hungry vagrant or some other fool sort. Just put a lock on it an' be done with it already."

"And I'm tellin' you no man is hungry enough to come back for a second helping after tastin' your food, woman!"

"For someone who hates my cookin' so much you sure don't look like you're hurtin' for food, mister." Wilma poked a finger into her husband's side and watched it sink a few inches before pulling it out.

"I consider it my patriotic duty to make sure there's none of that foul muck left to end up in front a' some other poor fool."

"Fine. You put out as many those durn traps as you want, but I'm callin' Sheriff Stanley."

Chapter Two

The promise of the beautiful morning having been fulfilled with a torrential down pour, Stanley was now squelching home and wishing he'd driven the two blocks to the office that morning. Normally, he'd be hurrying through the rain, especially a drenching one like this, but with nothing else to rush home to, other than the dreaded meatloaf, he decided he'd rather take his chances with pneumonia. He could only hope that maybe this time she'd made something other than green bean casserole.

It wasn't her fault, really, he reflected. She'd never cooked at all before she married Stanley, but at least she'd been willing to try it. She attacked it with her usual "If the poor can do it, I can probably do it better" mentality, but had yet to admit that being born into a family with money did not give her any special aptitudes in life outside of being able to buy bigger and better things. Cooking was definitely one of those skills not added to her slim repertoire of talents that, as far as Stanley could tell, consisted mainly of casting dirty looks, getting her father to take her shopping, and good hair. He wasn't even really sure that having good hair could be considered a talent, but he was willing to stretch a little. She was his wife, after all, even if she'd become so after only their third date.

He sighed as he reached his doorstep; there was an acrid smell in the air that was all too familiar. He opened the door with his soggy hand and was struck full in the face by a billowing onslaught of smoke trying to escape the house. He could hear the smoke detectors chirping in full force, despite the frantic yelling from Isabelle trying to order them to be silent. He pushed into the living room, fanning the stinging smoke away from his eyes.

"Honey? Izzy?"

She hadn't heard him yet over her own yelling and cursing, but a small whine from underneath the armchair caught his attention. He dripped his way over to it and peered underneath. Stanley gasped. "Good God! What happened to you?"

Mr. Cuddle Face hadn't had a good day. In shame, he buried his muzzle under his paws when Stanley reached under the chair to pull him out, but finally gave in to Stanley's gentle tugs and came on out. He was certainly a different dog from the one he'd been that morning, and it hadn't stopped with the baby blue rhinestone collar, either. He now had baby blue toe nails, blue ribbons on each ear that were matted from his attempts to remove them, and at some point Isabelle had taken it upon herself to closely shave all but the very end of the poor dog's tail, giving it a sad sort of poodle bob that resembled a molting palm tree. Stanley grimaced, wondering if she'd used his electric razor for the job.

"You poor thing," he said as he affectionately scratched the mutt's ear. "You didn't know what you were getting into when you wandered into this yard, did you? Come on, let's see what we can do about this."

Stanley was sitting on the living room carpet in a puddle of his own making and removing the offending bows from Mr. Cuddle Face's ears when Isabelle finally realized he'd come home after she silenced the smoke alarms.

"Stanley! What exactly do you think you're doing? It took me nearly an *hour* to get those on him! And look at the mess you're making all over the carpet. Really, Stanley, this is just not acceptable. I've been working all afternoon making you dinner and all you can do is come in here and make a mess of everything while the meatloaf is flaming in the kitchen! What did I do to deserve this?"

She collapsed into a chair in her best martyr's fashion and waited for Stanley to apologize. As usual, Stanley missed his cue.

"Then I take it dinner's ruined?" He asked cheerfully.

"Oh, don't sound so happy about it, will you? It's still perfectly fine. You just have to scrape away the charred bit on the outside."

A glance at the miserable pooch on the floor lapping at Stanley's puddle prompted him to ask. "Um, Izzy? Er..." he faltered as he recognized Dirty Look #37 glaring out from between her fingers. The subtitle to this one was the I'm Having a Bad Day So You Can Bet Yours is About to Get Worse look.

"Don't call me 'Izzy' again. You know how much I hate that. Now what are you trying to ask?"

"I'm sorry, Izz...I mean, Isabelle. I was just wondering, I was thinking–"

"Out with it!"

"Didn't you notice that the dog is a boy?" He asked quickly. "I mean, the rhinestones, ribbons, and nail polish are all a bit much, don't you think? And what happened to his tail?"

Dirty Look #37 was still there, but it was being slowly tempered with Dirty Look #68, aka the Keep Pushing Me, You've Got To Sleep Sometime look. Stanley looked down at his feet.

"Of course I know he's a boy, *dear*. That's why I used blue instead of pink."

He kept looking down at his feet. He could imagine a dozen other dirty names he'd rather be called than for her to call him "Dear" in that tone of voice.

"Just thought I'd ask," he muttered. Mr. Cuddle Face whined on the floor as his champion choked in the first round.

"Well don't. He likes his ribbons so just leave them alone." She sighed. "Come on and eat. But take off your wet shoes, will you?"

"Are you sure you wouldn't rather just eat out? I wouldn't mind if it's too burned." Stanley couldn't conceal the hopefulness in his voice as he slipped out of his sopping loafers. His socks weren't much drier.

"It's *fine*. And there's nothing wrong with the green bean casserole at all."

"Oh, that's...nice." Defeated, he followed Isabelle into the kitchen, avoiding eye contact with Mr. Cuddle Face out of shame.

He seated himself at the table while Isabelle chiseled through the outer crust of the would-be meat loaf, sawed off a doubly thick slice for Stanley, and heaped on the casserole. Stanley eyed his plate morosely.

"Aren't you eating anything, dear?" He asked as she sat down with only a glass of wine in front of her. She always seemed to have a half glass of wine with her at night, though he'd strangely never seen her actually pour a bottle.

"I don't feel well tonight. I had some crackers earlier."

"Oh God, you aren't pregnant are you?" He exclaimed with a manly lack of tact. He'd also forgotten for the moment that given the infrequency of their intimacy the chances were more in favor of her having already given birth than just now feeling the symptoms.

"I think we can safely say that's not the problem," she replied coldly. "Now why don't you eat your dinner?"

He tugged a green bean to freedom from its gluey sauce, absently noticing Isabelle's eyes were glued to the vegetable in anticipation as he raised it to his mouth. He stopped mid-air.

"I forgot the salt!" Salt could forgive all manner of culinary crimes. He practically leapt to the counter to grab it and made it all the way back to his seat before he realized the canister he was holding was definitely not salt. "Oops. Flea powder!" He chuckled amiably in the way that had always grated on Isabelle. Stanley returned the powder to the counter and grabbed the correct one this time. "That was a close one. Good thing it was empty, huh? What did you do, feed it to him to get rid of the fleas?"

"Not exactly," she murmured as she affected a deep fascination with the rim of her wine glass. While she wasn't looking Stanley slipped the green bean loose from his fork and dropped it under the table for the dog. A low growl emerged from under the table in a definite lack of gratitude after the preliminary sniff of the morsel. It wasn't encouraging.

"Well," he began after he'd dug a piece of something pliable out of the scorched meatloaf shell, "here's to good food and good company, right?" After all, there must be good food and good company out there somewhere, he reasoned.

Isabelle's eyes lit up as he lifted the fork to his mouth with a minimum of trembling. He closed his eyes, held his breath, and nearly choked as the sky came falling down.

At least, it sounded like the sky falling. Really, it was an answer to Stanley's fervent prayers to not have to eat this meal. It was Mad Mother Hinkle, but she happened to be answering Stanley's prayer and making a noise like the sky was falling all at the same time.

"You've got to be kidding me!" Isabelle threw her hands up in the air at the interruption, stomped into the living room, and threw open the door. "What do you...? Oh, I'm sorry, Mad Moth—I mean, Mother Hinkle." Her voice dropped from an outraged cry to a whimper in the course of a few stuttered words. One thing Isabelle shared with the average poor person from whom she distanced herself was a very real fear of Mad Mother Hinkle. Neither man nor beast stood in her way, and it was generally agreed in the town that even the gods themselves would have turned and run back up the mountain from whence they came when faced with an angry Mother Hinkle. Unfortunately for Isabelle, nothing made Mad Mother Hinkle madder than being called Mad Mother.

"Move aside, hussy! I need a word with your husband."

"Stanley! It's for you," she screamed and ran into the bedroom, slamming the door behind her before Stanley even came out of the kitchen. Mother Hinkle had just finished bringing all of her considerable self into the living room and was sniffing the air with disdain when Stanley arrived.

"Is everything all right, Mother Hinkle?"

"What have you two been doin' in here? It smells like a burnt outhouse." She sniffed again. "And flea powder."

"Oh, that. Isabelle made me dinner, you see."

She cast a distrustful look in the direction of the bedroom. Stanley was the one of the few people that she could tolerate, so she tended toward a protective maternal feeling for him that would have put most people off motherhood entirely.

"You watch what the vile hussy does, Stanley. Do! Her father is a snake and she slithered out of that same nest, I tell you."

"I'm sure it's all right, Mother. She's just never learned how to actually cook. Now have a seat," he gestured toward one of their sturdier chairs to support a woman of Mother Hinkle's vast dimensions, "and tell me what's bothering you."

"No time for that. No time at all. I need you to come with me and tell these men what for. On my property, no less!"

"What men?"

She had the exasperated look worn by someone who expected you to read their mind and was frustrated by having to actually express themselves. "Them circus freaks! They went an' had the nerve to put up on *my* property!"

"Oh dear," said Stanley, who'd been secretly hoping for something more exciting. "We'd better get going, then. Let me just get my rain coat." He quietly stepped into the bedroom and looked around for Isabelle. He didn't see her, so he rummaged through the closet until he finally found what would pass for a rain coat.

"Is she gone?" He heard a quiet voice ask from the vicinity of the bed. He still didn't see her, so he leaned over and lifted the dust cover.

"Isabelle?"

"I asked if she's gone!" Answered a more irritated voice, but definitely Isabelle's and definitely from under the bed.

"Um, yes and no. She's about to leave, but I'll have to go with her. There's trouble at her property and she needs my help. I'm afraid that means I won't be able to eat supper with you tonight after all. I'm really sorry," he lied.

"That's fine, just go!"

Isabelle waited for the bedroom door to close, and then waited to hear the living room door shut. She continued to wait for another minute just to be on the safe side before finally crawling out from under the bed. She dusted herself off and squared her shoulders as she walked back to the kitchen, daring the empty room to mention the fact that she'd just been cowering underneath a bed because of a middle-aged woman. Granted, that woman had been described as a brick wall and had been known to stare down raging bulls, but Isabelle still felt there should be standards. She picked up Stanley's plate from the table and scraped it into the trash can with a sigh.

• • •

Mr. Cuddle Face had been following the progress of the plate and lingered by the can after Isabelle left the room. He sniffed the base and cocked his head as he wondered what was making that strange hissing noise. If he'd been smarter than the average dog he might have realized that it was actually Stanley's intended meal disintegrating the plastic bag it had landed on.

• • •

"Watch, watch, watch where you're backing that elephant up, boy! I don't have time for another shower, so kindly point him the other direction, thank you!" Cyrus barked his commands proudly. No one could bark quite like Cyrus. "You, over there! My, you've got something of a marmoset face, don't you? Never mind, just get that bear to put down the damned poodle and get him back in his cage after he does his business. And will somebody tell me where the damned dwarfs are?"

As ringmaster and commander of Sir Cyrus Cleansby's Myriad of Marvels traveling show, he surveyed his collapsible realm with the pride of a pharaoh watching his pyramid being erected. The Egyptians might have been onto a good thing with the sphinx, but it was a shame that such a gold mine should be stuck out in the middle of the desert going to waste. If he'd been pharaoh, he'd have built one that could be torn down and rebuilt as a summer house in Alexandria over a weekend. A grunt from about waist level brought Cyrus's attention back down to earth.

"All right, keep moving! And remember, five minute breaks are for the unemployed!" He turned his attention back to the matter at hand. "Now, for you two—"

"Little people."

"Excuse me?" Sir Cyrus was very unaccustomed to being interrupted.

"I believe you called us 'dwarfs' a moment ago. 'Little people' is the preferred and accepted term."

"Is that a fact?" Cyrus chewed the end of his soggy cigar. The rain pouring in under his scant office tent made it impossible to keep it lit, but he felt having it in his mouth added to his air of authority. If he'd had a mirror he'd have realized that having a drooping, dripping cigar impeding your speech only added to your air of absurdity. "I'll try to keep that in mind," he continued with the tone of one who intended no such thing.

The more diminutive of the two little people seemed to recognize familiar stormy waters in his boss' demeanor. "Is there something we can do for you, sir?" He nudged his politically minded partner into silence.

"Well, I'm so glad you asked that. Snow White sent word to me five minutes ago that she refused to perform again as long as a certain dwarf—oh *excuse* me—*little person*," he spat the phrase, "was employed here. Now would either of you like to tell me why that is?"

The taller of the two, whom Cyrus had mentally named Slappy, was already reddening.

"She started it! She said she'd hang me up by my ankles and see if she couldn't stretch me into a man!"

"Really? That's just terrible! Why do you think she'd go and do a thing like that? Don't you even think about going anywhere!" He added to the other little person who'd begun edging away from the conversation after learning that it didn't have anything to do with him. He flinched and stopped in his tracks.

"Well," began Slappy, "I gave her flowers yesterday, kinda as a joke, you know, but I think she may have taken it the wrong way."

"No kidding? Would these, in fact, be the flowers trimmed out with ladies' safety razors that are lying on my desk right now?" Slappy's nod was barely perceptible. "Imagine that. I can't think of any reason why Snow White the Bearded Lady might take that the wrong way! Now, I want you to go apologize to her this minute and take her this box of chocolates. These have never failed me before. Now go!" He shoved the box of Belgian truffles into Slappy's hands as the little person took off at a dead run.

"As for you," he addressed the other one who'd managed to edge all the way to the tent flap again. "You seem much smarter than your little friend. What's your name?"

"Big Joe, sir," he replied quietly.

"Big... Ah! I see, one of those joke names. Irony, right? Because you're so short?"

"Um, not exactly, sir. The name has nothing to do with my height, actually."

Cyrus looked thoughtfully at Big Joe. "Son, you know this is a family circus, right?"

Big Joe wondered if his face were actually on fire or if it had suddenly just gotten much hotter in the tent. "Yes, sir."

"From now on, if someone asks you that while you're in my show, it's because of the height thing. Got it?"

"Yes, sir!"

"Good. Now here's your job. Keep an eye on Slappy for me—"

"Slappy, sir?"

Cyrus cursed his habit of mentally tagging people in place of remembering their names. "Oh, the one who just left. What's his name?"

"Little Joe, actually."

Cyrus looked at him again. "Because of the height thing, right?" He asked slowly.

Ever the quick learner, Big Joe replied, "Exactly sir! Because he's so short, yes. Nothing to do with anything at all but his height."

"Good. What I want you to do is watch Little Joe for me. If he gets it into his head to pull any more of his pranks I want you to come right back and tell me all about it. I can't afford to keep buying these blasted chocolates. Go on now, get started!"

"Yes sir!" Big Joe practically saluted Cyrus in his excitement to finally be released.

"Whoever heard of a prima donna with a beard, anyway?" Cyrus asked the empty air after both Joes had left.

Cyrus sighed and put his floppy rain hat back on before venturing out into the relentless showers soaking his empire. There were three huge tents that formed the main attractions, and these were encircled by a variety of smaller tents, booths, and games offering everything, including a penny chance for a goldfish, a peek at a heavily tattooed pig, and a fortune teller who claimed she was the reincarnation of Marilyn Monroe, despite the fact that she'd been in elementary school when Marilyn Monroe was born. Placed carefully between the tents that tended to get the hottest were the ice cream and lemonade stands, and dotted everywhere would be tantalizing displays of fluffy cotton candy, caramel apples, and lollipops the size of small children.

All of this would have been set up hours ago if it hadn't been for the rain. It had been pouring so heavily for so long now that the tent poles floated back out of the ground every time they made any headway in getting one sunk. It wasn't that he was afraid of not getting set up in time; the circus didn't officially begin until Thursday night, two days away. But Sir Cyrus Cleansby had learned in his many years of carnival barking that it paid to set up early and let everyone think about what wonders might be waiting for them under the enormous tents. The longer they had to think about it, the more they wanted to come. In his mind, every minute those tents weren't up was another $5.50 ticket they wouldn't sell.

He sloshed across the field in search of his assistant and favorite attraction. Even in this hazy downpour Goliath would be a hard one to miss.

"Ah, bingo!"

He squinted the water out of his eyes and made out a hulking figure on the back of an elephant urging it to pull a truck out of a mud hole. The orphaned elephant Gumby was Goliath's favorite mount, horses having a tendency to whinny and collapse under the behemoth. From a distance, the rider and his mount seemed to almost be about the right size. The closer one got, however, the more one realized that one had been sadly mistaken. And that one might need a change of trousers.

Cyrus, after years of acquaintance with both of the gentle giants, was no longer affected by the sheer enormity of their size. He'd learned that it paid to be wary when shaking Goliath's hand and not to stand directly behind him if there was any chance that he might suddenly back up, but anyone keeping these two things in mind was perfectly capable of having a wonderful working relationship with the man. Cyrus waited for the man and beast to finish hauling their load out of the mud.

"Goliath? Can you come down here for a moment when you have the chance?" Of all of his employees, Goliath was the only one to whom Cyrus made requests. Everyone else merely received his orders. The arrangement worked well, however. Goliath was typically happy to please his boss and Cyrus slept better knowing that the giant man with skull-crushing hands was also sleeping happily.

Goliath threw a leg over Gumby's rigging and hopped down into the mud, slapping the elephant on the rump to send him off. Happy that work was now over, the beast wandered amiably to the site where he'd last found the apple barrel.

"Someone's coming across the field, Cyrus. I saw them from Gumby's back."

"That's what I came to talk to you about. One of the lads warned me a bit ago that the old crone who owns this property is a little irate about our settling here and had gone to get the sheriff. I want you to sit in the negotiations with me when they get here." Another not so surprising benefit to having Goliath present in proceedings was that people became remarkably agreeable to whatever Cyrus asked. "Did you get a good look at them?"

"Only to see that one was very big and the other seemed small and puny."

"I see," said Cyrus. "The little old bat must have brought the biggest man they had to scare us off. Well! Won't they be surprised then?" Cyrus's smile gleamed even through the rain.

"I suppose so, sir," Goliath sighed. One of the many drawbacks to his enormous size was that there were certain roles that he was expected to play, intimidator being chief on that list. It was a role he detested and felt that it was terribly beneath him, but at least it paid well. Becoming Goliath the Giant at a freak show wouldn't have been his first, second, or even one-hundred-and-seventy-third choice in careers, but he'd been destined for the life the moment he reached six-feet tall in elementary school. All in all, he had to admit that it hadn't been a terrible life. The food was consistent, the pay was always on time, and it even gave him a roof over his head, despite the fact that it was made of canvas. Besides, though the costume was a bit embarrassing, it certainly saved him the equal embarrassment of trying to find a suit that didn't split as soon as he'd tried it on.

At the moment, however, more than anything he just wanted to go somewhere and find a dry corner with a good book.

• • •

"Stanley, is that man wearing a *loincloth?*" Mother Hinkle stared in disbelief and shock as the pair of men approached them at the edge of the encampment. At least, she would have said it was disbelief and shock if asked later. Of course it wasn't with even the mildest of intrigue, she'd have said.

"Wow, I believe it is. At least, it's part of one, I think. I always pictured a loincloth as somehow bigger." Stanley tried to focus his attention on the ground in front of him.

"Well! I hope they don't have any young ladies runnin' around like that as well!"

Stanley cleared his throat and tried not to look embarrassed. "Yes, that would be a terrible shame. If there were half-naked young ladies running around, I mean." He wasn't sure but he thought he saw the hint of a smirk on Mother Hinkle's face disappearing as he turned to face her.

"You should probably let me do the talking, Mother. I think I know how these sleazy types are."

"Yes, you ought to, bein' married to one and all."

Stanley had a mild sense of guilt that he wasn't jumping to Isabelle's defense, but he feigned a sudden case of deafness instead. As they reached the edge of the field where the pair of circus folk were waiting for them, Stanley noticed a look of poorly concealed surprise on the face of the smaller man. *Aha,* he thought proudly, *they must not have expected Mother Hinkle to come with the sheriff on her side.*

It was a kindness that Stanley didn't have any idea of what was really going through the minds of both Cyrus and Goliath at the moment.

"Well now!" Cyrus recovered himself and boomed an amiable greeting. "You must be the kind lady my assistants have told me about who had the charitable spirit to let us sit on a tiny corner of her fair property." Cyrus, a man whom no one could have called smart with a straight face, had been given extra helpings out of the shrewdness and cunning bins to make up for his lacking in areas involving history, spelling bees, and ethics. His way of telling people how kind they were being to him had the effect of making people want to go out of their way to actually be kind to him. This was a skill that had worked wonders for him in every town he'd traveled to, but that was only because he'd never met anyone like Mother Hinkle before.

"Is that a fact?" Mother Hinkle was not impressed as she looked down at the little man. "Only I don't recall ever havin' been asked by anyone to sit on any corner of my property, and especially not in the middle of my tater field!"

"My dear lady!" Cyrus applied his best look of shock and dismay and immediately followed it up with the look of humble apology he saved only for the most dire circumstances. "Please accept my deepest heartfelt apologies. I was under the impression that my staff had come to a mutually beneficial arrangement with you beforehand. Please, both of you, come into my office and I'm sure we can work something out that will send us both home smiling."

Cyrus led them between a scattering of collapsing tents and equipment to his "office." At the moment, this consisted of a giant tarpaulin stretched between two trucks with a small table anchored in the mud underneath. Despite the frequent drips from the canvas roof, it was still a tremendous break from the constant hammer of rain on their heads. He turned back to his guests.

"That's better. If you please, my name is Sir Cyrus Cleansby—"

"Sir?" Inquired Mother Hinkle skeptically.

"Yes, honorary."

"Honorary what?"

"I mean, I would be honored if you would simply call me Cyrus as my friends do," he rallied heroically. "My tall associate here is Goliath."

Stanley pulled the floppy hat from his head, dumping water from the brim all over his feet. "I'm Sheriff Stanley Grace and this is Mother...I mean, Mrs. Hinkle."

"That's Ms. Hinkle, in fact," she added gently.

"Charmed to make your acquaintance," rumbled a voice from somewhere near the ceiling. Both Stanley and Cyrus looked up. No one could have missed the look of awe in Goliath's face as he extended his hand toward Mother Hinkle, and certainly no one could have missed the look of awe in Stanley's face as Mother Hinkle placed her hand in his and giggled as the giant very gently kissed it.

As has already been mentioned, Cyrus was not a smart man. But he was no fool, either. "Goliath," he began innocently, "why don't you take Miss Hinkle over to the food truck and find her a lovely cup of coffee while the sheriff and I discuss matters? In fact, I believe there might even be a box or two of truffles still to be had. Find her one, won't you?"

"It would be my pleasure." Goliath beamed as he offered his arm to escort the woman from the tent. There was a shared moment of silence while the two men remaining in the makeshift office paused to digest the scene that had just transpired.

"Anyway, Mr. Cleansby," Stanley recovered himself first. "I think there must be some confusion. I've seen the field that was marked by the mayor for the circus to set up. It wouldn't be any problem at all for me to show you the spot if you need."

"Ah, you see, dear boy, that is precisely where the problem lies. We went directly to the location your mayor assigned to us upon our arrival this afternoon. Unfortunately, that field is currently, in fact, not a field at all. I believe it's actually a small pond at the moment. Might I offer the opinion that Merit's good mayor is not actually a fan of the circus, perhaps?"

"Oh no," Stanley shook his head. "The river must have flooded already. It has a tendency to do that in the spring. But you still can't just put up shop in the middle of Mrs. Hinkle's potato field! She makes her living from this farm."

"So all we're talking about here is really a few potatoes? I'm sure we could find a way to compensate the kind woman for any loss she may have in produce. How much does she sell them for?"

"Around fifty cents per pound, I think."

"Really? Well that's no problem at all! Why just one of our tickets here will buy eleven pounds of her potatoes, and I'd venture to say we should sell at least fifteen hundred this weekend. How many pounds do you think we're talking about here?"

Stanley took a quiet look around the chaos of the circus encampment. They had already spread themselves out over almost two acres, and everywhere he turned he saw more people—mostly people, anyway—frantically trying to drive huge stakes into the ground and shoveling mud away from spinning truck tires and the few tents or stands they'd actually managed to erect so far.

"Oh, probably at least 25,000 pounds from the looks of it so far."

"Really?" Cyrus' face continued smiling, but his voice had suddenly acquired tones of lead. "Let's think about this. My Myriad of Marvels is here on an invitation from your charming city, and we find ourselves suddenly homeless due to an unexpected act of nature and now are looking at $12,500 in rent for a single weekend? I'd be willing to go as high as $300 to help Mrs. Hinkle in the case of her *potential* losses, but anything higher than that and I'd have to starve my poor animals. Have you ever traveled with hungry bears and tigers, Stanley?"

Stanley swallowed. "You do have a point, there," he said reluctantly. "I'll still need to talk to Mrs. Hinkle and possibly the mayor about this before I can agree to anything."

"We're in luck then. Here comes the charming lady now with my assistant."

The sound of unfamiliar laughter reached Stanley's ears before he even turned around. Mother Hinkle and Goliath were enjoying what appeared to be a very friendly conversation.

"Really?" She was saying as they entered the office. "The whole bear right over your shoulders like that?"

"Just like that. You wouldn't think so, but they really seem to enjoy it. Bears are natural wrestlers. Besides, it's usually the crowd's favorite part of the show."

"Goliath," Cyrus cleared his throat. "I hate to interrupt, but we need to borrow your lovely companion for just a moment to discuss our situation here."

"Oh, that?" Mother Hinkle giggled again. "Don't you worry about that. Mr. Goliath promised me he'd make sure they were careful of my crops. I usually lose half this field to flooding, anyway. They're more than welcome to stay."

"Really?" Stanley was shocked. "Because Mr. Cleansby here just offered—"

"Stanley my boy, don't be such a damper!" Cyrus quickly interrupted before Stanley could get any dollar figures out of his mouth. "Don't you see this is a time for celebration? Madame, it is truly my pleasure to be working with you! I assure you that under our Goliath's supervision your field will be in safe hands."

Mother Hinkle blushed again. "We'll just be goin' now, but it was a pleasure to meet the both of you. I'll drop by sometime tomorrow to make sure you have everything you need."

"That would be a delight for me, Miranda." Goliath smiled.

Stanley waited just until they were both out of earshot of the tent before speaking.

"Miranda?" He whispered from the corner of his mouth.

"What?" Mother Hinkle answered hotly. "Don't look at me like that, boy. Everyone's got to have a first name, don't they? And I better not hear one word of this from anyone around town. Do you hear me, young man?"

"Yes, ma'am," Stanley mumbled.

• • •

Cyrus was still dumbfounded.

"Good God, Goliath, that woman was almost as tall as you are!"

"I know," he answered dreamily.

"And she was almost as broad!"

"Yes, she was."

"A real brute of a woman, too."

"I know," Goliath sighed. "Wasn't she wonderful?"

• • •

Four short but dreadfully yellow rain slickers and eight multi-colored galoshes were trying to approach the far side of the circus as inconspicuously as possible. They were about as successful as a flamingo hiding in a chicken coop. Fortunately for them, however, Cyrus had favorable views about children sneaking around the tents for a preview and had instructed his staff to pique their interest in whatever ways possible, short of potential death or dismemberment. To his mind, sending the amazed children back to school to tell all of their little friends about the wonders under the tents was the best advertising he could get. And best of all, it was *free*.

The four children in question were none other than the Upper Jelly River Gang, fresh from their afternoon naps to make up for their lost sleep from the night before. Tyler and Jordan led the way with Beazer and Bub dragging along behind, caught in the excitement of everything they saw. They had been unusually quiet since meeting up at their traditional spot behind the "Forest of Dred" at Old John's Christmas Tree Farm, and they were mostly avoiding eye contact wherever possible. There was an unspoken understanding that they were all being forced to wear the rain slickers and galoshes to be able to come out in the first place, but they were still afraid of their natural tendency to tease one another for looking like plucked daisies.

The children moved cautiously through this strange world. Once, Tyler had to stop to let a bear carrying a poodle by the scruff pass while his trainer chased after him with a tricycle. Beazer and Bub had to run to catch up with their friends after being detained by a soggy woman with a bushy beard who apparently thought they were her dwarves. She screamed at them until realizing her mistake and storming off. Even Jordan had nearly gotten herself lost when she started following a monkey who led her into a dark corner and tried to pick her pockets. It got mad and ran off when it found that all she had was a cracked blue marble and a soggy mint shoved in her jacket pocket.

All in all, the Upper Jelly River Gang were in heaven.

"Tyler," Jordan poked her leader, "look at that man! I think he's coming over here!" She stepped slightly behind Tyler as she spoke and heard Beazer behind her sniggering. She shot him a dirty look and stepped out in front of Tyler to meet the man first. She had a reputation to protect, after all.

As the man drew nearer, all of them realized almost at once that what looked like a brightly colored shirt and mask were actually none other than the man himself. He looked as if he'd gone to sleep at a graffiti competition and awoke at a scrap metal workers meeting. Not even his face was free of the amazingly detailed tattoos, and some of those were hidden by the incredible amount of piercings his face supported. Where most people were concerned with acne or wrinkles, he looked as if his biggest concern might have been rust.

"What do you kids think you're doing here?" He leaned over them and spoke in a slightly foreign accent. Jordan was suddenly regretting her decision to be brave.

"We're just—we're, I mean..." she faltered. Her eyes were wandering over some of his more exotic tattoos and she suddenly had some questions she wanted to ask her parents when she got home.

"We just came to see if we could help!" Tyler, as nervous as any of them, let out the words like a shot.

The tattooed man laughed, causing certain of his tattoos to twitch in ways that the boys were very uncomfortable with. Thankfully, Jordan had already stopped looking.

"Help? You thought little mites like yourselves could help here? What would you do exactly? Feed the tigers? Brush the bears? Tie the elephants' shoe laces?"

"Elephants wear shoes?" Beazer exclaimed in wonder.

"Ours do," he smiled grimly, baring a mouth full of teeth filed to a point. "It makes it easier for us to clean their feet after they step on little children!" He nearly bent double in laughter as the kids bolted away, leaving the sounds of squeals streaming behind them.

"Jimmy? What's going on? What'd you say to those kids?" Little Joe had been trying to drag his miniature pony by when he heard the ruckus.

"Aw, nothin' much man," said Jimmy, the tattooed man, now in a casual mid-west accent. "I just gave them the old elephant shoe gag."

"Ah, yes." Little Joe nodded sagely. "That one gets 'em every time. I'll bet we get twice as many up here now tomorrow night."

• • •

Stanley was just sliding his badge into place when he suddenly became aware of an animal attempting soulful puppy eyes at his feet. Mr. Cuddle Face waited until Stanley looked down before adding what he hoped was a heart-wrenching whine and tail wag.

"What is it, Mr. Cud...um, boy?" Stanley couldn't bring himself to say the dog's full name at the best of times, but especially not when he was wearing his badge.

Mr. Cuddle Face sat up and begged in reply. Stanley crouched down and scratched the dog's mangy ears.

"You wanna go with me, doncha' boy? You want to get out of here before you-know-who wakes up." Stanley looked around conspiratorially for any sign of Isabelle approaching and whispered more quietly. "I don't blame you. That's why I'm going to work early."

"Stanley?" A husky sleep-ridden voice from the hallway behind him caused him to straighten up far more quickly than his back would have liked.

"Yes! I mean, good morning, dear." He grimaced as he tried to stretch his spine back out of a question mark.

"Weren't you going to wake me up before you left? What's Mr. Cuddle Face doing?"

"You looked so peaceful. Asleep. Like that," Stanley said, faltering. He glanced at his feet again and found that the dog was apparently trying to hide himself behind Stanley's legs. "Um, I think Mr... he—the dog, I mean—wants to go with me."

"Well," Isabelle said with disinterest, "his leash is on the coat rack. Don't let him eat anything he might throw up later."

"But I can't..." he began, but she'd already left the hallway and headed for the kitchen to seek out coffee.

Stanley sighed and reached for the shiny blue leash, which quickly stopped the sound of a tail rapidly thumping the floor.

"I'm sorry, but I have to. You heard her."

Mr. Cuddle Face did the equivalent of weighing his options in his doggy mind. He looked toward the kitchen where the object of his horror waited with the promise of more high-fiber beef lumps in gravy.

He didn't even pretend to growl when Stanley put the leash on him.

• • •

Bertie Betters was deceptively fat. He walked to work every day after his morning calisthenics, never overate, and always said no to dessert. He was simply one of the people whom Nature had intended to be well insulated against cold weather, possibly even a nuclear winter. Unfortunately for Nature's best laid plans, he lived in a part of the country that hadn't seen snow since the soap flake truck flipped on the overpass in '83.

This morning, as every morning, Bertie was bouncing happily on his way to the sheriff's office and juggling his newspaper under his arm while he periodically launched a strike in his ever-present war with his shirt tails. Part of Nature's gift of insulation had brought with it an inability to keep a shirt tucked in evenly for more than twelve full steps at a time. With the fifth and sixth steps after his last attack he came even with the sidewalk to the familiar sight of the building which housed the one-cell, three-room sheriff's station. Everything seemed largely in order; the mossy oak tree on the north corner was standing in its normal spot, the vines creeping up the brick exterior were still thriving on the dark soil made rich by the seeping septic tank, and the shining silver words proclaiming their purpose were still missing the telltale letters. What had once read To Serve and Protect now read To Ser e and P ote t. Despite the friendly and familiar sight of all of this, Bertie was acutely aware that something was still wrong with the scene, and he had a strong feeling that it had something to do with his boss standing on the front stoop having what appeared to be a heated conversation with a dog.

"Stanley?" He asked carefully. "Um, is everything okay?"

"Oh!" Stanley shot upright in embarrassment, shocking his

back straight for the second time that morning. "Everything's fine. Just fine. It's just the dog here. He ate most of what I think used to be a cat on the road before I could stop him. Do you think it'll make him sick?"

Bertie cast an appraising look at the dog. "I get the feeling that this dog's had his share of road kill dinners before. Is Isabelle taking in strays again?"

"You guessed it."

"How long did this one last?"

"All of a day."

"New record, I'd say. What are you going to do with it, Stanley?"

"I don't know yet." The dog, seemingly aware of its place in the conversation, cocked his head endearingly at Stanley. "He's kinda grown on me though. It's almost as if he understands me. Maybe I'll try to keep him if Isabelle lets me."

If Isabelle lets him. The thought strayed across Bertie's mind and he shook his head, following Stanley and the dog inside. Bertie knew better than to say a word against her because Stanley's formidable sense of honor and loyalty wouldn't allow him to tolerate it. Still, he wondered if Stanley didn't deep down really know that he was even more under the woman's thumb than her own fingerprint. He started the coffee pot and settled down to unsleeve his newspaper when another thought struck him.

"So what's his name anyway?"

"Well, that's sort of a problem. She named him Mr. Cuddle Face, but I can't really go around calling him that, can I? He seems to already know his name, though."

"What about just Cuddles?"

Stanley gave Bertie a Look he'd borrowed from Isabelle's enormous collection. He'd been practicing it in front of the mirror and was anxious for his first chance to try it out.

Bertie recoiled.

"Okay, so maybe not." He took another look at Stanley's dog,

who had thrown his back leg high into the air and gleefully engaged in a form of loud bathing that would be unlawful and shocking in the human world. In public, at least.

"Here's a thought," Bertie began. "How about just Cud?"

Stanley stared thoughtfully at the dog, who had suddenly and
forever become Cud in his mind. "Isabelle will hate it, you know."

Bertie detected the hint of a smile on Stanley's lips. "Yes, but—"

He was cut off by the phone ringing. Stanley reached over to
answer it.

"Merit Sheriff's Office, Sheriff Grace speaking. Excuse me? No,
I don't have any comment to make about the...wait, what racial
tension? What paper are you with? No, I think you must have the
wrong number, goodbye." Stanley hung up. "That was the damned-
est thing. A reporter from the Jostlem Daily Word just wanted to
know what we intended to do about the 'unbridled racial tension'
in the city. What on earth do you think that could be about? The
last problem we had over race was when Mother Hinkle didn't
want to hire a Mexican to work at her store. It turned out he was
Asian, anyway."

Bertie had unrolled his newspaper while Stanley was on the
phone and was scanning the front page with a dark face. "Stanley,
I hate to say it, but it looks like we might have a problem after all.
You'll want to see this."

Stanley took the paper from Bertie and quickly skimmed the
first few lines.

"Oh. Crap."

• • •

"Thank you, as always, Barbara and Jim. Yes, we are on location in
the seemingly quiet and peaceful small town of Merit. Children are
playing, dogs are barking, and the sun is shining on clean streets
and beautiful gardens. Yet, thanks to this young citizen who was

brave enough to speak out, we've learned now that the sickness of racism is festering here like a slumbering giant. Erwin Mayer of Miss Douglas's third grade class is here to tell us the story. Erwin, please tell us what's happening in your home town that's caused you to seek help from the outside world?"

"Well, Dana, the root of all of our trouble is the gang problem that I talked about in my editorial to the Jostlem Times. I'm surprised that it made front page news, but hopefully the world will take notice and learn from our problems."

"Right. Now can you tell us what *specifically* the gangs are doing here in Merit for our viewers who don't read the paper?"

"Well, they fight. They fight everywhere and it's only because they're different from each other. They told me so themselves when I interviewed them in prison."

"These gangs have criminal records as well?"

"Oh yes! They must be a mile long by now! There's always at least one of them in detention, but usually more. Nobody does anything about it, though. It's like they just sit back and hope they kill each other off so it won't be their problem anymore or something."

"You heard it here first. The gang violence has gotten so bad in Merit that the good citizens are actually hoping that they 'kill each other off.' Yes, I believe the world will definitely take notice, thanks to this brave young man. Already there are activists and celebrities heading for Merit to strike out against racism and gang-related violence. Reporting for K-ACTN News, I'm Dana Perki. Back to you, Barbara and Jim. Aaaaand, we're out. Thank god," she sighed as her perfect smile melted into a yawn.

"Ms. Perky," Erwin began, slipping his glasses from his face in the slightly more debonair manner he'd been practicing all day. "I really want to thank you for coming all the way down here and—"

"Sure kid, but the 'i' in my name is silent, okay? It's just pronounced *Perk*. Christ, I just said it two seconds ago. Allen! Give the boy the twenty bucks we promised him and, and… ATCHOO! And find me a drug store already!" Sniff. "If I don't get some allergy medicine soon I'm not going to make the five o'clock spot with the reverend. Blast this place and its beautiful gardens!"

• • •

"Hey, turn that TV up!"

"…believe the world will definitely take notice, thanks to this brave young man. Already there are activists and celebrities heading for Merit to strike out against racism and gang-related violence. Reporting for K-ACTN News, I'm Dana Perki. Back to you, Barbara and Jim."

"That's it!" Monty spilled his whiskey across the bar when he jumped out of his seat. "I have to go to Merit! Everyone who's *anyone* will be there and I have to get there first. People have to know the truth about me and this is my chance! You, bartender guy, whatever your name is. Where the hell is Merit?"

• • •

"Did you hear that, Goliath? Celebrities and activists are coming, and now more will come just because they heard others are coming. Oh yes, this will be the most profitable stop on our tour or my name isn't Sir Cyrus Cleansby! Quick, get the hawkers in here. I've got to tell them to raise the price of everything by a dollar!"

• • •

Stanley finished reading the last lines of the article and dropped it in his lap.

"Oh crap!"

Chapter Three

"All right, calm down everybody! We're gonna have to go one at a time, okay?" Tyler was tired. It had been one of the longest days of his life. Even longer than the day he spent with his sister at the mall last week. But he'd called the meeting between the Upper and Lower Jelly River Gangs for an important reason and he had to keep them on track. They'd agreed to meet after they all received a surprise detention even though they had been doing their best to be good all day. Currently, they were all trying to talk at once in one of the secret neutral places in the north woods.

"Brewer, you start. Have your parents been weird today? Or bringin' weird people over to the house to talk to you?"

"Well, my mom's been crying a lot today. She keeps saying that she doesn't know how she's raised a..." His face screwed up with the effort of recalling the word. "A *erasist*. I didn't know I'm erasist. I don't even know what it means. She's got some lady from church coming by tonight after dinner to talk to me about it."

"I was afraid of that." Tyler looked around the wooden shack. It had previously served as an electrical shed and was still full of interesting equipment, but the power had been off for years. "Has anyone else been called racist by their parents?"

There were glum nods from Jordan, Carrie, and Crow.

"Not just that," Crow admitted. "Some old man tried to spit on me today and called me a cookie, or something like that."

"Was it cracker? I got called that in gym class today by Jamal, but I thought it was a compliment." Brewer shifted uneasily at missing his chance to respond to an insult.

"Yeah, that was it. Cracker. What's it mean?"

"I don't know exactly, but I think it has something to do with being white. My mom had some reverend come to talk to me at school today, and he explained a lot of things to me."

Everyone looked at Tyler in amazement.

"Is that why you missed recess?" Jordan asked.

Tyler nodded. "He and Mom said that it had to do with me, Beazer, and Spike being black, and that white people was always going to be racist against us for that. That the white folks, which I guess is you guys, are trying to keep us down. He said it's a problem everywhere, and that the only way to fight it is to band up and stand up for ourselves."

"I don't get it." Carrie looked flustered. "I don't *feel* racist, and Spike and I have always been friends. Does this mean I have to fight with him now?"

Jordan jumped to her feet. "Whoa, hold on. Tyler, why does it have to be *us* against *you*? How come you can't be racist against us? I don't wanna be the bad guys."

"I don't know," Tyler shook his head. "That's just how the reverend explained it to me. I don't think he'd lie to me. He's supposed to be big and important to the cause, Mom said."

"So what do we do now?"

Bub finally spoke up. "I think there's only one thing we *can* do."

• • •

It was still a beautiful afternoon in Merit; gardens were in full bloom all over town, and nowhere were they more beautiful than in Charity Park at the heart of the town. Tulips, lilacs, daisies, and every imaginable spring bloom were bursting into life with the help of the heavy rains from the day before. Of course, along with this colorful burst came an extraordinary pollen count, which was causing the tremendous amount of sniffling and sneezing from an extremely frustrated reporter with a silent "i" in her name. And it was almost five o'clock.

Dana was frantically dabbing makeup over her red eyes and nose while accidentally stripping off every other dab by blowing her nose again. She was also swaying slightly.

"Dana, I really think you need to lay off the antihistamine for a while. You look a little drunk."

"Don't be dumb, Allen. Just sway the camera with me and no one will notice. It's not working, anyway. I think I need to take one more just to get through the interview."

"Ms. Perky–"

"Perk!" She caught herself. "I'm sorry, Reverend. It's just that the 'i' at the end of my name is actually silent."

"It's all right, child. I was just going to suggest that since you're feeling so ill maybe I should just read a statement instead of an interview. I have one prepared just in case–"

"Nonsense, I'm fine! I just wish I knew whose idea it was to do the feed from this blasted park."

"It was the network, actually." Allen finished a little hesitantly. "Also, they asked me to tell you to lay off the prose a little this time. They said the morning interview was a little syrupy."

"Excuse me?" She responded acidly.

"Don't blame me! I'm just the messenger. Okay, looks like we're on in twenty seconds, so get ready."

The reverend straightened himself and his suit ceremoniously while Dana sniffed deep and hard one last time while applying the last layers of powder to her red nose. "Syrupy my ass," she muttered.

"Okay, on in three, two, one." He pointed at her and her distinguished guest.

"Yes, Barbara, we are still here in Merit where the situation continues to worsen. I'm here with the esteemed Reverend Elliot Simmons, better known in some circles as 'The Boxer' due to his tireless fight against racism with Jostlem's youth. Reverend, what was it about this story that made you decide to offer your services to this strife-ridden town?"

"That's quite simple, Dana. It was the Lord who called me down here, and it's the Lord who wants me to stay and help His children. I can tell you that I know our Lord Jesus cries when He sees His children fighting, and I will be here in Merit until all have seen the error of their ways. I have the support of my faithful congregation at the Blessed Sacrament of the Holy Church of the RISEN Savior in Jostlem, services Sundays at eight and ten and Wednesdays at seven, and they will be collecting donations for our work here on my behalf. Checks can be made out to Christians Against Merit Madness. Please, help us in the fight against racial rage and resentment; your prayers and checks do make all of the difference in destroying this evil forever!"

"Wow, Reverend. Thank you for your, um, *powerful* message to our viewers. I think I see two residents approaching us now. Let's see if we can get their opinion on Merit's struggles. Sir? Sir! May I have a word with you?"

"Um, I don't see why not."

The resident thoughtfully scratched his chin, his neck, and then his groin. Dana felt regret pouring over her immediately, but it was too late to turn back.

"Sir, what do you think about the problems in Merit? How did your town become such a den of inequity?"

"Shoot, well, I don't know 'bout no den of iniquity 'round here. They closed down the whorehouse ages back. I should know!"

"Dagnabbit, Albert!"

Dana hurriedly gestured the camera back to her while the wife of the citizen grabbed him by the collar and dragged him down the street, fussing loudly.

"There you have it, Barbara. Not only racism, but prostitution and adultery as well. What is our world coming to?"

Pause for a two second empathetic shake of the head.

"Back to you in Jostlem, Barbara!"

"We're clear!" Allen said. "Good recovery with the whole prostitute thing. I had to hold my breath to keep from laughing."

"Really? I had to hold mine to keep from crying. That was awful!" Dana scanned the park and found that the reverend was out of ear shot talking with the citizens he'd cornered in the playground, but still leaned in closer to her camera man to whisper. "And the network had the nerve to call *me* syrupy? I think I can still smell the brimstone from that guy!"

"You're not the only one. On the bright side, I think I see a cop heading this way."

"Oh brother! Where was he two minutes ago when I needed an intelligent commentary?"

• • •

Sheriff Stanley was walking to Sal's to pick up dinner when he noticed a television reporter conducting an interview. *Oh no.* He'd hoped against hope that this whole fiasco Erwin caused with his editorial would just blow over, but after dealing with numerous phone calls from parents, reporters, activists, and others all day long he was starting to think that an avalanche was coming. Bertie had fielded as many of the journalists as he could while Stanley spent the better part of the day consoling the worried parents that he was doing all he could to control the racial problem. Just as soon as he figured out what the problem was, that is. Still, he'd hoped that the media wouldn't start pouring into the town just yet, despite what he'd heard on the news about the celebrities and activists. That could have just been for ratings, right?

Well, he figured, the least he could do is establish some ground rules for the newcomers, and it might as well start here. He crossed the street and passed Mr. Stiller being dragged out of the park by his wife.

"I'll show you some iniquity when we get home, Albert, and you ain't gonna like it! Oh! Hi, Stanley," Mrs. Stiller said as she nearly bumped into the sheriff. "Don't mind us, I'm just taking Albert home."

"I can see that." He cast a meaningful look at Mr. Stiller. "Just let me know if you need any help and I'll be right there."

"Thank you!" Mr. Stiller called out as his wife picked up the pace and her verbal assault. The Stillers used to be a frequent source of activity for Stanley in the evenings, but since the town had forced Mrs. Stiller to hand over her collection of rolling pins, things had been much quieter. He hoped she hadn't held onto one for a special occasion.

Stanley turned back toward the newswoman and her cameraman and found that they were already hurrying toward him. He puffed out his chest and sucked in his already slim gut in preparation for a fight.

"Officer! I'm Dana Perki with K-ACTN news in Jostlem and I'm so glad to see you!"

"Really?" This was the second time Stanley had prepared for a fight and been caught off guard. And this one was playfully extending her hand toward him palm down as if she expected him to take it and kiss it. He awkwardly took her hand and started to bend to it, then decided that kissing her hand might send the wrong message, so he instead gripped it firmly and shook it.

"Oh! What a strong grip you have there, Officer," she said, rubbing the color back into her hand.

"Actually, I'm the sheriff. Sheriff Stanley Grace. I was hoping–"

"Why, you're absolutely right, I'm sorry! It says right there on your badge... Wait, you do know there's only one 'r' in sheriff, right? There are two on your badge."

Stanley reddened and cleared his throat.

"Yes, there's a long story to it. We keep it that way now for sentimental reasons." Because the engraver sentimentally ran off with the florist before Stanley could get him to fix it. "Like I was saying, I was hoping we could have a talk about your plans here in Merit."

"That's exactly what I had in mind, too! I was hoping you could tell me all about your charming little town. What do you say we do dinner tonight and talk about it?"

"I don't think that's—"

"Now please, don't say no." Dana said. "It'll be short and you'll do me a world of good. Please?"

"Well, all right. Maybe you can help me understand what exactly is happening around here. I have a terrible feeling that this whole misunderstanding is just about to get out of control, and I need to know how to stop it before it begins. Hang on here for a minute. I'll call my wife and let her know I'll be home late."

As Stanley walked away pulling a bulky and outdated cell phone from his pocket, Allen leaned in to whisper to Dana.

"What on earth was all that about? Were you flirting with him?"

"Give me a break. I may be able to use him for a better story. He's the freakin' sheriff, didn't you hear? That's got to be top dog in this town, if you ask me. Small town sheriffs always have more power than even the mayor. If I have to flirt with him a little for it, so what?"

"He's married. You did catch that, right?"

"Prude. It's not like I'm trying to steal the bumpkin from his wife." She cast Stanley an appraising look. "Though, he's not bad looking, really."

Allen smiled. "Uh-oh, I know that look. Look out Sheriff Stanley!"

• • •

Sal's Hot Table was the premier restaurant in Merit, arguably because it was the only restaurant in Merit that had waiters and tables rather than paper hat-sporting teenagers and counters. It was therefore crowded every night and, since everyone in Merit knew everyone else, always full of lively conversation. Tonight, however, Stanley noticed it was strangely muted when he and Dana walked in. Then, somewhere between the first beer and the appetizer, Stanley became acutely aware that he had acquired a devoted audience. While Dana told him at length about her dreams of making it to the networks and getting out of local news, he noticed that people were even shushing their neighbors for talking too loudly. By the time the entrée arrived he realized why and nearly stabbed himself in the mouth with the fork.
"Oh my god, I'm at dinner with another woman and everyone's going to know it!"

Dana froze mid-sip, banging her wine glass into her teeth. "What are you talking about?"

"Shh! Not so loud!" Stanley barely moved his lips, but gestured madly with his eyes, which for some reason made Dana think of a boiling tea pot with a rattling lid.

"Stanley, you called your wife, right? This is just business, after all. I don't know why you're–"

"No, you don't understand. *You* know it's business. I know it's business. But this town *thrives* on gossip! You could have a briefcase in your lap right now and be giving me contracts to sign, and tomorrow someone will still be saying, 'Heh heh, did you see the way he handed her that pen?' Gossip is currency around here. You know how people used to trade goats and produce for what they needed? Here you can trade the knowledge of where old Mrs. Beck's tattoo is for it instead. It doesn't matter if it's not *entirely* true. In fact, the less true it sounds the more people love it. And now I'm sitting in a restaurant in front of everyone with an attractive woman who's not my wife, and by tomorrow the story will be that we've run off to raise our children in a nudist colony!"

"But that's just—wait, you think I'm attractive?"

"No!"

"Gee, real charmer you are."

"I didn't mean it like that. I mean, crap. Yes, you are an attractive woman, but, being a married man, I couldn't possibly, myself married and all, be attracted to you."

"Okay, I see your problem. But why are we whispering still?"

"So they can't hear us! Can't you tell they're dying to listen?"

"Yes, so let them hear. Don't you think whispering to an attractive woman who's not your wife in a restaurant looks more suspicious than loudly talking about the terrible gang problem in Merit to a reporter? We could even pretend it was an official interview. That way if anyone says anything later you have a perfect cover story. I wouldn't even mind going along with it if it would help you out of this terrible predicament."

"Really? You'd do that?"

"Of course," she said sweetly. "But you'd better try to get into it and really talk about it so people believe it's for real. Just tell me every little thing that pops into your head. I'll start by asking you a few questions. Ready?"

Stanley nodded eagerly.

"Great, Sheriff, let's get started," Dana began loudly, grabbing her notebook and pen out of her purse. "What would you say, in your professional opinion, is the root of the problem with Merit's youth? Would you say it's the fault of the parents for not taking greater pains to educate their children about their differences?"

"Well, Dana, I can't say that I think there really even *is* a problem with our kids. They're high-spirited, yes, but no one's really getting hurt in all this. Thank you, by the way..." He cleared his throat noisily. "For taking time out of your busy professional schedule to talk to me. It's very *professional* of you."

She silently mouthed the word *overkill*. Stanley closed his mouth.

"Then let me ask you this. How do you know that the problem isn't just that no one's been hurt yet? What will you do then, when it's already too late?"

"I just think everyone's being a little silly about this whole thing! I mean, I remember what it was like when I was ten and–"

"Wait!" Dana slammed her notebook down on the table and leaned forward. "How old?"

"Uh, ten?" Stanley said, trying to figure out if her sudden shift in tone was part of the show.

"You can't seriously mean to tell me that what we're talking about is two gangs of ten-year-olds!" She nearly hissed.

"Well, not just. I believe Tyler's almost eleven, but Carrie and Bub are both only nine."

She laughed bitterly, her eyes taking on a look of glazed shock. "What kind of town *is* this? Do you realize there are already six news vans, a flock of journalists, and God knows how many tag-alongs that just want a chance to get in a quip on the six o'clock news? When the motel filled up they started bringing campers, and now they're even pitching tents." Her expression was mixed. "And I'm the only one who knows that they aren't even real gangs!"

"Um, are you all right?"

"I don't know. I'm trying to figure out if this story is a career killer or a Pulitzer, but I can't see the angle. Seriously, just kids? Why didn't anyone tell us?"

"Are you really asking me that? *Now*? Because that would make you the first! Think about it. An eight-year-old-boy writes an article condemning the racism in his hometown, and no one even thinks to find out if there's even anything to it? How many eight-year-olds know many kids that much older than they are? Of *course* he'd only write about kids his age. If it sounds like big news it's only because it's big news to him and his imagination. This makes me think it's not just Merit that thrives on gossip. Don't people even care if the news is true?"

"No, not really. Well, the only things they really want to be true are the weather forecasts, and there's no hope of one of those ever being right, so I guess the rest just follows suit. They want interesting. A hotbed of hatred masquerading as a simple small town is interesting. A few kids getting into squabbles at recess…I just don't know what that is."

"It's life. Just like anywhere else, I promise. The most interesting thing to happen in Merit this week was Arnie Smith's kid getting a whole quarter stuck up his nose on a bet. Trust me on this; you won't find your big break here. I'm sorry, but that's just the way it is."

She regarded him carefully for a moment, disappointment apparent in her face. "You might be right. I don't know what to think right now. Can we get the check? I need to figure this out."

"Ma'am?"

The waitress, who'd been accidentally lingering closely enough to hear everything for the last few minutes, nervously approached them. "I'm sorry, I didn't mean to be nosy, but ain't you that reporter from the news on TV?"

Dana brightened a little and nodded prettily.

"I knew it!" Tina, as her pink badge proclaimed, ran back over to the bar and grabbed a wine glass and proceeded to bang raucously against it with a fork.

"Excuse me! Everybody! I just want to bring to y'alls' attention that we have a celebrity in the restaurant tonight!"

The few diners who hadn't already been actively staring at Dana and Stanley now also turned their attention to them.

"Sorry about this," Stanley whispered. "This is what passes for dinner theater in this town."

"That's all right. I think it's kind of sweet."

Tina continued proudly. "This is Miss Dana Perky from the TV news show right here in our own Merit!"

"No!" Dana groaned. Restaurant patrons froze mid-smile and stared with renewed interest.

"I'm sorry," she tried to recover sweetly. "It's just that the 'i' is silent. So it's pronounced Perk."

"What'd she say?"

"She said there's something wrong with her eye, I think."

"She said it's silent, her eye is silent."

"Ain't they supposed to be silent?

Oh brother, Dana thought. "Do they think we can't hear?" She asked Stanley.

"My brother's eye wasn't. He could make a really funny noise by cupping his hand over it and squeezing it like this…"

Stanley stood quickly. "All right, everyone, it's been really fun, but I think it's time to call it a night." He hurriedly paid the check and escorted Dana outside.

"Did you hear that? They're going to call it a night!"

"Uh-oh! I hope nobody tells Isabelle!"

"Okay, so I see what you mean now," Dana said when they made it to the sidewalk. "Stanley, I want to thank you for being honest with me. Just so you know, I'm going to call my producer tonight and let him know what you told me, and they'll probably tell me to get back to Jostlem first thing in the morning. Once word gets around I imagine all of the others will disappear quickly, too."

"Well, that's a relief."

She shot him a sideways look.

"I mean, it's a relief that all of those others are leaving now before things get worse. But it was nice meeting you, Ms. Dana Perki with a silent 'i.'" Stanley turned to her and extended his hand for another of his trademarked handshakes. Small men tended to overestimate just how firm a handshake should be and end up delivering a circulation-denying grip. Dana, having already experienced this once today, sidestepped his extended hand and gave him a quick peck on the cheek.

"It was nice meeting you, too, Sheriff Stanley with two R's."

The sound of children's voices was a much needed relief to

Stanley's sudden feeling of awkward embarrassment. He looked across the street and saw both the Upper and Lower Jelly River gangs exiting the park together. The fact that they weren't brawling struck him as odd, but not nearly so important as the rescue that they meant for him.

"Hold on, you might get to meet our two little gangs after all. Brewer! Tyler! Come over here for a minute with everybody, will you?"

All eight of the children stopped dead in their tracks in a mixture of fear and automatic guilt. Each of their minds were quickly filing through the afternoon's events to make sure that they hadn't done anything that they should be punished for. Most of them were at least sure that they hadn't been *caught* doing anything they should be punished for.

"Yes, sir?" Tyler took the lead as he usually did, being the oldest.

"Kids, I want you to meet Ms. Dana Perki. She's from the news station in Jostlem and she came all the way out here just to hear about the eight of you. Dana," he pointed out each one, "meet Tyler, Jordan, Beazer, Bub, Brewer, Carrie, Spike, and Crow. Together they make up the vicious Upper and Lower Jelly River gangs of Merit."

"Actually, sir," Jordan started shyly, "we're not the Jelly River Gangs anymore. We came up with some new names after school."

Stanley belatedly noticed that the kids weren't standing in their usual groups this time. "Okay, so what are you called now?"

Brewer answered for them. "Well, Tyler, Beazer and Spike are their own gang now called the Brothers. Me, Carrie, Jordan, Bub, and Crow are in the other gang and we're called the Crackers. And our truce ends in about twenty minutes, so we need to get home before we have to start fighting again. Our moms'd really be mad at us then. Nice to meet you ma'am."

As the kids walked away and Stanley remembered to close his mouth, he realized that Dana was starting at him hotly.

"The Crackers and the Brothers? You lied to me! You said there was nothing to this story at all!"

"But there really isn't! Look, I don't know what just happened there, but I'll go talk–"

"You can do whatever you want, but I'm *staying* and I'm going to break this story before anyone else does. You thought you could run me and everyone else out of town? Ha! Well, I've got news for you; this town hasn't seen *anything* yet! Before we're through the whole world will know what's happening here, I promise!" She turned on her heel and started to walk away from him. She made it three steps before turning back again.

"I can't believe I let a jerk like you charm me into thinking this was just a quiet little boring town. Ugh!" She stomped down the street in a huff.

Stanley's brain was working slowly as brains do when shocked. It filtered the torrent from Dana and allowed only the least offensive part of her tirade to completely register.

"You thought I was charming?"

Luckily for him, she was too far down the street already to hear. Not so luckily for him, the restaurant patrons who'd glued themselves to the windows and doorway were not.

"Crap. Crap, crap, crap!"

Chapter Four

Cyrus was smiling broadly at everyone he saw this morning. This made the carnies nervous for a very good reason: Cyrus only smiled when he was making money or making someone miserable, and the circus didn't open for another eight hours so making money was obviously out of the question. Everyone he encountered instantly became a very busy person, even if they were only busy looking for something to busy themselves with. It could be quite terrifying, being smiled at like that.

Then, quite unexpectedly and completely without warning, he began to *hum*. Big Joe was the first to witness this turn for the worst and watched his boss carefully for a few minutes. It was when he saw Cyrus telling Snow White how luxuriant her beard looked that he knew it was time to do something. He ran straight for Goliath.

"I see what you mean," said the giant as they watched Cyrus's meanderings from behind a tent flap.

"It's got to stop! Nobody can get anything done because they keep looking over their shoulders. He nearly gave the Fat Man a heart attack, and the String Man almost bent himself into a knot he was so scared! Even the animals are restless around him. It's bad enough that all the durned reporters running around are making a mess of things already. Can you do something?"

"I'll try," he said and sighed.

It wasn't that Goliath minded having to go talk to Cyrus. He was well aware that he was the only one in the circus that could speak openly and honestly to the man without fear of Cyrus's famous temper. It was just that he had finally found a comfortable quiet place where he could think clearly enough to compose his love letter to Miranda. Before Joe had come for Cyrus, he'd gotten as far as "My Dearest Miranda," and even just that had taken him nearly half an hour to get onto the paper. He was no stranger to writing, either. In fact, he wrote a weekly column under his real name, Lynus Minor, on the issues of parenting. He didn't have children of his own, but it was simply amazing the things one could learn about raising them while working in a circus. Specifically as to how *not* to do it. Hopefully, he would have time to finish it before tonight, but for now it would have to wait.

"Cyrus..." The gentle giant delicately approached his boss. "Are you...okay?"

Cyrus wheeled around at the sound of Goliath's voice and began talking excitedly.

"Aha! Goliath, my very dear friend, I've been looking all over for you!" His worried cigar edged nearer to escape with each word. "Wait until you hear what I've done! This is going to be the greatest show on earth!"

• • •

"Good morning, Barbara and Jim. There was quite a surprising turn of events here in Merit last night as this reporter was the first to discover the true nature of the town's problem. Far from the familiar story of race-related gang violence, this story begins with the very heart of the town: their own children. These young children, ranging between the ages of nine and eleven, are suddenly the unlikely focus of the nation. What could have poisoned them at such a young age, and what lessons can we learn from their suffering? More at eleven."

"All right, Allen, don't even tell me that had too much prose for the network. That's as cut and dried as I can make it without sounding like a robot." Dana rescued the handkerchief from its hiding place in her cleavage and dabbed at her eyes, fending off the ever-threatening flood. Since arriving in Merit she'd been walking a delicate balance between antihistamine-addled zombie and allergy afflictions. To help mollify the constant attacks she had taken to spiking her water bottle with liquid allergy medicine. She was starting to think the network was punishing her by demanding only outdoor shots.

"I think we're good with that lead in. Any luck on getting the school to let the kids talk to us for the lunch spot?"

"Not a chance. They've got those kids under lock and key. So far the only one who's getting in there is the Boxer, and I'd *kill* to get a peek at that show." She snuffled again and noticed a man hurrying toward them over Allen's shoulder. He bore little similarity to Merit's other residents, whom she had finally given up interviewing. In fact, in his lime green trousers and lilac silk shirt she pegged him automatically as a crackpot—either an activist or just plain looney—who'd come to Merit to join the media frenzy. Except, there was something terribly familiar about him as he got closer...

"Oh my god! Mr. Gregory?" She exclaimed in shock.

"Yes!" He exclaimed, panting theatrically as he did so. "Yes, I am he and I am just so happy to see you, my lovely Ms. Perki." He pronounced it perfectly. "I have such fabulous news, and I can't think of a more beautiful woman with whom I would rather share it first."

As he reached for her hand and bent over it for a most cavalier kiss she found herself stuttering. "B-but, but, Mr. Gregory! I mean, really, I thought you were—"

"Dead?" He interjected suavely. "Yes, but it was but a trifle. I have far too much passion for this life yet to go gently into that good night."

"Oh yes, dead. That, too. But what I meant was, actually, I thought you were gay. I mean, your mother even said—"

"Gay. Really." Monty snatched his hand away from hers and tried to contain his crumbling dignity by ignoring the soft choking from Allen, who'd nearly dropped the camera in an explosion of silent laughter behind them. He managed to recover himself and smiled again, using his patented Playboy/Lovable Scamp/Casanova smile that always worked for him on beautiful young women. Well, at least a solid thirty-five percent of the time.

"Well then, my enchantress, I'm glad to be able to tell you in person that you've been cruelly mislead by events at my funeral. I have to say, however, I'm terribly disappointed that a fellow manages to literally come back from the dead to save his career and his good name, and the first thing that people focus on is a crude rumor without a mote of truth to it. That blasted colorist only wanted his fifteen minutes of fame, and for that meager quarter-hour he cast a permanent shadow across all of my accomplishments!"

He paused to rest his face dramatically in his hands, all the while peering slyly between his fingers for signs of sympathy. Seeing only bewilderment from Dana, he continued. "Anyway, I didn't come here to burden you with my troubles. I've come here to share with you my triumph! I've only been here since last night and I, Montana Gregory, have already secured the first ever post-mortem acting engagement!"

"Dana!" Allen hissed at her while gesturing wildly at the camera. He had quite obviously salvaged his wits far more quickly than she had, and his instincts were already screaming "newsworthy" at full alert.

"Oh! What am I thinking? Mr. Gregory, would you mind if we taped an interview with you for the eleven o'clock slot?" She had already begun powdering her nose again and had stuck the microphone awkwardly under her arm.

"Of *me*? Why, I'd be honored!" Monty barely even bothered to cover the irony in his voice. A dead celebrity approaches the reporter most starved for a decent story and it takes this much prompting to get her to do an interview? No wonder television gets blamed for ruining attention spans.

"Great! Okay, before we get started, can you give me an idea of what we're talking about here? Is it a movie or TV show?" She gestured to Allen to hurry up with the camera.

"Actually, this marks a triumphant return to the stage for me. I have not performed live in some time, and I do believe this may mark a strategic turning point in my career."

"Um, just to clarify, can we really call it a 'live' performance? I mean, given the whole death thing and all."

"I don't believe I should have to quibble over terms," Monty said, petulant. "Doesn't being murdered give an artist a certain prerogative?"

"Speaking of," she suddenly looked hungry, "do you know who did it? You could solve the whole case and I could help you break it!"

"If I could have, that would have been my first move, I assure you. Unfortunately, the event has been wickedly stripped from my memory. The last thing I remember was dancing in my favorite club absolutely surrounded by gorgeous women who were fighting over the right to dance with me and buy me drinks. If I hadn't known any better I'd have thought I was already in heaven. The next thing I knew, I was hovering over my own dead body."

"Mr. Gregory, it sounds to me like you were drugged."

"Please, my dear, call me Monty. As for the drugging, you should know more than I do. I've tried to avoid the reports of my death since all of them seem to be focused on that blasted colorist. Haven't the police said anything yet to that effect?"

"Not yet. Right now they're sitting on everything they have. The rumor is, due to the compromising position you were in when you were found, that a lover might have been involved...." She left the suggestion hanging.

"Really?" Monty cleared his throat loudly and his voice cracked just a hair. "I can't imagine what that would be. Shall we get back to the interview about my triumphant return now? I doubt the public would want to dwell on the dark and depressing."

Dana's eyes crossed. Then he really didn't know his public. "Of course, Monty. Allen?" She looked to her cameraman, who nodded that he was now rolling.

"I'm here with the recently deceased—yes you heard me correctly, *deceased*—actor Montana 'Monty' Gregory, who has just informed me that even death cannot tarnish his shining star. Mr. Gregory, please tell us more about your plans for continuing your career after your vicious murder. Are you turning your sights now to Broadway?"

"Not yet, Dana. However, that may be next for me. First, I'm going to start by giving back to a community where my peaceful voice is most needed. I'll be performing right here in Merit!"

"From the big screens of Jostlem to small town local theater, what a change! You must truly be a generous soul to offer your talents to Merit at a time such as this."

Or he just knew how to read the winds of public interest and knew where to stage a career revival.

"I do what I can, as is the responsibility of every actor, to lift up the communities that support them. In this case I'm even joining the circus! I have been booked for the world's first post-mortem engagement, and in this ground breaking event I'll be joined by the very children of Merit who have been the cause of all of this ruckus."

"Whoa, wait, CUT!" Dana nearly dropped the microphone. "Do you mean to tell me that you've actually gotten to talk to these kids? I've been trying all day to get at them!" She had blown her only chance last night when they were right in front of her.

"Well, no, not exactly. We'll be co-starring together in a dramatic retelling of their story on the main stage, but we haven't been introduced yet. The circus owner, Sir Cyrus, is the miracle worker who made it all happen."

"A circus show. About racism? Surely this is all some big joke. How on earth did he get the parents to agree to this?"

"Oh, that part was easy. He said they signed..."

• • •

"Permission slips, Cyrus? How did you get them to do that?" Goliath read over the papers in his hands. They appeared legitimate, but he had still known his boss to gloss over the occasional nefarious detail hidden beneath impressively complex legal jargon.

"Yes, yes, and what's best is they are performing practically for free! The only thing I am paying for is the meager cost of the costumes, and I've already set our best seamstresses to the task. You should have been there, Goliath. It was my masterpiece! I have actually managed to convince these parents that it is only through art that their poor misguided children can work together to overcome their malicious prejudices and return to the proper path of the straight and narrow. And just wait until you see the drivel of a script I presented to them for it. I wrote it out last night in a frenzy when the idea came to me, but I never dared to dream that they would buy it! You just have to love these small towns, Goliath. There is indeed money to be made here, my boy. Money to be made indeed."

Goliath recognized the glint in Cyrus's eye. "Boss, are you sure this is completely legal? Is there something in here that I'm not seeing?"

"What?" Cyrus drifted back from his reverie. "Well, they may not have noticed that the permission slips and contracts bind the kids to a minimum of thirty shows, whether those shows are here in Merit or whether we move on to Jostlem, where we can easily double the price. Of course, defaulting on that part would result in a fee, but only a nominal one so that I can make up for my potential losses, of course."

"Good grief! These are just kids, Cyrus! You can't go dragging them about the country and exploiting their problems just to make a quick buck. It's immoral."

Cyrus was irritated at the first break in his mood. He paused for dramatic effect and lit the short remainder of his cigar and chewed on the end reflectively before he responded. "Goliath, my friend, let me see if I get this straight. You object on moral grounds to my objectification of these flaws, quirks, and otherwise abnormal problems in order to make money?"

"Yes, sir, I do."

"Well then. I'm glad you were able to get that off your chest. In fact, you're probably right." He stood, poking his cigar hand into Goliath's broad chest. "But it's a good thing the rest of the world doesn't share your moral compunctions, otherwise the entire freak show industry would cease to exist and you and I would both be out of a job!" He started to put his cigar back in his mouth before realizing he had mashed the soggy end of it against Goliath in his anger.

"Now," he continued more calmly, "would you like to hear what the show is going to be?"

Goliath sighed. Some days it just didn't pay to be a gentle giant. "Sure, Boss. Tell me all about it."

"Ha! I'm glad you asked!" Cyrus was already returning to the excited frenzy in which Goliath had found him. "It's an epic piece set in Roman times! The children are gladiators, fighting each other for different lords, though they know not why." Cyrus leapt onto the bench in an icon-clashing swashbuckling position. "Then suddenly a monster is among them! A monster none of them has ever seen and could never defeat alone. Now they must work together and put aside their differences to slay this unknown beast. And what do you think that beast represents, Goliath? I'll tell you. Racism!"

"Wow, I don't know what to say. That sounds really...deep. I suppose I'm the beast they fight? God knows you can't put kids in a ring with real beasts, no matter what their parents signed."

"Oh, don't be such a sour grape. Originally, yes, I had planned for you to be the beast the children faced. Who would have been more obvious, of course? But then, another amazing stroke of luck happened as I was on my way back here from the meeting with the parents and the principal. You and I both know this town is already starting to fill up with celebrities and newshounds, but somehow the fates managed to put none other than Monty Gregory right in my path!"

Goliath was thoughtful. "You know I don't follow celebrity news at all, but it seems like I heard recently that he—"

"Yes, yes, he *died*! Don't you see how that makes it even better? He's the undead beast that the children must fight...that adds to the symbolism! Now he represents an *eternal* symbol of racism, as an ancient evil that must be overcome!"

"He died? I was going to say that I thought I'd heard he was gay."

"What?" Cyrus stamped the miserable remains of his cigar into the ground. "Well, not in *my* circus he's not. It's a family show, after all. I may have to write that into his contract."

"Sir, I really don't think you can do that."

"Goliath, haven't you noticed that I specialize in doing things that I can't do?"

• • •

Somewhere, Bertie knew, was a police station that wasn't filled with the sound of a dog noisily licking its private parts. Assuming, that was, that dogs had anything which could be remotely considered private. It wasn't that Bertie didn't love his job; quite the contrary. But the less than appetizing sound of hygiene slurping away at his feet only made him wish he could hurry Stanley off the phone so he could give him the news and put his ear plugs back in.

"No, dear," Stanley was saying. In fact, he'd said nothing but variations on "no, dear" and "yes, dear" for the majority of the phone call. Bertie could hear the telltale tones of a Stanley not paying one bit of attention. The past two days had worn Stanley down considerably, and it was showing on his boss's face. He wouldn't have said that Merit's young sheriff was usually a chipper and sunny fellow, but he was at least amiably aloof. Now he simply looked miserable and haggard, and Bertie had a good feeling that there was more hag in his haggard today for a reason.

"No, dear, I'm sure I don't know where Mrs. Gordon could have gotten that idea. She must have been watching those corny daytime TV dramas again." Suddenly Stanley had a look of inspiration and leaned away from the desk, rapping his foot three times against the wood. "Oh goodness, I have to go. It sounds like there's another reporter at the door." He winced then as if in pain. "No, no, I'm sure it's a different reporter, a male one. Yes! I can see him out the window, dear. It's a big, fat, balding male reporter, and I'd better go talk to him since Bertie isn't here right now."

Bertie looked up at his boss with an eyebrow raised and was met by a look of pleading helplessness to stay quiet.

"Yes, dear, I'll call you back as soon as I'm finished. You, too. What? No, I'm not afraid to say it, I'm just at work and... Okay. Wuv oo, too, Boo-boo." Stanley hung up the phone in defeat.

After giving Stanley a few seconds to collect his trampled dignity, Bertie ventured, "Isabelle got some fool idea about what went on last night during that dinner...um, interview?"

"No, not just Isabelle. The whole fool town has some fool idea, and I'm a fool for even letting it happen. Mrs. Gordon is the third person to call her this morning, and each time someone calls her about it I have to go through the whole thing with her all over again. I can tell people must be talking about it everywhere, too. The details are getting thicker. This time I was apparently looking at Ms. Perki with 'smoldering eyes of passion.' Bertie, my eyes have *never* smoldered, even at my wife. Why would I smolder my eyes at a total stranger? I'm not sure I even know how to smolder my eyes," he finished pathetically.

At this point Cud decided to help ameliorate his master's mood by hopping into his lap and licking his face excitedly. Bertie fought a rising gag in his throat and decided kindly to not point out to Stanley Cud's extremely recent activity with that tongue. He forced himself to look away from Cud's show of affection.

"Somehow I fully believe that. Still, it could be worse."

"Really? How? Aliens landing in the park and demanding all of our paperclips or they blow up the earth?"

"Uh, no." Bertie was caught off guard by the uncharacteristic sarcasm from his boss. "We could be police in Jostlem. I just read in the news where one of them disappeared this week without a trace. They suspect he might have been killed."

"Wow. Okay, so you were right. I may have an entire loony town obsessing over my lack of a sex life and non-existent affairs while the rest of the world calls us backwards racists, but I'm not at the bottom of the river somewhere. Yet, that still fails to comfort me somehow."

"Oh, cheer up! At least everyone will forget about this and start talking about something else as soon as something more interesting happens around here." Sensing a good way to break bad news, he continued as though a thought had only just occurred to him. "Hey! I know just the thing that will take their dirty minds off you right away. The circus opens up tonight and that's probably all people will want to talk about for days now."

Stanley looked only half-hopeful. "I forgot about the circus. Still, I doubt that's going to be big enough to distract them. Don't forget that it took a cow being struck by lightning to make people forget about Mother Hinkle's son taking off to Jostlem with the mayor's wife."

"What about a celebrity? I just found out that some big movie star has agreed to do a show with the circus right here tonight and all weekend!"

"Are you kidding? Bertie, that's perfect! This is better than I could have hoped. It will make these people completely forget about that dinner AND the kids! There's nothing they love around here better than a famous person. Bring a movie star to Merit and the whole world will forget all about our supposed 'gang problem.'" He leaned back and scratched Cud, who promptly wriggled over in his lap for a belly rub.

"Ahh, well, you see..." Bertie nervously fidgeted with his ever-escaping shirt tails. "I'm sure it'll fix that first part, the part about you having dinner with the pretty reporter. Folks'll forget about that one for sure. I think the second part, about the kids, I mean, will be a problem."

"Oh God, just tell me. It's not like this day can get any worse. What is it?"

Bertie slid the flyer that he'd been crumpling and uncrumpling over to Stanley, who uncurled it with the delicacy of a nuclear technician with a particularly tricky bomb. Bertie watched Stanley's reaction as he scanned the hastily sketched pictures of the Coliseum and the tiny gladiators fighting a giant monster with sharp fangs.

"You see, the actor is only part of it. The kids are actually the stars."

• • •

Completely unbeknownst to Stanley, at the very same moment he was banging his fist against his desk in frustration, he just happened to be in perfect beat with the pounding coming from his house two blocks away. His kitchen floor was being battered mercilessly under the relentless pacing of two very sharp heels, and the room was filled with the clacking of angry designer shoes venting the rage of their owner. The only thing that could be heard over it was the occasional muttering of various acrimonies such as "Lousy Rat" and "Rotten Jerk." A larger than normal number of "How Dare He's" had been thrown into the mix as well.

Isabelle was in what Stanley, and most of the town, would have referred to as a "mood." That these moods occurred often was plainly evident by the worn path around the kitchen floor where she confined her pacing. She chose this particular path because she felt the acoustics in the room more properly matched her mood. To accurately render an assessment of her current level of anger would require a bit of math. On an average day with average irritations, Isabelle traced this pacing path around eleven times. Today she had already covered her route one-hundred-forty-three times, which meant that she was roughly twelve-hundred percent angrier than usual and still gaining.

Another easy way for those who knew her to tell what sort of mood Isabelle was in was by the size of her hairstyle. Fortunately for Stanley, he'd left the house before she fixed her hair that morning, otherwise he'd have known she was rapidly approaching supernova.

Much to the relief of the kitchen floor, a knock at the door took Isabelle's attention away from her pacing as she raced to answer hoping for a wayward salesman to make suffer. She opened the door and glared at the newcomer.

The newcomer in question, already a very slight man, became even slighter as he shrank into himself away from her Look. He also quickly learned that apologies for his intrusion worked about as well as a cocktail umbrella in a hurricane.

"I'm awful sorry to bother you, Mrs. Grace, and I wouldn't if it weren't important."

"What is it, Charlie?" She asked with the tone of someone who hoped they wouldn't be answered. Charlie Fountain was one of the poor people who worked for her father in a roundabout way.

Currently, Charlie was the caretaker of the old Youngblood family mine just outside of town. The mine had been closed for years since the rubber plant had proven more profitable, but it was still an important family asset and Charlie was responsible for keeping it accessible and keeping his eye out for troublemakers. Being the former foreman of this particular mine, he took his job to heart and had expanded the mine quite a bit over the years with just the help of his two sons.

"Well, ma'am, I needed to let your husband know that we'd be dynamitin' again around lunch time, and since we got into all that trouble last time we blew stuff up and scared everybody so much, I figured I'd better run over here first and let him know. Not that anyone goes around there much anyway."

"Charlie, my husband is in his office right now. I just spoke with him. Why don't you just run your little legs right up there and tell him yourself?"

"I would, ma'am, but there's all those reporters around there trying to talk to everybody who passes by, so I thought it'd be best if I just came to you instead. I don't want to end up on some news show somewhere."

"Did you see these reporters? Was there a pretty one there with brown hair? Well, not really pretty, she's too skinny to be pretty. And her hair is positively hideous. But did you see her? Tell me!"

Charlie's eyes widened and he took a few cautious steps backwards and answered as carefully as he could. "No ma'am, I didn't see anyone like that. Well, I best be back to the mine now. Thanks!" He turned and ran away, wishing he'd faced the reporters instead after all. Especially if there was a pretty one there that he'd missed.

Isabelle closed the door behind him and froze before she'd even taken her hand off the knob.

"That's it!" She exclaimed happily as she jerked the door back open. "Charlie, you may have just earned a raise," she said. This may have surprised the little man scampering away had he lingered long enough to hear it.

• • •

Enjoying the lovely spring morning just outside of the sheriff's office, Cud was busily chasing his tail between chasing butterflies. He'd had quite a full morning already; he'd bathed himself, cheered up his master, eaten something he'd found in the trash can (which, incidentally, had earned him his current exile in the yard), sniffed the ankles of a few reporters, been kicked by a few of those same reporters, and had scared two dirty old cats away from the bushes under Stanley's window. He was just beginning to think of taking a nap in the sunshine for a while when a familiar and scary scent caught his attention. *She* was approaching and it was too late to run away. She'd already seen him, so he tucked his tail between his legs and hung his head like he'd been scolded already. When she passed him by without stopping to inflict him with some torturous new glittery accessory, he celebrated by eating the remainder of what he'd scared the cats away from and left hidden in the bushes.

"Oh, Stanley dear, where are you?" Isabelle called out in a singsong voice. She counted the reporters hanging about outside and smugly noticed that the only female present was the old shrew from the Jostlem Times's self-help column. Satisfied with that, she marched into the office with a bright smile on her face.

Stanley had just stepped out of the restroom and almost bumped into that bright smiling face and sizeable hairdo, and managed to stifle a scream. Well, most of a scream. The bit that escaped was enough to catch the attention of one of the reporters, who had to shoo away a certain smelly dog to get behind the bushes next to Stanley's open window where he could eavesdrop.

"Oh Stanley, I'm so glad you're still here. Oh, and there's Bertie, too. Did you just get back, Bertie?" Isabelle was being sweet *and* charming. Both Stanley and Bertie were suddenly afraid to speak. Bertie managed to nod before hurrying back to a study of the newspaper he'd read once already that morning.

"Well, Stanley, I've got some news for you. Old Charlie from the mine came by and needs your help. He said there are kids hiding in the mine looking for gold and he needs you to meet him down there and help ferret them out. Here..." She reached into her large purse and pushed a flashlight into his hands. "I brought this for you from the house. You'd better hurry! He's on his way there right now."

Still slightly dazed, Stanley took the flashlight. "Looking for gold? Don't they know it's a coal mine?"

"Oh, you know kids." She laughed nervously. "All mines are gold or diamond mines to them. Now go, get a move on. Those kids might need help if they're down there all alone."

Bertie finally found his voice. "I'll go with you. I used to play down there as a kid so I probably know the mines pretty well."

"No!" Isabelle interjected with an edge of panic. "I mean, I think somebody should stay here to fend off the reporters, and that mine has gotten a lot bigger than it was since you were a child, Bertie. Need I point out how *very* long ago it was that you were a child?" She added with a peevish mind-your-own-business tone. "Besides," she continued sweetly, leading Stanley to the door by his arm, "I think this could be just what you need to take your mind off things. Just think. Go find those little children in the mine and the town will forget all about that little dinner date of yours last night."

"It was an interview! I was just doing my job! I learned some things from her, too, you know."

"I'm sure you did, you weasel," she muttered bitterly beneath her breath. Audibly, she called behind him, "Just go on in when you get there if you don't see him. He already had a good head start on you."

Stanley trudged out the door with a flashlight in hand, belatedly wondering why there were kids in the mine in the middle of a school day. Lost in thought, he missed the sounds of a man struggling to shake off the dog who was extremely interested in the remains of the carcass that were still sticking to his shoe from standing in it underneath the window.

"Smith!" The reporter called quietly but urgently to his camera man, who'd been dozing on a bench in the sun. "Smith!"

He finally shuffled his sticky way over to the man and shook him rudely awake. "Quick! Find out where an abandoned mine around here is and get ready to head to it. I've got a scoop that I don't want anyone else to get to first. It sounds like those kids have sneaked off from school and are lost in that mine, and the sheriff is on his way to save them. Get busy. I've got to go change shoes first."

• • •

"Dana!" Allen rounded the corner to the pharmacy with one arm flailing to keep him balanced and the other arm struggling to hold the bulky camera equipment. Dana was just stepping out of the small drug store reading the directions for her latest allergy trial when she saw him barreling toward her.

"What's wrong? What happened?" She braced for impact as he skidded to a stop inches in front of her.

"We've got a scoop," he panted. "Gotta hurry, to a mine some-where. Gotta find it first!"

"Allen, slow down and breathe! What are you talking about?"

"Aagghh! Just go back and ask where," he gulped for air, "the mine is! I'll tell you in a sec." He dropped down on his haunches in the middle of the sidewalk to rest while a confused Dana ran in to get directions to a local mine from the pharmacist.

"All right." She returned and helped him to his feet as they jogged together toward the van. "It's just about five miles north of here. Will you tell me what's going on now?"

"Apparently the kids sneaked out of school and are hiding out in the mine! I'm not clear on the details, but I think they're in trouble, maybe even hurt. At any rate, the sheriff is riding to the rescue at this moment, and we have to get there before anyone else does!"

"Oh my god! How did you find out about this?"

"That camera hack Smith from WPEW was asking for directions and I promised him I'd tell him where it was if he told me the scoop."

"But you didn't know where it was, did you?"

Allen smiled. "Of course not. Remember that old closed gas station we passed on the way into town about fifteen miles before we got here? I told him it was down the dirt road that veered off beside it. It seemed as plausible as anything else. I guess he believed me because he took off like a shot to get his guy and head out there before I could find you. He's going to be so mad when they get back!"

Dana practically squealed with delight as Allen sped the news van closer to the mine. "Allen, I'm sure I don't tell you this enough, but you're the best!"

"Yeah? Just try to remember that when you're collecting your Pulitzer Prize money this time next year." He almost hesitated before moving onto his next thought. "Er, there's a bit more, though."

"To the story?"

"No, more to your sheriff."

"Hold it," she snapped. "He's not *my* sheriff. But tell me what you mean by 'more.'"

"Well, it turns out that his father was a sheriff in Jostlem before the department got so big." This hadn't been very long ago, either. Jostlem had experienced growth in spurts, and the spurt that pushed it to its current limits had been more of a growth-eruption than a spurt.

"That's interesting, but I get the impression there's more here. Don't drag this out for dramatic effect. You know I hate that kind of thing." She sighed. Growing up with a name mistakenly pronounced "perky" tended to make a person very serious.

"All right, all right. Think back about twenty-two years to the last person who went by the name Sheriff Grace. Ring any bells?"

"You're doing it again!"

"Fine! You have no imagination. *Anyway*, Sheriff Grace Senior was the sheriff who was murdered during an investigation into the drug cartel that had moved in from Byaz that year. The Byazis were vicious. Do you remember any of this?"

"Kind of. I was just a kid then, and I guess he would have been just a kid, too."

"He was. His mother moved him here to be safe and they lived with his grandparents until they died. She died when he was only twenty, as well. He really doesn't have anyone left."

"Except his wife." She realized she sounded almost bitter and hated herself for it.

"Funny you should mention that. It actually brings me kind of to my next point."

"There's *more*?"

"You better believe it. You said yourself that Stanley seemed unnaturally concerned that his wife might hear something about your...ahem...*interview* last night—"

"Don't start."

"I'm not. Complete slip of the tongue, I'm sure. Pun intended. Well, it turns out that he had reason to be. First, he was right about this town being a gossip haven. Actually, that's not the word for it. 'Haven' sounds like a place where something comes to rest. This is more of a gossip factory, a breeding ground, whatever. Rumors here walk, talk, grow up, and have families and make more little rumors. Here are just a few of them that I've picked up today. You see, there have been these 'accidents'..."

Merit did thrive on rumor, as has been mentioned, but one of its favorite high-calorie treats was the subject of Isabelle and Stanley. They had achieved a veritable personality cult status among the most romantic gossips, their day-to-day troubles culminating in the tabloid version of an epic saga. Allen delivered to her the abridged version of some of the town's favorite episodes in the Grace Affair, as it had come to be called.

It was quite widely known to everyone in the town that Isabelle was trying to kill Stanley. Oh, of course it was always an "accident" of some sort, but no matter what purely innocuous seeming injury Stanley appeared with, it had always turned out that she was found at the root of the matter, brimming with innocence and virtue under her tall hairdo and painted smile. It was the same manner in which a mosquito might have appeared had you caught him drinking a cocktail of your blood.

Most of the town's favorite anecdotes began, "There was this one time when she was *really* mad, and I do mean really mad..." and ended with some variation of Stanley being treated for some mild abrasion or other injury. The most frequent method of attack usually involved her seafood surprise, the surprise being that some sneaky little mollusk had found its way into her chicken casserole, despite Stanley's deadly allergic reaction to shellfish. The doctor had taken to keeping a syringe of epinephrine handy in case Stanley fell into anaphylactic shock. The most recent inclusion, and one granted numerous style points by even the harshest critics of Merit, was her relocation of her prized cutlery collection to the extremely wobbly top shelf of the coat closet where Stanley kept his uniforms. This was one that had resulted in thirteen stitches for Stanley, and would have been more had he not been wearing a bandage around his head already for the concussion he had received when he discovered the bottom of the tub had been polished with vegetable oil because she claimed it made it shiny and pretty.

"But that's all just rumor, right?" Dana finally asked when Allen had finished his story. She had taken on a glazed look.

"Here's the thing about rumor. The ones you weed out are the ones that are completely different, and I heard plenty of those, too. But I also heard these same stories from completely different people. Those tend to be the ones with a grain of truth to them."

"And he just lets it happen? *They* just let it happen?"

"That's the funny part. They say it's none of their business."

She somehow didn't feel inclined to laugh.

• • •

If you were the sheriff in a small town where everyone came to you to solve all of their problems, it would be easy to sometimes find yourself feeling sublimely powerful and in a position to save the world, or at least your small corner of it. Then there were the other times, like now, where you might find yourself standing doubtfully in front of a mine entrance with nothing but a flashlight and a small multi-breed stray dog, as did one Sheriff Stanley Grace.

This particular mine wasn't at all what one might imagine of a mine that had been shut down for two decades. There were no rotted boards barring entrance; no ominously faded signs saying Keep Out; no rusted and abandoned tools. The sign at this entrance read Youngblood Mines, with a smaller sign underneath that read "Tours Arranged, $5. See Charlie at the foot of the hill" with an arrow, painted on as an afterthought, pointing toward his house below the hill. The sign had even just been repainted in bright blue and red. Far from the abandoned mine of ghost stories, this one could even be described as charming, especially with the row of gerbera daisies planted at both sides of the entrance.

"Charlie?" Stanley called into the mouth of the mine a couple of times and waited for a response that didn't come. There was no sign of him except for a line that fed into the mouth of the mine leading from somewhere else in the woods. Probably some sort of tether so you don't get lost in the mine, Stanley decided.

He looked down at Cud who'd followed him all the way from the office. "You'd probably better stay here in the car. I don't think you want to get lost in there, boy." Cud cocked his head at him, and then started walking toward the mine before looking backward toward his master and sitting back down closer to the mine's entrance. Stanley suddenly had the feeling that dogs only pretended they didn't understand you when you gave them a command they didn't want to follow. Testing the flashlight in the palm of his hand, he moved into the darkness ahead. Cud followed, but only after grabbing a quick mouthful of the lovely daisies on the way.

• • •

Charlie Fountain was about to do what he did best. He and his sons had spent a beautiful sunny morning blissfully in the dark passages of the Youngblood mine placing dynamite in carefully selected locations and double checking the integrity of the bracing they had erected throughout the mine. The sign on the front might say that it belonged to Rupert Youngblood, but in his heart this mine belonged to Charlie, and he was proud of every cultivated inch of it. He'd spent his entire adult life working this mine, as had both of his sons. They knew it so well that the brothers' favorite game was for one of them to hide an item in the mine in a tunnel and send the other in after it without even a flashlight. It was rare that one would turn up empty handed.

Still, even with years of familiarity, the mine wasn't without dangers. In fact, the area they were blasting today was subject to a cave-in that would have resulted in a very flat version of Charlie had he not just wandered out in search of his mallet moments before. The mine could be a very dangerous place when you were least expecting it. This was why the care Charlie and his boys took on blasting days approached near religious zeal. They ran the lines to the charges from over a quarter mile away from the cave entrance, and Charlie was especially proud of himself today for remembering to let Stanley know so no unfortunate soul could get hurt, whether they were trespassing or not.

"All right, my boys. It's time. Are we ready?"

Both sons nodded in unison, and Charlie continued with what had become a deeply meaningful tradition to the Fountain family.

"Delbert, have the charges been placed and secured?"

"Yes, sir," Delbert answered with a heavy formality. "The charges have been placed and they are secure."

"Baxter, have the lines been run, long and true?"

"Yes, sir, the lines have been run and they are long and true."

"My sons, what we are about to do must never be taken lightly. With our capable and respectful hands we have placed dangerous tools into the mouth of darkness, deep in the belly of the beast. Are you prepared for what comes next?"

"Yes, sir, we are ready." The boys answered in unison.

"Well then. Fire in the hole!" Charlie yelled at the top of his lungs as he dropped with all his limited weight onto the handle to ignite the charges in the mine.

"Thar she blows!" shouted Delbert, and they waited. And waited.

"Uh, guys?" Baxter started after a few moments. "Nothing happened."

Charlie flashed his eldest son a brief scowl until something else caught his attention. "Did you just hear someone sneeze?"

• • •

"I guess there's a bright side here. We're definitely first on the scene." Allen kicked a loose stone into the mine's vacant opening while Dana looked frantically around for any signs of life or, more importantly, a story. She put her hand on the hood of the sheriff's car. It was still warm.

"Hellooo-oooo! Is anyone out here? Oh, good grief! If there's a story to be had," she turned toward the mouth of the mine, "it's happening in there right now. We should go in and find it. How strong is the spotlight on that camera?"

"In there? That dark and scary place where people might be trying to rescue other people who didn't know their way around and might be lying under rubble in a deep hole, never to be seen or heard from again? I think maybe 'No' would be an appropriate answer here."

"Oh, don't be so dramatic." Dana sneezed and turned her irritated gaze toward a recently mauled bed of daisies. She took a swig from her antihistamine-laced water jug and cast her gaze around for clues. "What's that?" Dana pointed toward a length of wire on the ground trailing from the mine's entrance.

"Good question. Maybe it's like a lead line that you follow and don't get lost." He followed the line from the entrance until it ran underneath the tire of the news van. He gave it a sharp tug to try to pull it free and it snapped loose in his hand, nearly whipping him across the face.

Dana couldn't help but laugh at him as he danced away from it. "Way to go, slick. If it was a lead line it won't do them much good now. Let's tie it off to something so it won't get lost."

While Allen tied the line off to the sign Dana wandered further along the trail following the end of the wire beyond the van leading into the woods. If she hadn't been sneezing every few steps she would have been able to notice how lovely the dogwoods and redbud trees were rather than seeing them as vicious purveyors of pollen.

"Blast this town, blast this story, blast these flowers, blast it all! Blast, Blast, Blast!" Her muttering frustrations mounted in one big yell as she used her final tissue with no pharmacy in sight.

"Hey! Did it blast? Did you hear it? You shouldn't be here!"

Startled, Dana looked up to see an older man with two men in their early twenties running down the trail toward her. She started to back up in fright, but recovered her journalistic nerves.

"What do you mean I shouldn't be here? Who are you? Are you trying to hide something from the press?"

"Me? I'm the caretaker!" Charlie suddenly stopped in his tracks and looked stricken. "Oh no, are you one of those reporters what been hangin' about?" Just then he noticed what his two sons had already noticed judging by their sudden chest puffing and preening. This reporter was a very pretty brunette. He wondered if this was the one that Mrs. Grace had seemed so worried about and secretly felt a bit of pride for Stanley.

"Yes I am 'one of those reporters.' I'm the reporter who broke this story, in fact. My name is Dana Perki and I have every right to be here. The whole world has a right to know if those children are safe or if they have fallen victim to the negligence of a slipshod caretaker." She felt herself slipping into full investigative journalist mode.

"What children? And just who you callin' slipshod?"

"The children in the mine, of course! Sheriff Grace himself came down here to rescue them. I assumed he was in the mine already."

"In the mine! Oh no!" All three of the Fountain men began to scramble under Charlie's orders. "Boys, get the lights and get ropes just in case! We have to get them out of there before it blows!"

Dana tried to run after the men and found she could only keep up with Charlie. "What's going to blow? Is there a bomb in there?"

"You might say that. We wired the mine up this morning to do some blastin' around a new seam. See that wire?" He pointed to the wire Dana had followed into the woods. "That goes to the dynamite in the mine. We just dropped the lever so it shoulda blown already. I don't know why it didn't go off."

"Oh." Dana looked sheepishly toward the broken wire they'd tied off. "In that case, I have good news."

• • •

Despite the charm of the entrance, the staleness of the cave was attacking Stanley's nostrils and the dankness was downright oppressive. Even Cud seemed to be hovering closer than usual to his master's legs as they walked together, while Stanley continued to call for Charlie. The feeble light of the flashlight swung ahead of them. As it flickered dimly he wished he'd checked the batteries before he left the station.

Stanley hadn't realized just how much work the Fountains had done here over the years. He had sneaked in here many times as a child, as had all the Merit children as a rite of passage, but back then the mine hadn't seemed quite so endless. He'd been moving from room to room now for at least twenty minutes without really getting a grasp of the layout. Some of the rooms he entered had only one other connecting them, some had two or three branching off, and some came to dead ends. None of them were quite the same, though, and sometimes when he thought he was doubling back he found himself in rooms he hadn't seen before.

It was time to admit it. Stanley was hopelessly lost.

Here and there in the cave he encountered signs of people, usually in the form of some kind of trash or graffiti. There were beer cans and food wrappers scattered loosely in all of the rooms he'd seen so far, but the further he'd gone he noticed fewer and fewer of them. Stanley assumed he was in an older part of the mine now because the only trash he was seeing was nearly rotted, rusted, or otherwise choked with mud. If he were on the track of a kids' hideout, then he would have expected candy wrappers, soda cans, or something else to indicate the presence of children, but there was nothing to be seen. He was just in the process of calling out again when his light fell on a very peculiar patch of graffiti leading into the next room. He scanned his flashlight across it and found himself feeling a little frightened, the mine becoming a much darker and lonely place.

Across the room from him was what looked to be a campsite that was thankfully empty for the moment. A cot with a blanket and pillows, a battery powered lantern, and a small cooler were tucked neatly out of the way. Stanley cast his eyes back up to the wall and decided quickly that this did not belong to one of the Fountains.

Covering the wall from top to bottom, written sideways and crossways, filling the wall all the way around the room, was fresh graffiti in red and blue paint. The same phrase was written over and over again.

• • •

After having first sent his sons to ensure that the explosives were not going to detonate, Charlie agreed to let Dana and Allen join them on the search for Stanley and the missing children. Allen kept the camera rolling and Dana continued an impromptu interview going with Charlie between intermittent calls for Stanley.

"So you were really completely unaware that there were any children down in the mines when you set these explosives?"

"Of course! I've been working this mine my entire life and I never once had an accident, Ms. Perky." Dana smothered the impulse to correct him. "We always check the place the day we blast and you can mark my words, weren't no kids in here when we set those charges!"

"Then if you didn't call Sheriff Grace to come help, how did he know there were children lost down here in this labyrinth?"

"It's no labby...laba...maze down here if you know it like we do. One of the parent's musta called him about it. Times past, if a couple of youngsters ran off this was always the first place they checked. If there's kids down here, and I'm not saying there is, we'll find them out and get them a scolding like you never seen!"

Just at that moment they heard a distant voice call Charlie's name.

"Stanley!" Dana cried out, feeling thrilled despite herself. She tried to remind herself that he had just insulted her the night before, but a story was a story. "Stanley! Where are you?"

A muffled yell and thud came back in reply, followed by running footsteps. Angry barking began echoing through the mine.

"It was this way, c'mon!" Baxter and Delbert both took off at a dead run toward the barking, leaving the other three trailing behind. Luckily for Dana and Allen, Charlie seemed to know the right direction to run as well.

It sounded like someone had been hurt. Hopefully not poor Stanley. "Oh god, it must be the antihistamines," she muttered to herself as they came upon the two Fountain brothers helping a still breathing Stanley to his feet, while a small terrier-ish dog hopped and barked excitedly around their feet.

"He hit me and took off," Stanley was saying. "I'm not sure which way he went." He was still rubbing his head and looking bewildered toward each of the three openings to this particular room.

"Don't you worry, Sheriff Grace, we'll catch him at the entrance. There's still only one way out of this mine and I doubt he can get past all of us." Charlie preened, becoming aware of the camera in Allen's hand once again. "Baxter, you stay with the sheriff and we'll go find those children!"

"Didn't you find them yet? I hoped you had them already." He struggled for a moment to stay on his feet.

"Sheriff, I didn't know about no children until Ms. Perky here told me you came lookin' for 'em. But you can bet we'll find 'em!"

"What do you mean you didn't know? Izzy came to the office to tell me you needed me to get down here right away to help find them."

Charlie looked perplexed. "Mrs. Grace told you that? That's awful funny. I asked her to tell you to make sure nobody came down this way because we was gonna be blastin' some new rooms today. I didn't mention no kids, though."

"Yes, that is…funny. She definitely didn't mention any blasting to me. She just told me to hurry up and get down here."

Suddenly no one in the room could bring themselves to look Stanley in the eye.

"You know, Sheriff," Delbert ventured, "you could've been killed if those charges hadn't messed up like they did."

"The charges were already set?"

"Yes, sir," Charlie took over. "We already hit the switch, but lucky for you the line got cut."

Stanley swallowed hard. "So there are no children lost in the mine that you needed my help to find." It was more a statement than a question.

"No, sir, I'd say it's safe to say there's not."

"Well. I guess she was just confused then." Stanley was met by silence. "She's had a lot on her mind lately, you know," he finished lamely.

"Right." Dana changed the subject deliberately. "I'd say it's safe to say that someone has been down here for a while, though."

While trying to avoid looking at Stanley during the awkwardness, her gaze had wandered toward the walls.

"Wow, Dad! I think we know what happened to all that paint that went missin' now."

"Someone has definitely been living here, and it's got to be whoever hit me, Charlie. Have you ever seen this before?" He gestured to the makeshift campsite.

"No, sir! I'd've kicked this squatter from here to Timbuktu if I'd seen it before."

"This is terrifying!" Dana directed Allen to bring the camera closer to the wall. "Whoever has been living in this abandoned mine must be a very disturbed individual, apparently plagued by some ghost from his past. What could have haunted him so to drive him to the point of hiding in the dark and ruminating obsessively over just one thought?" Dana cleared her voice, looking dramatically at the writing from one end of the room to the other.

"*Why won't he die?*" she read aloud.

• • •

How did they find me already? His blood thrummed in his ears as he tried to run through the pitch black of the mines as silently as he could. He'd been so careful. He hadn't left any trash behind and he'd only ventured out at night. It was impossible that they'd seen him. Yet he had just found a cop standing in his campsite. Without other options, he'd punched the cop and run as quickly as he could in the darkness, feeling along the walls he'd gotten so used to over the past few days. He was lucky enough to find a room to dive into when he heard the footsteps of the rest of the group running toward him.

How did they find me? What did I do wrong?

So carefully he'd sneaked into town last night for supplies just like the other nights. That was when saw the dead man casually enter the bar. He couldn't be there, but he was.

Did he follow me? He must know I'm here. The man sneaked out of the mine and ran away into the woods. He squinted in the harsh daylight. It seemed so long since he'd seen it.

Did he come for me?

Why won't he just die already?

• • •

There were footprints everywhere, leading in all directions and back again in circle upon circle. Charlie and the Fountain boys scattered and ran everywhere trying to find the squatter who'd hit Stanley, but turned up nothing. Now the footprints were a mess of tangled paths leading everywhere. Stanley tried to peer through them and find something unique that yelled "Here I am, I went this way!" through the mess. Even Cud had added to the footprints considerably since he seemed to think it was a game of chase the shoe as the brothers ran back and forth.

He was suddenly feeling very inadequate as a sheriff. Merit didn't have actual crime so he'd never had to look for clues or solve a mystery, and didn't have the slightest idea as to where to start. Before this week he'd simply thought his job was boring; now he was beginning to think it was also pointless if he was going to be useless when something big did finally happen.

He was still walking in circles, looking through the dust and the items they'd hauled out of the mine, when Dana grabbed him by the arm.

"Stanley, stop! This is madness. It's not like he left a nametag behind or anything. This really isn't going to help you. You should probably be sitting down after a blow like that anyway."

"He's out there somewhere. He's out there in my town and I should be doing something about it. This man, whoever he is, has been hiding out here doing God knows what, and I didn't know about it. I should have. I just should have known."

"How could you possibly have known? He didn't leave a trace of himself anywhere."

"That's where you're wrong. I've had little reports all week here and there about things disappearing. Food from the Braden's freezer, Mr. Geyser's fishing boots, a blanket here, milk there; it all adds up to someone stocking up on supplies! But I've been ignoring these tiny thefts because of the insanity everywhere else in the town. I let it slip right by me while I was busy not making any progress whatsoever in making everyone calm down and getting all of the media out of here so things can go back to normal. What else can go wrong that I probably also can't fix?"

"So that's what this funk is about? That you can't make everything go back to normal?" She looked at him incredulously. "Stanley, you really have to step back and think about this. There is nothing you can do to make this story die down yet. You told me yourself that this town hasn't had anything interesting happen to it in years and that they thrive on gossip. This place was practically bursting with pent-up energy, just dying for something like this! Add to that an entire nation full of reporters like me dying to get their break on a story that could be as good as this one and you've practically dropped filet mignon into a piranha tank. Right now, Merit is a media darling and all of the residents are eating up every second of the attention. You can't tell me that every one of them isn't glued to the TV news stations right now and calling all of their friends every time they see each other in the background of some interview. Even your mayor is thrilled about the economic boon caused by this affair which you call 'insanity.' I interviewed him this morning and he told me that the local businesses are killing themselves to stay stocked enough to meet the demand, and even local residents are renting out spare rooms to make more money themselves. Stanley, not even the president himself could stop this. They want it too badly. They *need* it too badly!"

"Is telling me there's nothing I can do supposed to comfort me?" He looked even more vulnerable than before. She found that his sad eyes had a strange effect on her. He was attractive, even if his ears were a little too big and he wore his pants too close to his rib cage.

"I'm sorry. That probably all came out wrong. What I'm really trying to get at is this: You can't stop it, that part is true. In reality, anything you do to try to counter it will probably just fan the flames and make people even more interested. So the best thing you can do is probably ignore it wherever possible and don't get suckered into making any inflammatory comments. Trust me when I say that some of those reporters wouldn't think twice about making you look like a hot-headed redneck on national TV. But here is the good news: This Will Pass. I mean that. People will get so tired of this before long that they'll be sick of hearing the name Merit every time they turn on the TV or read a headline. It will be replaced with something else that people will also only get excited about because it's new. That's why they call it the 'News,' you know? If you're not new anymore you're not News."

"So in the meantime you just want me to ignore the fact that there are people picketing town hall with signs that say Merit

Makes Me Sick, sending letters to my office from all over the country telling me I'm a racist bumpkin, parents pulling their kids out of classes because they're afraid of racial violence, and hardware stores offering specials on replacement windows in case of drive-bys that have never happened? I don't think these kids even knew what racism was until you and the rest of the world came to town and told us we had a gang problem, when what we really had were a bunch of kids who've grown up together having fun. Now they think they can't even be friends because people like you have come in telling them the difference between them is a problem!"

"Don't you dare try and blame this on me! I didn't make this problem for you. You should be grateful that this little pollen-infested town is getting any attention in the first place! Merit? Please! Whoever heard of Merit before this? I know I hadn't, and I'm starting to wish I still never had!"

"Um, guys?" There was an awkward moment as Stanley and Dana both realized they'd had an audience for their latest little argument. Allen was standing nearby, stifling a smile. For a moment he'd seemed much smaller to Stanley, then he'd realized that this was just the first time he'd ever seen him without that hulking camera attached to his shoulder. He noticed that Allen walked a bit lopsided without it.

"What is it, Allen?" Dana made a mental note to punch Allen in the arm later when he smirked at her.

"I just thought you might be interested to know that Charlie and his boys found something up the hill."

"What is it?" Stanley finally felt himself coming to life again. A *lead!*

Allen's smirk turned serious. "I think you should come see."

As they walked up the hill to find the Fountain family, Stanley found himself watching Dana. She wasn't so bad, really. She just didn't understand how things were supposed to be in a small town. Then he realized he'd forgotten that he was still mad at her for... well, for something.

They met the Fountains halfway up the hill. Charlie was standing over something reverently.

"Oh my god. Charlie, is that what I think it is?" Stanley sputtered.

"Yes, sir," Charlie said mournfully. "I believe it is. Says here 'Jostlem Police Department' on the sleeve. There's a badge there, too."

"Is that really a uniform?" Dana was trying to edge closer for a better look.

"Yes," Stanley's brow creased. "And it's covered in blood."

•　•　•

Not too far away from the mine at least someone in Merit was having a good time. If you asked anyone in town, the people of Merit weren't big drinkers. But if you asked them when they were completely alone with no visible windows where anyone they knew could see them and had at least three feet of concrete to avoid eavesdroppers, then they would tell you that yes, they did like to tip a few back from time to time. They would also tell you that the best place to go for a drink or two was either Duncan's or Porter's, which also happened to be the only two bars in town. It was also quite convenient that they were located right next door to each other.

They had a very unique set-up insofar as their entrances went. The primary way in was through a shared entrance around the back that was only accessible by an alley on the far side of the block. The reason for this was not to encourage secretive espionage, as the arrangement might suggest. It was merely a brilliant business maneuver. After years of patchy sales, Duncan and Porter both realized their lack of business was due to the large Baptist church on the corner with office windows that faced the front doors to the bars. The secretary had taken to keeping track of who she saw patronizing these places of ill repute during the day, and published the list on the bulletin board weekly. Creating the hidden rear entrances had since tripled business. Some of their best patrons now were even church elders.

Currently, there were very few people in either bar at this early point in the day, but that didn't stop Monty from making the most of the audience at hand. He'd just made his hopeful way into Porter's from a disappointing round at Duncan's. There were usually only two sorts of bar patrons this early in the afternoon—those with something to celebrate and the utterly depressed. Unfortunately, Duncan's only had the latter sort of customer and Monty was looking for someone to rabble rouse with. His first live, sort of, stage performance was looming near and he was actually nervous. Anxiety over a performance was something he was utterly unfamiliar with...but then again, so was performing post-mortem.

"Another round, Porter! Another round for me and my friend here. What'd you say your name was again?"

"It's Albert. Albert Stiller. Listen, I really don't think I should be havin' another beer, Mr. Monty. My wife'll be right irate if I come home liquor'd up."

"Ha! Like she needs a reason to be irate," said Porter, familiar with the Stiller saga right down to the rolling pins.

"Oh, come now," cajoled Monty, who was desperately trying to have fun. "One beer won't hurt. It's on me! I'm celebrating and one can't celebrate alone. Porter, two more!"

"Comin' right up! And another empty glass with yours like last time."

Monty tried to ignore the last bit. He'd gotten better at trying to drink. He'd managed to take a drink and hold it in his mouth long enough that he was almost sure he could even taste again, but swallowing was still out of the question. Trying that resulted in something that looked like a serious *faux pas* on his pants. Still, some would have suggested that the pastel plaid pants he was wearing were a *faux pas* in themselves, not to mention the magenta button down with the bow tie.

"A toast! To victorious comebacks!" He cried as he lifted the beer Porter had just placed in front of him. He hoisted it to his mouth, gargled and swished, then spit it into the other empty mug at his side. *Not quite the same,* he thought, *but close.*

"Yeah, to Victoria's comeback!" Albert tried to parrot, then for some reason spat the beer on the floor beside him. It was possible he'd done it out of a sense of social conscience, but probable that he'd forgotten to take his chewing tobacco out before drinking again.

The bell dinged, indicating a new patron was coming. In previous years this would have been obvious by the flood of light as the door opened and everyone would have turned to see who had just entered. Now the bell was the sole herald for a new patron as they wound their way through the back alley, through the cellar door where the boilers were always blazing, through one of two doors marked either Duncan's or Porter's, and up the stairs to find their way to the bar, by which time they were very thirsty indeed.

Monty nearly spilled his beer in his spin toward the door when he heard the bell. His anticipation did not go unrewarded.

"Ms. Perki!" Monty leapt from his bar stool and had momentary trouble getting his feet to touch the floor again. "I'm so glad to see you! It would be my pleasure to buy you a drink if you'll help me celebrate with my friend here." He gestured toward Albert at the bar.

"Hey, I remember you! You was that lady asking about the whorehouses t'other day. Say, I hear you got something wrong with your eye. It ain't c'tagious, is it?"

Dana stood thoughtfully for a moment and weighed her options. She, like Monty, had started off at Duncan's but was instantly put off by the man sobbing at the bar. Option number two had started strong but was ending with a belch.

"You know, I think I need a drink *that* badly," she said to herself. "Monty, I'd be honored to join you. What are we celebrating?"

"Someone called Victoria, I think," Albert answered before succumbing to a hiccup with some food matter behind it.

"No, my comeback. My *victorious* comeback," Monty said testily. "I think there was some error in translation. My first show is mere hours away!"

"That's right! So much has happened today that I nearly forgot about it. Hey, isn't it bad luck to toast a show before it's over? It seems like I heard that before from some of my friends in theater."

"Oh my god, *is it*? I've never heard that before. Is that really true?"

Dana laughed. "I think it's just an old wives' tale. You really shouldn't believe everything you hear. It'll make you superstitious."

"Oh, you're absolutely right. Let's see, so far this week I've only died and come back from the grave as a semi-substantial ghost trying to break back into theater. There's nothing there that could possibly make me superstitious, is there?"

She blushed. "I'm sorry. It's just that it's really easy to forget that you're dead when I'm sitting here talking to you. I still don't understand how this is possible."

"It's all a matter of will," he said and sighed. He lifted his beer mug to taste the beer, then spit it into the now filling up mug. "You're actually surrounded by more of us than you know. The others just quit trying to be seen. I just wish it were so easy for me to forget it like you can. If I stop focusing for even a moment I lose touch with reality again. Just like now. I haven't figured out how to drink again yet so I can't forget and try to swallow again otherwise I end up wearing my drink. And if I don't focus on walking I end up floating, and then people run away screaming. Do I really look that scary?"

Avoiding the obvious dilemma with that question, she answered, "Of course not! Not in a scary, haunty, ghosty kind of way, I mean."

"I don't know," piped up Albert. "I was a little scared when you walked in. I always been afraid a' clowns. It's okay now that I know that you ain't a mean clown like some of them others I seen."

Monty glared, while Dana choked on the martini Porter had just served her. "Why would you think I'm a clown, Albert?"

"Ain't it obvious? You been talkin' about a show at the circus and you came in here wearin' your costume already. I ain't that dumb, you know."

"Gee, just when I was beginning to have doubts. Thanks for clearing that up for me."

Monty turned toward Dana with a pleading look. She caved, wiping her mouth with her sleeve. "Okay, I'm only saying this because I just downed that entire martini, but he does have a point, Monty. That outfit is a little, uh, loud, for a town like this, don't you think?"

The bell dinged again. Monty, now feeling more melancholy than celebratory, looked toward the door dourly.

"But it *has* to be loud," he said. "My wardrobe has always been my signature, kind of my gimmick, I suppose. Gary, my agent, said I had to have a way to stand out in the crowd so I wouldn't be forgotten. He was the one who wanted me to pretend to be such a Casanova, too. I think even he knew I wasn't really that good of an actor to begin with." Monty sighed and tried to taste his beer again as he looked to the door. Whoever had entered from the alley must have gone to Duncan's instead.

"Wait, does that mean all the drinking, the womanizing, paternity tests, all of that was his idea?"

Monty nodded glumly.

Dana continued, "Well, what does he think now that you're a ghost? That has to be far better publicity that these dreadful outfits."

He flinched. "Mmm. So that's what they mean by rubbing salt in a wound."

She blushed. "I didn't mean–"

"Yes, you did. And you're right. They are horrible. I guess I just got used to them after a while."

They were interrupted by Albert yelling at Porter. "It's just one more! What can she do 'bout it anyhow? I ain't afraid a' her."

"Well, what does he think you should do now?" They tried to ignore the continued arguing as Albert descended into a one-sided mumbling rant.

"Hell if I know. I tried calling him once I was finally able to pick up the phone, but as soon as I said 'This is Monty' he screamed and hung up the phone. I'm on my own now."

"But you've been all over the news in the last couple of days. Have you tried calling him again? It seems like he'd enjoy the media thrill of having a murdered client who doesn't remember anything about his murder."

"No. I don't think I will, either. Honestly, I always kind of got the feeling that he didn't really like me."

She watched him adjust his argyle bow tie. "I think I can see why you'd say that."

"Not afraid a' her at all," the muttering continued in the background.

"I probably shouldn't have gone along with him in the first place. I just didn't feel like I was getting anywhere on my own before. If you don't make it in this business pretty early in life you won't make it at all."

"Now that," Dana began while taking a deep long drink from her second martini, "is something I can completely understand. My business is the same way. I've been trying to work my way into an anchor position for years now and it doesn't seem like I can ever get out of this human interest crap. You can grow older as an anchor, but, for a woman, you can't begin as an older anchor. It's so unfair. I'd been hoping that this place might give me my break, but it just keeps getting more confusing. I came here to do a story on racism in a small town that become an issue of childhood racism, and now I've interviewed the ghost who's funeral I covered earlier this week, and just filmed a spot for the five o'clock news on the discovery of a Jostlem police uniform in the woods. Stanley may be right. Something strange really is going on here."

"Did you say a Jostlem police uniform?"

"Yes. It was covered in blood, too. They think it may belong to the cop who disappeared earlier this week. It looks like he may have been murdered."

For the first time in a week, Monty felt that strange tugging at his shoulder again. He shrugged it off. "That sounds somehow... familiar. I probably read it in a paper somewhere. Anyway, a murdered cop story sounds like it could be a bigger story for you than the kids."

"It could, but something still just doesn't feel right. I can't put my finger on it yet, though. Besides, nobody here seems interested in it yet. They seem to think of it as a foreign problem despite the fact that the uniform was found right here in Merit. All they seem to be able to focus on is this farcical show with the kids. It's all so strange."

"You know, I don't get it. I've met them now and they seem like awfully nice kids to be wrapped up in something like this. The whole town seems nice, really. A little crazy, maybe, but nice."

"I think you're right. They are nice. I just hope we haven't ruined them." She finished her second martini in a swallow. "Speaking of, I need to be headed over to the circus now, too. Are you—?" She stopped for a moment, listening. "Did you hear that?" She asked Monty, pointing to the empty doorway.

"Hear what?"

"I thought I heard something. I thought I saw a shadow, too, but I guess I'm just letting my imagination get the best of me. Are you coming?"

Monty gargled, spit the last of his drink, and flopped a handful of bills on the bar.

"No time like the present, I suppose."

• • •

The alley behind Duncan's and Porter's was one of the few places in Merit with what could be called dark and spooky corners. One of these corners was currently occupied by a watcher who had slipped into the dark alley from his hiding place in the stairwell to the bar. Deathly silent, he listened to them now as the ghost wished the woman luck finding her story and the missing cop. When he left the mine he'd gone straight for the bar to find and confront the ghost. It wasn't a tough guess; the ghost was always at a bar. He'd planned to try to find a way to make him stay dead, but he hadn't expected to find the ghost with a journalist. That complicated everything. What was she doing with the ghost? What had the ghost told her about the cop? She was nosy and that was dangerous. He held his breath and pressed himself farther into his hiding spot until they both left, and then he slipped quietly into the street. He had one more stop to make tonight.

Maybe the ghost can't die...but she can.

Chapter Five

"Nobody says a word, got it?" Tyler was furious and it showed. First, they'd spent the entire day in detention and couldn't even go to eat lunch in the cafeteria, and everyone was acting like they'd done something wrong. They hadn't even fought this time! Then he'd had to try to keep that mean Reverend Boxer from talking his mother out of letting him be in the circus. What kid didn't want to be in the circus? Just because that old preacher said he was being sploited or something didn't mean he couldn't have some fun. It wasn't hurting anyone.

But the worst part didn't happen until they got to the dressing room and saw the costumes. They were fine for the girls, but enough was enough! He didn't know what gladiators actually wore, but he was pretty sure they didn't wear *dresses!*

"Not one single word!" He growled to the assembled members of both gangs. Or all four gangs, depending on how you looked at it. Feelings were still pretty mixed about the new gangs, and out of habit the Crackers and the Brothers kept accidentally lining up as the Uppers and the Lowers and forgetting about their new divisions. It was a good thing that the truce they'd come up with today declared simply that nobody fought anybody for any reason. The only two who'd become comfortable with their new alignment were Carrie and Jordan. They were even fixing each other's hair in the headdresses they'd been given to go with their costumes.

"Man, get over it. You're not the only one of us stuck in a dress." Brewer was sulky now.

"It's not a dress," Bub said. "This is actually a tunic. It's what all the Romans wore. They had to wear 'em around town, too."

"Well, whatever it's called," said Spike, "at least they gave us swords!" He pulled out his wooden sword from its plastic scabbard and took an aggressive pose with it. He struck out at the tent pole with a fierce battle cry that faded as the sword clonked against the pole and fell right off of the hilt. He dropped the hilt on the ground and looked disgusted as he realized some of the gold spray paint had come off on his hands.

"Kids, kids! Be careful with that equipment now. Do you know just how hard it is, even for a worldly man such as myself, to come across ancient Roman tools of warfare?"

All of the kids stopped what they were doing and stared. This was a *real* ringmaster! It was the beginning of a dream come true. Cyrus was exactly as they would have envisioned a real circus ringmaster, right down to the long and curling mustache. Each of them, deep down, harbored the hope that if they could impress this man enough with their talents they could possibly be asked to join the show permanently. They imagined their lives with midgets, freaks, vicious animals, being laughed at in sideshows, living day to day on scraps of junk food between performances. Nothing could have made them happier.

"My name is Sir Cyrus Cleansby, but I hope you all will oblige me by calling me Uncle Cyrus. How do you like your costumes? We had them made especially just for you." Cyrus was laying on his paternal act with molasses thickness, the way he did all of his new attractions before he had them on contract.

"They're awesome, sir! I always wanted my own t-tunic," Tyler jumped to answer first, stumbling over the word he'd just learned from that fountain of knowledge, Bub. Brewer and Spike both sulked that Tyler had gotten to suck up first, but Beazer got in the next words.

"It's such an honor to be working with you, sir! I'm a huge fan."

"Well now, that's nice of you to say, young man." Cyrus smiled, realizing how easily he had these children eating out of his hand. "You all look like such ferocious gladiators," he boomed in his ringside voice. "How easy it will be to believe that you will slay the fearsome beast!"

"What beast exactly is that, Mr. Cyrus?" Jordan asked anxiously. She and Carrie were holding hands like sisters in their nervousness.

"Why, I'm surprised you don't know! It's the beast that got you into the mess to begin with. The beast is Racism itself!"

The kids cast dubious looks at one another.

"So, is it like a tiger or something?" Spike asked hopefully.

"No, of course not! I wouldn't put you dear children in a ring with a tiger." He saw not only disappointment but also confusion on the kids' faces and another thought occurred to him. "Tell me, you do know what racism is, don't you?"

"My mother and the reverend said it's about our skin," Tyler spoke for the group as usual. "They said that since some of us are black and some of us are white that we can't really be friends."

"But you were all friends before they told you about your skin?"

"Well, sorta. We were in gangs, but we were the Uppers and Lowers before we had to be the Crackers and the Brothers. Spike and I were friends," Crow said bravely.

"Yeah, and Tyler, Beazer, and I were friends," Bub said.

"Oh dear." Cyrus shook his head, feeling the faintest tinges of what he might have called guilt had he ever experienced it before. "I think that actually is racism, children. Not the part about your skins, but the part about your parents telling you that you're different and can't really be friends just because of your skins. Don't you see?"

Carrie shook her head. "No, sir. Can't you tell us what to do? We just want to be friends again and stop being in trouble."

"Racism is...I guess it's, I mean... Oh my."

"It's hurtful and pointless, that's what it is." A deep new voice entered, a voice that awed the children. Goliath had been dressing on the other side of the tent flap and overheard Cyrus's failing explanation. "All you can be is who you are, take it from me. It doesn't matter if you're black, white, tall, short, fat, skinny. None of those things can make you who you are, and none of those things can tell you who your friends should be. The choices and decisions you make are what make each of you unique and define your character. That's the only thing that should ever make you really different. Nothing on the outside matters to anyone who truly cares about you, and you can't let the outside dictate who you choose to care about. Do you understand that?" The children nodded slowly.

It was apparent to everyone, Cyrus included, that Goliath was speaking from deeply personal experience.

"All right, everyone, it's time for you to head to the main tent so you can meet your co-star and get some rehearsals in before show time. Are you ready?" Cyrus effectively herded the children out of the tent and turned toward Goliath hesitantly before he went with them.

"I would disagree with you on one point, my friend. What you are on the outside did shape part of who you are." He continued before Goliath could argue. "It gave you compassion and empathy. You were able to understand what those children were going through in a way I never could. So maybe a part of what really makes you who you are is what you choose to learn from what you are on the outside." He left the tent and Goliath could hear his voice following them to the main tent, introducing them to the other acts and trying to get them excited again for the show.

"I'll be damned," Goliath said, dumbfounded.

• • •

On the other side of the potato patch from the excitement of the preparing circus, a large middle-aged woman was in the middle of picking out a dress for the evening. Unfortunately, as Mother Hinkle discovered in a moment of panic, her years of farming in solitude since her husband died had reduced her dress collection to the dress she wore on her wedding day to the late Mr. Hinkle twenty-four years and around seventy pounds ago, and the black smock from the Death costume she'd worn to a Halloween party at the church almost a decade ago. She'd heard women talk about how a "little black dress" was good for any occasion, and she eyed her old Halloween costume. It certainly wasn't little, but it was black. *Very* black. Without the skeletal mask and hood it wasn't really bad, she supposed. Perhaps with a new hem to raise it no higher than just above the ankles (it wouldn't do to prance about like a tramp at her age) and a belt to cinch the waist... On second thought, forget the belt. She hitched up her work pants and remembered that she no longer had a waist to cinch. Instead, perhaps a cinch to the sleeves to make them puff. She eyed the smock again and narrowed her eyes. All right, so maybe the right jewelry could still make this work.

She found herself wondering if Goliath would like it and giggled again, a sound that had been very unfamiliar in her house until now. In fact, she had giggled at least twice in the last week, and that was two times more than she had giggled or laughed in the last two decades. Mother Hinkle sighed to herself. How unnatural this feeling seemed now after all these years. She busied herself with getting her dress ready and found a lovely silver ribbon she could use as trim and began cutting off the extra length to turn it into a proper dress.

She'd read books where women made ball gowns out of curtains. If curtains would do the trick, then this smock should be easy. Right?

• • •

The circus was a life in and of itself. It was a sprawling, living creature composed of a myriad of bold colors, dancing lights, lively music, enchantingly high-calorie smells, sticky sweets, the mad calls
of carnival barkers, the rustling of animals, the marvels of acrobats,
and the spinning and winding rides which coursed through it like
veins. What completed the circus, what gave it a heartbeat, however, were the thrumming steps of a crowd coursing with awe and
excitement from tent to tent and stall to stall. All of the collected
wonders of the most brilliant circus in the world were meaningless
without an audience. This was as firm as the laws of physics as far
as Cyrus was concerned. In fact, he'd have sworn he'd first read it
in the *Bible*, had he ever actually read one. The audience was the
heart and soul of the circus.

And such an audience this was! Normally Cyrus avoided small
towns unless they just happened to be on the way to larger cities.
He typically only sold enough tickets in towns this size to cover
the cost of setting up and performing. His only two reasons for
stopping in towns like this to begin with were to help advertise the
circus for upcoming shows in neighboring cities and to give his
performers an adequate chance to try out new routines on small
audiences.

Tonight, however, was a different story altogether. They had
run out of tickets within an hour of opening and had resorted to
stamping patrons' hands with a small heart-shaped correspon-
dence stamp that one of the performers used to sign her letters
to home. The games were thronged with people to the point that
Cyrus had been forced to improvise and had even set up horseshoe
stations to help keep the massive crowd entertained. And they
were even PAYING to play horseshoes! At least two of the cotton
candy stations would be emptied before the night ended, and he'd
already sent two of his crew on an emergency resupply trip to Jos-

tlem for hot dogs, buns, and caramels. He'd begun watering down the lemonade, more than usual anyway, as soon as he saw how quickly the tickets were going, so hopefully that would hold out through the weekend.

It didn't seem possible to him that this town could hold so many extra people. He kept his eye out for anyone who looked official. The sort of official, that is, who'd be inclined to use the words "capacity" and "fire code" in the same sentence. Where had all of these people come from? Where were they staying? If he had the extra canvas to spare he'd have ordered the seamstresses to sew small tents together and stitch the circus logo onto them for sale on the midway.

The prices people were paying just to see these children!

●   ●   ●

Kicking in the door had been no problem at all. It was obvious that no one in this town ever suspected that someone might rob them; he'd found only the most minimal of locks on every building and home that he had entered so far. Most of them hadn't even been locked, but those that were he'd picked within moments. It would have been just as easy to pick this simple lock had his set of picks not been confiscated from the mine that morning, but a broken door would send a better message anyway.

He opened his duffle and moved quickly through the rooms to find what he needed. Wherever he moved he randomly knocked over lamps and stacks of papers, and then he overturned tables and chairs.

He packed additional flashlights that he found and raided the kitchen cabinets for food. He hadn't eaten since his food had been taken that morning, but even that hadn't been a total loss. The casserole he'd taken from that freezer barely qualified as "food" as it was.

There was a whisper.

He stopped in his tracks. Silently he turned and hunted for the source but found nothing. *My imagination,* he decided. He continued his search into the next room, shaking off the feeling that someone was watching him. Someone angry. That blasted ghost had made him paranoid.

What he found was a cabinet with a padlock on it. Fortunately, his investigation had already delivered a set of bolt cutters from the utility closet. He opened it and smiled as the light caught what lay inside.

Somewhere from the back of the same room came a low growl, barely audible. He backed slowly through the door with his new-found prize and closed it behind him to separate himself from the owner of that growl just as it was elevating to a snarl.

He zipped his now-full duffle bag and took another look around him. He was pleased with what he saw. Small-scale destruction may not be satisfying to most people—the lamp he'd knocked off the desk hadn't even broken—but to those with a sense of order that a drill sergeant would envy it was nearly the equivalent of a mortal wound. He was in a rage, but it was a calculated and carefully directed sub-dermal rage that had not even registered on the surface yet. This was the kind of man who could make a cup of tea for his grandmother while internally plotting a killing spree.

He tossed his duffle over his shoulder and turned to leave when a reflection of light caught his eye from the wall.

"*Look,*" said a whisper.

His blood froze in his veins as it always did when that voice came back, and it seemed to come more and more often since he'd set foot in this blasted town. He grabbed the picture off the wall and stifled what would have been a scream from someone less in control of their emotions.

The picture hit the opposite wall with a shatter of glass as running footsteps pounded in the opposite direction.

A few moments later there was another sound. It was what the idea of a great struggle and strength might sound like if human ears were equipped to hear it. It barely trembled at first, but slowly the door knob turned as the latch shuddered open and a small dog trotted out.

He looked up at his liberator with a friendly whine and rolled over for a belly rub.

· · ·

"Bertie, who *are* these people?" Stanley was mystified. He'd expected the entire town as well as all of the media who'd infested Merit to turn out for the circus, but he barely recognized one out of every five faces he saw. People had come from all over to see this show. But the circus wasn't really the show they were coming to see, was it? He frowned. Even without the added chaos of the real circus being in town, the media had already created a side show with his citizens as the stars. Cyrus's appearance and manipulation of the situation just helped complete the catastrophe. As much as he hated to admit it, Dana was absolutely right about the inevitability of all of this. He'd been trying to single-handedly stop an avalanche with a towel.

Just when he thought he couldn't feel any lower, a clown dashed in front of Bertie and Stanley and paused just long enough to honk a horn in Stanley's face.

"Wow," he said. "That was all it needed. You can't have a truly complete nightmare without clowns."

"Don't forget the monkeys," Bertie added as he shivered. He'd had a completely uncontrollable fear of monkeys since childhood. His only theory was that his very loud and constantly drunk Uncle Theo had looked quite like a chimpanzee. He also smelled quite like one.

"At least the only one of those we've seen so far was that tiny one with the organ grinder," Stanley consoled him.

"But did you see the look in his eyes? That one had murder on the brain, and I'll swear to it."

Stanley thought the monkey was rather adorable, but he wouldn't have put much past the organ grinder. The man was made up in a gruesome style that put him in mind of Jack the Ripper.

"All right," he shrugged off the thought. "Back to work. I have to meet Isabelle and her father soon, so we need to make a few more passes through here before the kids go on."

"Right. But..." Bertie stalled. "Explain to me again what it is exactly that we're doing?"

"We're looking for anything abnormal and suspicious."

"Right. We're looking for anything abnormal. At a freak show."

"You know what I mean! I just have a very bad feeling about this. We didn't catch whoever hit me in the cave, which means we've at least got some kind of deranged vagrant running around town wanting someone to die. And then the bloody uniform turning up and the cop still missing? I doubt any of this has anything to do with the kids, but if you were wanting to commit a murder in a small town, it seems to me that this chaos would provide a great smoke screen for it."

"Stanley, I'm sure that shook you up. It would've scared the bejesus out of me, I know. But you don't know that this guy is some sort of murderer. He could just be another crazy bum passing through or another kid run away from home for a while."

"The only thing I saw of him was his fist coming toward me, and what I saw were huge hairy knuckles. It definitely wasn't a kid. And it wasn't just the words on the wall that scared me. The campsite he had set up was full of stuff straight from survival magazines, and he had buried every last bit of his trash like he was trying to cover up any trace of his existence. This man was no bum. He was set up like someone who was deep in hiding and intended to stay that way for a while. Can you think of any good reasons that a man would want to completely disappear like that?"

"Oh, Stanley! We're over here!" Stanley paled slightly as he heard Isabelle calling to him from a little distance off.

"You know," Bertie said with a slight grin. "I do believe I could think of one or two."

Stanley sighed. "You go on, Bertie. I'll catch up with you in a few minutes."

"I'll just be over by the funnel cakes then. That's within screaming distance if you need me, you hear?"

"Go!" Stanley hurried Bertie away and went to meet Isabelle and her father. He was not comforted by the fact that she seemed even more cheery than the last time he had spoken to her that day, just before he went down to the mine. He walked over to Isabelle and Rupert Youngblood and tried to smile.

"Hello, dear. Hello, Rupert." As usual, his father-in-law was standing back with one hand in his interior pocket and the other grasping his expensive cigar. It was a pompous, disconnected stance. Aside from that, Stanley had always liked his father-in-law and found him to be a very warm and witty man. Posturing, Stanley had decided, was the only thing Isabelle had inherited from her father.

Suddenly, Isabelle put herself inches away from his face. If he hadn't been left at the station with a bowl of food and water, Cud would have been whimpering in empathy for Stanley. She was wearing a Look that Stanley didn't recognize. He would have to number and name it later when he was more himself, but at first glance he would have called it Overly Concerned and Brimming with Contrived Innocence.

"Stanley, honey, I got the worst call from Charlie just before we came! He told me that I'd completely misunderstood him about children in the mine. I'm so sorry I sent you off on that wild goose chase. How silly of me!" She giggled almost whimsically. "Now that we're all here let's find our seats and get some popcorn." She nodded dismissively and turned as if waiting for Stanley to follow her.

Before Stanley had to summon the courage himself his father-in-law came to the rescue.

"Isabunny," as her father had called her since childhood to her immense displeasure, "Charlie called me yesterday and mentioned that he was going to be blasting in the mine today. Did you just say you sent Stanley down into the mine to look for children?"

Isabelle maintained the innocent part of her look while her eyes widened slightly in panic. "Daddy, it was all just a silly mistake. Stanley knows that and he's just fine. Aren't you Stanley?"

She turned to Stanley expecting him to answer as he normally would have. Today hadn't been a very good day for Stanley, however. Isabelle's position between Stanley and her father allowed her to instantly turn the look of innocence and charm that had just been showering her father into a scowl of menacing proportions as Stanley didn't respond in the expected way.

"I said, 'Aren't you, Stanley?' Just *fine*, right?"

He swallowed. "I could have died today, Isabelle. I would have, in fact, if it hadn't been for a malfunction. I guess I just don't feel like calling it such a 'silly' little mistake."

He was sure he imagined it, but her hair seemed to get even larger suddenly, as if it had gasped at the same time she had.

"How dare you! What are you trying to suggest, Stanley? Charlie came down to the house talking about kids and the mine and you know how hard he is to understand, don't you, Daddy?" She turned toward her father seeking corroboration, and frowned when she found none. "Anyway, it was all a simple misunderstanding and I won't hear anything more about it. We're at the circus to have fun!" She stormed off toward their seats in her typical huff that aimed to leave any innocent bystander feeling as though they'd done something terribly wrong. In times of war, this would be called "friendly fire."

To his complete surprise, Stanley looked up to see Rupert suppressing laughter.

"Well, it took you long enough, didn't it?"

"I'm sorry sir, but I don't know what you're talking about." He was completely bewildered and slightly frightened for some odd reason. It could have been the whiplash from Isabelle's Just You Wait Till We Get Home look that she threw at him before stomping off.

"It took you long enough to grow a pair!" The big man boomed in laughter now, startling small children. "Look, Stanley, I've always liked you a lot. I normally wouldn't have let my daughter marry a man I liked so much, but I always thought you might have what it would take to teach her a thing or two. I just never thought it would take this long! But I see it coming now. You've got the look of a man who's reached his limit, and boy would I like to know what that limit must be for you to have been married to my daughter for this long without reaching it!"

Ever the pacifier even at the worst of times, Stanley plunged on bravely. "No, Rupert, you've got it all wrong. We're perfectly happy. It was just a terrible misunderstanding, that's all." He hated lying. And he knew he still wasn't any good at it by the way it set Rupert off on another laughing fit.

"I'm sorry, Stanley, you just don't know how long I've been waiting to hear you stand up to her. I've tried to help you out with her here and there where I could without interfering, but there's only so much a man can do without stepping on another man's pride. You know, 'You can't wear a man's balls for him and you can't give him your own, neither,' my mother always said."

"Your mother always said that?"

"All the time! You have to understand something, though. My father was quite a lot like you, Stanley. No offense, of course, but he was unbearably nice and patient and always so helpful to the point of being walked on and treated like a doormat by all of his business partners. It took my mother's strength to strike fear in the hearts of his partners, though I doubt he ever had a clue that she would follow-up all of his negotiations with a little visit of her own. He always seemed shocked when they would call him a day later after a negotiation and capitulate to his every demand."

"I get it. You took after your mother, then."

"I only wish. My mother was twice the man I am." He suddenly turned a wary look on Stanley as though he'd over-spoken in his reverie. "But if you ever repeat that to anyone I'll make sure you're half the man you are now, if you follow my meaning."

Stanley instinctively dropped his hands to his crotch. "Don't worry, sir. I wouldn't dream of repeating those words in that order, with or without the threat."

"That's my lad! Listen, I'll keep her occupied for a while and get her back in a good mood. Why don't you join your employee for a while and enjoy the sights? Whatever you do, don't forget the feeling you had back there when you get home tonight, Stanley."

"What feeling?"

"You weren't afraid. I don't know what happened, but you were finally not frightened by her."

"I think I know what happened. I think I found something more frightening than even her."

• • •

A person with allergies could learn to cope by finding just the right balance of antihistamines, decongestants, tissues, and enough powder to cover up a bright red nose. However, this balance, as unfair as it may have seemed, tended to shift with the wind. Quite literally.

Dana had finally managed to breathe through both nostrils at the same time again through heavy experimentation with all of the modern marvels of the over-the-counter allergy section at the drug store. She had even thrown in a few local remedies offered to her by the kind townspeople who had watched her suffering, though the most potent of those home-grown remedies had unfortunately just given her gas. Still, she'd finally found relief in her regimen of pills and her spiked bottle of water, even if it did mean she had to endure a constant fog of medicinal grape syrup on her breath.

Allen had even remarked to her earlier that day how much better she seemed to be doing and she had agreed wholeheartedly. This, she realized too late, had been one big mistake. The last thing you wanted to do when things were going well was actually acknowledge the fact. In her mind there was a law far more powerful than Murphy's Law: Karma Is Always Listening. Though it had started out as a joke when she was in college, it had become a rule to her through more than sheer repetition. Coincidence has a strange way of reinforcing what was already suspected. As surely as ever, Karma had heard Dana boasting of conquering her allergies and had thrown a new twist her way in the form of animal dander by the boat loads. She may have been able to handle a few dogs or cats, but this was a circus after all. We're talking big animals with big dander.

She reflected between sneezes on this latest twist of fate. A little person, who was disturbingly close to groin height for someone who introduced himself as "Big Joe," had been lingering annoyingly close to Dana ever since she and Allen had arrived at the circus. Being the enterprising young reporter that she was, she bribed him to show her where the kids were rehearsing with Monty. The tent he had taken them to was a perfect hiding place and overlooked the entire rehearsal. It also happened to be the tent that held all of the caged animals in between acts. She sneezed again and cast an accusatory look at the nearest defenseless camel. The camel, as coincidence would have it, chose that moment to spit with what seemed to her to be absolute contempt. Truth, however, would have it that the camel simply found a piece of something particularly untasty in his mouth at that moment. Reality was seldom as poetic or romantic as coincidence.

Currently, Allen was filming what was proving to be one of the most remarkably strange rehearsals in the history of live theater while Dana tried to muffle her sniffles behind him.

"It's undignified, that's why!" Monty was yelling at a flabbergasted Cyrus. "I've never done my own stunts in the past and I don't know why I should be expected to now. I am an *ac-tor*, not a stuntman!" He enunciated the word "ac-tor" in the especially grating way that people did when they believed inflating pronunciation equated to inflating importance.

"But it's not a stunt! The script clearly calls for you to 'loom up out of the darkness and hover behind the children' for your entrance. It just means that you should float for a minute. You're a ghost, for Pete's sake, that's hardly a stunt for you!"

"That's practically racism! Just because I'm a ghost doesn't mean I should be exploited for the fact. You'll have me wandering around rattling chains next. I won't float, and that's final!"

"But look at you, you're doing it now!" Tyler chimed in happily. He was the only one not engaged, at the moment, in a mock war with the swords they'd been given.

Monty erupted in a yell of frustration as he tried to wave his arms and legs enough to make his way down. He looked like a swimmer drowning in reverse.

"It's not the same thing!" He yelled when he got his feet firmly on the ground. "It happens when I get upset. I'm still learning how to walk all over again."

"Mr. Gregory..." Cyrus was in his let's-make-a-deal mode. "I'm not suggesting that you should do anything unprofessional. You have, let's say, 'special' talents now and I think it would be an awful shame if you didn't put them to use. It gives you such an edge! I might even venture to suggest that it's an award-winning edge, if I may be so bold." Cyrus moved in closer and slid his arm around Monty's shoulder and walked him away from the children.

"This is the stuff that legends are made of, Monty. We're making history, you and I! Can't you just picture it now?" He waved his hand slowly across as if gesturing toward an imaginary crowd. "The audience dead quiet in anticipation as the narrator introduces the beast, and here you come out of nowhere in a fanfare of trumpets! They will be terrified, there will be screams! I can't believe you would want to walk away from such a triumphant return, but if you must, you must. I'm sure Goliath won't mind filling in for you." Cyrus dropped his arm from Monty's shoulder almost dismissively and started to turn away from him.

"Wait, what do you mean 'walk away'? I never said I was walking away." Monty, who was only a moment ago full of affronted outrage, was now subdued and downright plaintive.

"Oh, but I thought you did. It must have been my mistake. I was under the impression that you wanted to break your contract by not performing the script *exactly* as written, so I thought you must be willing to throw it all away."

"That was in the contract?"

"Yes, indeed. On page fourteen in paragraph IV.a, sub clause iii.b, if I do remember correctly." It took a twisted and ingenious business mind to actually speak in Roman numerals.

"Oh. I guess then, sure. I mean, I guess it won't really hurt anything. I don't want to be difficult or anything. Should we just start over?"

Cyrus practically gleamed, his cigar twitching in self-applause. "What a great idea! Let's take it from the beginning. Children! CHILDREN!" He yelled over the sounds of clashing wooden swords and clacking plastic shields. "Let's get back to our places, shall we?"

In the shadows Dana was busily pinching the bridge of her nose to stop the progress of an approaching monumental sneeze.

"Allen, I can't take it anymore! There's nothing I can do here, anyway. Keep filming for a while and maybe we'll at least get some good footage for an intro. I'm going to go wait outside and see if I can find anything else going on."

"Sure thing. Oh, when you find Sheriff Stanley be sure to tell him hello from me." He had his back turned to her but she was certain she could see his grin wrapping all the way around his head.

"I never said I was looking for Stanley...I mean, the sheriff. I'm just going to see if there is anything else worth filming, got it?"

Without waiting for a response she turned toward the distant entrance, milling her way through the myriad of allergy agitators. The nerve! To suggest that she had a thing for this small-town cop, let alone a married man! She harrumphed to herself and mumbled unkind things about Allen all the way to the tent exit where...

"Hello?" She was certain that there had been something in the darkness, something that didn't move like an animal. Something that moved like a man. Did they have gorillas here? She didn't know. Still, was there someone else in here?

Suddenly she was fuming. It had to be another reporter! "I said hello! I know you're in here, there's no use in hiding. Just come on out. This is MY story!"

"Dana? Who are you talking to? Nevermind, we gotta move! They're on the move now." Allen came dashing not-so-nimbly among the crowded rows of animals and nearly slid on a pile of what he was really hoping was mud.

"But there was someone else in here snooping. Didn't you see anyone?"

"All I saw was you standing there talking to yourself. Let's move!" He dashed out of view through the tent flap. She hesitated before following him. *There was someone in there, wasn't there?* Dana peered into the darkness between the cages and had another thought. *If there is someone hiding in here, do I really want to be alone in here with them?* She ducked out quickly behind Allen and nearly ran into the back of his camera as she turned the corner.

"Jesus! What are you doing? You could've killed me with that thing!"

"Just look. See why I stopped?"

To her horror she saw Barbara Chase-Howard, the female anchor of K-ACTN news in Jostlem, not to mention her own personal nemesis. She had cornered Monty and the Ringmaster on their way out of the tent with the children and looked primed to begin an interview with her own cameraman.

"Barbara! What are you doing here? This has been my story from the beginning. Why didn't anyone tell me you were coming down here?"

"Well, you know how it is, dear." Barbara tossed her overly-teased blonde hair over her shoulder as she turned up the level of condescension to max. "We had a meeting with the Network this morning and they decided it would be best if I took over from here. Oh, not that you haven't done a simply *charming* job, but you really are more suited to those quaint little human interest stories that you do, don't you think?"

Dana knew what that meant. Barbara Chase-Howard was one of those dreadful people who wielded her success like a deadly weapon. She would use it against anyone who tried to achieve any success of their own for fear that it would take away from hers. She regularly stepped on Dana's hopes, and had even ordered her to get a bagel with cream cheese for her in front of the Network executives at staff meetings. This sort of person made for a terrible loser. Barbara must have begun scheming the second Dana's Merit interviews began to gather more interest.

Barbara smiled evilly, turning away from a speechless Dana and back toward Monty and Cyrus, while her cameraman took a moment to wave a crude hand gesture at Allen. Yes, cameramen have nemeses, too.

"Now, gentlemen, I'd love to start the interview with a question for Mr. Gregory. I can see that your recent demise hasn't affected your acting career, but how have you been coping with the recent public discovery of your homosexuality?"

"What's *wrong* with you people?" Monty groaned as Cyrus

threw his hands over the ears of the nearest child and nearly choked on his cigar.

"The star of our show is not a *homosexual!*" Cyrus whispered the word. "This is a family circus. It's in his contract that he isn't gay—"

"It's *what?*" Monty's jaw dropped.

"—and Mr. Gregory wouldn't dream of breaking his contract," Cyrus finished

"That's quite an answer! How do you respond, Mr. Gregory?"

Monty shifted his stupefied glare between Cyrus's righteous indignation and a smug Barbara before taking a long look at a crestfallen Dana who still managed to give him a nod of encouragement. *Be yourself*, she mouthed.

"I don't," he replied, still looking at Dana. "I'm afraid I've promised an exclusive interview to Ms. Dana Perki, so I guess we'll just have to end this interview, don't you think?"

Barbara nearly dropped her microphone before turning a stormy face toward Dana and back to Monty. "To *her*? To a fluff story second-rate reporter?"

"No, to that talented young lady right over there." Monty emphasized the "young," surmising correctly that Barbara was at least ten-years older than Dana. It achieved the effect he'd hoped for. The older anchor was positively shaking with fury.

"I hope you know that this amounts to career suicide! If you want to be interviewed by a nobody then you will *be* a nobody! Bobby, let's go!" She called her bewildered cameraman. Bobby started to follow her when Allen called out.

"Oh, Booby...I mean Bobby? Take care now." Allen's amiable smile and farewell were countered by the fact that he was only waving one finger at him. The one not suitable for a family circus.

Cyrus, feeling that he'd just missed something important, suddenly realized that he was about to let free publicity stalk away from him. "Wait! I haven't promised an exclusive to anyone. I can promise it to you, though! Come back!"

"Stuff it!" Yelled Barbara in a most unladylike fashion.

I really must be dreaming, Dana thought. She smiled broadly at Monty, her hero.

Then she sneezed.

. . .

Some people in life seemed to be doomed to having sticky bits of food stains on their clothes wherever they went. These were the unfortunate souls who were constantly afraid to eat in public, knowing that the ice cream would practically leap off the cone, the soup would dive from the spoon, and the juice would soar out of the cup all in an effort to find a new home down the front of their favorite shirt. Erwin Mayer was one of these souls. Right now he was hiding behind the animal tent spying on the interview Dana was conducting with Monty, Cyrus, and the kids, while trying furiously to rub the gooey brown blotch from the caramel apple off his shirt.

He was also wishing he was old enough to curse properly without being grounded. "Dang" and "Darn" just didn't seem to capture the full range of the emotion he was feeling. It was so unfair! *He* was the one who'd broken the story and brought everyone to Merit. *He* was the one who'd had the guts to stand up to the Jelly River Gangs, and if it weren't for *him* Merit would still just be a quiet town where nothing ever happened. But now he couldn't even get a reporter to pay any attention to him. Let alone give him his own weekly column. No one cared about little Erwin, the geeky kid with the glasses and the notepad. They all just wanted to talk to the delinquents, the activists, and now the darned old actors! Who cared about them, anyhow? He kicked the dirt in front of him, sending up a cloud of dust that made him cough. It was just so very unfair.

He listened to the voices around him. Everyone else was having the time of their lives, it seemed. There were more people here than he'd ever seen in one place in his life, and he tried to feel good about being part of the cause of that. They all seemed to be having fun, after all. Maybe, just maybe, he could go out and join them...

He looked down at the spreading blotch of goo and decided with a sniffle that he'd be better off just hide back here for the rest of the night.

It was never like this on TV. He should be carried into the center ring on someone's shoulders while everyone cheered and told him he was a hero. "Thank you, Erwin," they would say. "What would we do without you, Erwin?" Instead, he was in the back of a tent realizing that underneath the straw he was sitting on was a pile of fresh donkey crap.

"Story of my life," he mumbled to himself and wandered into the tent, hoping to find a bucket of water or something to wash off with.

Inside the tent he came face to face with the largest zebra he'd ever seen in his life, not to mention the only zebra he'd ever seen in his life. He gasped as the huge animal dipped its head down toward him as though it wanted Erwin to pet him. It was amazing! He'd always known he'd be a natural with animals. He scratched the creature behind its ear and smiled for the first time all day. He was practically a zebra-whisperer.

The zebra leaned closer, sniffed the strange brown patch on Erwin's shirt, and discovered a hitherto unknown allergy to caramel. It sneezed. And when an animal with a nose as long as a zebra's sneezed, any innocent bystander without an umbrella would suddenly develop an obsessive compulsion to shower anytime they heard a sneeze, possibly even a sniffle.

"Hey, kid."

Ernie spun around, momentarily forgetting that he was now mired in an entirely new kind of goo. The voice had come from behind the pens and sounded exactly like something from one of his TV shows—the creepy, foreboding voice you wanted to avoid.

"Need a towel?" The owner of the voice stepped into the light and Ernie felt himself shrinking into his sticky clothes. His parents had told him not to talk to strangers, and this was a stranger with a capital STRANGE. The man was smiling, but only with his mouth, and there was something very desperate in his eyes. Nevertheless, someone with Erwin's tendencies learned to never turn down a wet towel when it was offered. He sighed and reached out for it with a trembling hand.

Sensing Erwin's fear, the stranger tossed him the towel and took a step back away from him.

"See? It's all right. I'm not going to hurt you."

"What are you doing in here, mister?" A loose goat wandered in front of him, and he realized there were several others loose in the back already. "Hey, did you open those cages?"

"I just felt so bad seeing them in their pens. They should be free, don't you think? No creature deserves to be in a cage. Hey, since you're here, think you can do me a favor?"

Sensing that saying "no" would have been dangerous, Erwin nodded slowly.

The stranger's smile somehow looked scarier now. "Great, kid. I'm looking for my friend and I'm hoping you can help me find her."

• • •

The interview had consisted of Cyrus grandstanding while trying to keep the kids from jumping in front of the camera making gladiator poses and what they thought were battle cries, and Monty trying to strike overly masculine poses and trying to make his voice sound deeper. He sounded like he had phlegm in his throat. Still, it was the interview that no one else got. That made it a million-dollar interview.

Cyrus had just ushered the children off to the main tent after forcibly taking away the fake swords to get them to follow him. Monty hung back for a moment to speak to Dana.

"I just want to say thanks for not asking me, you know. *The* question. The whole world is like a dog with a bone over this. I may not have been the best actor, but I *did* win some awards in my time. And now here I am, back from the dead to resume my career, but none of that matters to them. It's like they won't be satisfied until they hear me say I'm gay." He looked down at his feet. This was the first time she'd seen him look so helpless. Her image of the cocky, arrogant, and selfish movie star had completely evaporated today.

"Are you—No. You know what? It doesn't matter. And it shouldn't matter to anyone else unless it matters to you. Screw them, Monty. You *are* a star and you don't have to let them dictate your story. Besides, I should be the one thanking you. You really saved the day for me with Barbara. I've never, ever been able to stand up to her. If it weren't for you, I'd have gone home with my tail between my legs and started my next report on another local garden show, I'm sure."

She saw a familiar lanky figure approaching behind Monty. "Hang on, there's someone you should meet. Stanley!" She caught his attention and Stanley turned her way. A plumper man following him was fighting to tuck his shirt in as he walked.

"Hi, Dana," Stanley said sheepishly, his ears reddening slightly. He was remembering that he'd never actually apologized for their argument by the mine.

Dana suddenly remembered the same. "Look, can we just forget about earlier? We were both pretty stressed out."

"Yes, definitely stressed out! We'll pretend like it never happened and not another word about it." Stanley was dreading having to explain this one to the sniggering Bertie. Allen was already whispering in Bertie's ear. He cast them both a dirty look.

"Great, that's settled. Now there's someone I'd like you to meet. Sheriff Stanley Grace, meet Montana Gregory, the actor."

Monty smiled and extended his hand to a bewildered Stanley. "It's a pleasure to meet you, Sheriff," Monty said gallantly.

Stanley took his hand and stammered a bit. "Um, you too. It seems I just heard something about you recently, though. Aren't you–?" He looked to Dana for back-up.

Something in Monty snapped. There was only so much a ghost could take.

"Oh, let me guess! Could it be that you heard that I was *gay*?" He practically snarled. "Fine! Go ahead and say it just like everyone else. What is *wrong* with you people? You thought I was gay. Well you know what? Maybe you're right! Maybe you're not! I don't even care anymore. Go ahead and tell the whole world anything you want! Tell them I might be gay, gay, gay, gay! What do you think of *that*, huh?"

Fate has a way of turning the volume down on everything else just when someone is saying something that they would never want to be heard by other people. That was the case just now. Monty realized that he could hear a pin drop for a moment when he finished his tirade before the music on the speakers moved on to the next dizzyingly cheery song. Bertie and Allen quit whispering and looked like they were attempting to catch flies in a very unhygienic way. Dana stood still with her eyes closed and her hand over her mouth.

Stanley faltered. "Actually, I was going to say that I'd heard you were dead. Funeral and everything. You know, kicked the bucket, gave up the ghost. Well, maybe not that part." Not knowing a good place to stop, his mouth continued on autopilot. "So, you're gay, then?"

"I'm...no, it's...GRRAPHTK!" He gurgled his frustration. "No! I'm not gay. All right?"

"But you just said–"

"NO! It's called sarcasm. Sar-Casm," Monty enunciated. "It means to say something you don't mean with ironic intent. Get it?" He was met by blank stares. "Whatever. Get a dictionary and figure it out. I have a show to perform!"

He turned and wheeled off with only a brief struggle when he realized that he was floating off the ground again. He touched down with only one person running away screaming this time. It was progress, at least.

"Did I just miss something here?" Stanley was the first to pierce the shocked silence.

"It's kind of a long story. He'll be all right, though. Did you find out anything about the uniform?"

"Not great news. I talked to Jostlem PD and they said the badge definitely belonged to the missing cop. A courier picked up the uniform and they'll do an analysis on the blood."

"That doesn't bode well. Where do you think the body is?"

"Not a clue. I just hope it doesn't wash up in the river somewhere for some poor kid to find."

Bertie felt something tugging on his pants leg and looked down. His velocity as he left the three standing there would have surprised any nearby physicists. That much mass simply shouldn't be able to move like that. They may have even noticed a slight tint of red and the dropping of his scream as he sped away.

Where Allen and Bertie had been standing together sharing whispered jokes, it was now Allen standing next to a chimpanzee who was as surprised as the rest of them by Bertie's reaction. The surprise quickly wore off, however, and he decided to squat down and investigate his armpit for fleas.

"Oh dear," Stanley said. "He's deathly afraid of monkeys. How do you suppose this one got out?"

Before Dana or Allen could answer, a donkey brushed past them at a fast trot, followed quickly by a trio of seals looking woefully out of place, half-hopping, half-dragging themselves to freedom from the tent.

Without warning, the sound of a gunshot rang out over the circus, making Stanley's stomach churn. Immediately following the shot was the sound of panic coming from the animal tent. Where there had been a slow trickle of animals wandering out of the massive tent there was now a stampeding flood of terrified creatures of all sizes, trampling everything in their path.

A gunshot in a crowd is the last thing a policeman wants to hear in his life. A stampede is, undoubtedly, the second to last. A stampede is essentially one tremendous animal with hundreds of pairs of legs, assorted teeth, fangs, talons, claws, and the ability to sound like the 1812 *Overture* as played by a full demolition team.

For the first time in his life Stanley actually heard the trumpet of an elephant and found himself wondering why it was referred to as a "trumpet" instead of an "angry shriek of violent death." He was also very aware of the earthquake-like rumbling of the ground as it charged close behind them. Searching for safer ground, he grabbed Dana just as she was hopping out of the way of a kangaroo, and headed for one of the semi-trucks parked a short distance away.

"Allen, come on!" She yelled behind them, realizing that Allen, ever the loyal camera man, was busily filming while backing away from an approaching bear. The bear's snarling seemed in stark contrast to, and possibly was caused by, the cheery pointed jester's cap and tutu around its waist. Stanley left Dana safe high on the side of the truck and ran back for Allen, dragging him by the shirt collar away from danger to the truck. Disappointed, the bear instead charged and knocked over a caramel cart and began gorging on the sticky goodies inside.

It was pure chaos of colossal proportions. Camels, horses, zebras, parrots, bears, monkeys, and even old, nearly toothless lions had poured out of the tent so quickly that they'd torn most of it down around them. The ground trembled and the air was rank with the smell of frightened animals. The thundering of hooves, screeching of the animals, screaming of the people trying to get to safety, and the crashing of stands and carts being overturned was too much for Stanley.

He had to *do* something for a change.

He reached for his side and suddenly cursed himself for the idea of going plain-clothes to the circus. His gun was locked up in his office with his uniform. He'd have to do what he could without it.

Dana could sense the resolve forming in Stanley and tried to reach out for him just as he leaped off the side of the truck.

"What are you doing? You'll be killed down there!"

He tried to ignore her while he spun out of the way of a speeding giraffe. What could he do? He needed higher ground. Just then he spotted a zebra that had come to a stop to inspect some cotton candy he'd found half-trampled into the ground. Stanley approached it stealthily and grabbed it on both sides of the neck before it realized someone was sneaking up on it. He managed to swing one leg over the back of the zebra and pull himself upright. All those years of riding horses were finally coming in handy.

Feeling more confident on his mount, Stanley held on to the animal's mane and clicked his feet into its rib cage, yelling "Giddyap!"

This was when he discovered that "Giddyap" in zebranese must actually mean "Buck Like Hell."

In the span of a few minutes this zebra had endured a small child, a gun fired in his ear, a monkey biting his ankles, and now an idiot on his back kicking him. He snorted, then arched his back and began kicking his back legs in an effort to unseat Stanley. The zebra was so angry that he wasn't aware that his burden had been flung off with the first buck. He didn't even hear the "Oomph!" as Stanley hit through the canvas wall of the nearest tent and landed in a pile of rank straw.

Stanley pulled himself up and rubbed his sore crotch, hoping above all that no one saw what happened.

Now what? Apparently herding them on horseback wasn't going to do the trick. He saw one of the dwarves across the fairway from him grab a parrot out of the air and rush toward the cages with it. Maybe grabbing them one by one was the only way.

A spider monkey holding someone's wallet ran around the corner and right into his boot.

"Gotcha!" Stanley cried out as he snatched the monkey off the ground and recognized it as the organ grinder's. It wriggled in his hand for a moment and turned toward him, baring needle-like teeth, and delivered the most inhuman and ear-piercing screech, like talons scraping across every blackboard in the world. That alone almost caused Stanley to drop the monkey in shock, but it clinched the deal when it sank the aforementioned needle-like teeth into the soft part of his hand between his thumb and forefinger. Stanley screamed and shook the evil little creature off his hand. It fell to the ground and screeched at him a few more times before turning back into the madness. *Maybe Bertie was right about monkeys all along*, he thought as he tried to rub the pain out of his hand.

"Out of my way, little man!" A familiar voice bellowed in his ear. "You're about to see why they call me 'Mad Mother Hinkle'!"

"No, don't, you'll be hurt, maybe," Stanley called weakly behind her as she pushed past him through the melee, shoving overturned carts and pushing animals out of her way. "Mad" didn't do her justice at this moment; she was practically steaming with rage. The thought occurred to him that he should be more worried about the safety of the animals than of Mother Hinkle in this sort of a fit.

Stanley watched her as she yanked the loose reins of a stampeding show horse and quickly tied one of them to a post and used the other rein to snare the zebra that had just humbled Stanley. Neither of them knew what had hit them. He cautiously followed in her wake while she subdued animal after animal, and it suddenly hit him that there was something strange about her. His brain had for some reason decided to bring to his attention that Mother Hinkle was wearing make-up. No, not just make-up. A dress, too. Well, sort of a dress. It was more of a very large black bag of puff with silver ribbons. And her hair was up. *Way* up. In fact, as she stormed through the pandemonium he began to think of her as a Valkyrie on a battlefield. She was...

"She's magnificent!"

This was not the word Stanley was looking for, but he wasn't about to argue the fact with the voice rumbling above him. From atop Gumby, Goliath was dragging a rope with several cowed animals tied to it, calm now from either fear of the giant or pure exhaustion from their temporary freedom. He slid off Gumby's back and followed after Mother Hinkle, leaving the rope tied to Gumby's harness. The bear waddled along at the end of it, his tutu encrusted with bits of caramel from the now empty stand. It belched loud and long, leaving Stanley in the wake of the foul breeze carrying obvious signs of gastronomical distress.

Stanley held his breath and hurried behind Goliath toward the main tent.

• • •

Erwin cowered underneath the truck. A large lizard was creeping stealthily closer to him, flicking its tongue at intervals, and he was trying in vain to make it go away by blowing in its direction. He knew Ms. Perki was clinging to the side above him; he was only too aware of it, in fact. His mother would be so mad at him if she found out that he sneaked a peek up Ms. Perki's skirt when he dove for cover. But right now he was too frightened by the stampede to call out to her to deliver his message.

Besides, the Stranger had told him specifically to wait until she was alone.

• • •

"Will somebody get him down from there? Where are my trainers? You! And you! Get up there and get him down before he hurts someone! We dropped the insurance policy two months ago!"

Cyrus bellowed across the center ring as the gorilla bounded from riser to riser as if searching for something lost. The few people still remaining in the stands were clambering over the sides to get away from it, even though it wasn't a particularly fearsome ape. In fact, the gray in its fur along with the playful sounds he made as he explored the risers made him seem as gentle as a kitten. But it was still a vast amount of ape, and a gentle nature didn't make a half-ton creature weigh any less when it playfully sat on you. Therefore, people, being of a particularly squishable nature, tended to run when they saw a large gorilla coming toward them and covering the ten-foot space between the stands in one leap with a smile at them. After all, it had such an awful lot of teeth to smile with.

The ape was somewhat aware of an annoying noise from below where Cyrus and the other circus staff were yelling at him, but he was far more interested in the small, pinkish creature in the top row of the stand that kept making wet noises with his mouth. The small man, tiny next to the ape, was completely paralyzed with fear and his lips were working as though he were trying to remember the way to form words. In this case the word was probably "help." The other pink creatures had run away too quickly for the ape to see them properly, but he saw something glittering on this one's face and was fascinated by it. The ape, as it turned out, suffered from severe astigmatism.

Realizing that the ape was heading right for him, the lone man began trying to improve upon his failing vocabulary and had worked up to "Da-da-da-da-da-da." The man's trembling doubled and tripled as the curious gorilla closed the distance between them. This caused his glasses to bounce all over his face and turn the glinting into a veritable light show for the excited ape. The ape clapped its hands happily as it reached the man and smiled broadly, pushing the man's shoulder back and forth to make the lights flash faster. Finally the lone spectator fainted, a fact he would never admit to anyone so long as he lived. As he slowly fell backwards the ape lifted the glasses from his face and placed them across his own nose. This caused the arms of the glasses to snap and fall off, but brute strength had wedged the glasses firmly across his broad nose and there they now sat as spectacles. As luck would have it, the spectator, who would never again set foot in a circus or any other event with animals larger than a guinea pig, was also astigmatic. For the ape, the world was...in focus.

Stanley entered the tent behind the human barricade of Mother Hinkle and Goliath and dove to the ground as a tiger was making the leap down from the stands above his head.

"Aaarrrgggghhh!"

He cowered in traditional earthquake position until he realized that he hadn't actually been disemboweled. He peered from the corner of his eye and saw that the tiger was indeed still there, and so was a large yellow ball. The tiger nudged the ball toward him with his nose, its purring a deep bass that made the hair on Stanley's neck stand on end.

"Leo, this is not the time for fetch. There, that's a good boy, aren't you?" Goliath was scratching the tiger under the chin and tossed the ball in toward the center ring where the trainer was trying to call him back. Leo sprang after it with a hunting growl that probably ruined the pants of any circus-goers remaining in ear shot.

Mother Hinkle helped haul Stanley to his feet while Goliath headed for Cyrus, who was shouting commands from the safety of the center ring.

"Chaz, you get down from there right now, do you hear me? Chaz! There's a nice juicy banana in it for you, but only if you put him down *right* now!"

Chaz, the aforementioned astigmatic ape, was enjoying new, sharper sights from his seat in the stands. The man whose glasses he was now wearing had woken up to a nightmare; the ape had pulled the man onto his lap like a doll or small child and was patting him on the head and rocking him while chattering and pointing at all of the activity around them. The man looked as though he were trying to burrow into his own neck before passing out again.

Then Chaz caught a glimpse of something that his master was waving at him. It was yellow, curved, and it looked *delicious*. He jumped up, causing the gurgling man to tumble from his lap, and made his way down the stands, crushing the chairs indifferently beneath his great feet. Cyrus smiled and coaxed the ape further down by tossing the banana up and down tauntingly. Chaz was intrigued and most of all hungry, but something else was tugging at the fringe of his hearing. It sounded like beautiful music to his ears.

"You get your stupid tiny hands off me, runt! I can take care of myself just fine, thank you!"

Snow White the Bearded Lady was pushing her dwarfs away. They were trying to get her away to someplace safer, but she'd be damned if the knight in shining armor rescuing her was going to be four feet tall. She pushed Little Joe away with an unladylike snarl.

"Uuhhnnkkh?" Chaz grunted and looked around for the sound and his eyes fell upon an angel with a beard. "Uuhhnnkkh!" He forgot entirely about the banana and bore down on Snow White, his knuckles pounding the ground as hard as his feet.

Little Joe and Big Joe turned away from her and ran, leaving her smugly certain that the dwarfs were afraid of her, but then a primordial sigh of longing filled her ears and blew her hair into her face. She turned slowly, her nose wrinkling at the stale banana breath that followed.

"Oh. My. God." She mouthed. Chaz, inches from her face, was giving her the gorilla equivalent of puppy eyes, which was actually more charming than one might think.

"Don't move! He's blind as a bat; he'll lose interest in a minute if you don't move." Cyrus hissed toward her as the trainer sneaked quietly behind him.

"But he's wearing glasses!" She hissed back out of the corner of her mouth.

"Glasses?" The trainer asked aloud before he could stop himself. He slapped his hands over his mouth and stood frozen in place, but it was too late. Growling, Chaz turned on him and punched the ground, challenging the newly entered rival male.

"Easy now, fella. It's just me, buddy. Remember ol' Davey? Just take it easy and leave the girl alone." He tried to move cautiously toward Snow White.

Chaz remembered ol' Davey, all right. He remembered clearly that there had been whips involved at some point.

Ol' Davey cleared the organ box and landed about ten feet past Cyrus when Chaz finally quit swinging him around by his feet and let go. Then Chaz threw Snow White over his shoulder and made for the highest ground he could find. With his burden kicking, screaming, and punching him in the back, he climbed the ladder to the gymnasts' tower where the high-wire and trapeze acts launched and perched himself on the platform overlooking the people below. Usually people were just a kind of blurry pinkish, whitish, or brownish haze to him. They brought him food and that was the extent of his interest in the human race. Now he finally saw the truth. They had *teeth*. And they had women.

Only the members of the Upper and Lower Jelly River gangs were pleased with the new show.

"Cool, did you see him pick that guy up?"

"Guy? But he's wearing a dress!"

"Dude, that's a girl with a beard!"

"But what's he want with a bearded lady?"

"Pick fleas? I dunno."

"Hey, we should do something. Like save someone or something!"

"We could save Jordan and Carrie!"

"We don't need savin'! Maybe we should save YOU."

"Don't be dumb, girls can't save boys!"

"Oh yeah?"

And so it continued with the rest of the adults completely unaware and uninterested in the children for the first time all week.

By now Cyrus had worried his cigar so violently that it hung in soggy shreds from his lip. "Goliath, *do* something!"

The inner Lynus Minor rolled his eyes. Part of the trouble with being the largest and strongest man anyone knew was that it was always assumed that you would save the day when push came to shove. Then the outer Goliath pushed up his sleeves, or would have had he been wearing something more substantial than a loincloth, and grabbed the bottom of the ladder.

Chaz saw a new rival male approaching. This one was *big*. He reared back with Snow White firmly grasped in one arm and bellowed across the tent, issuing his challenge to Goliath on the ladder below. With his newly acquired vision he noticed more movement near him and swatted at the trapeze artist who was reaching a hand to Snow White to grasp so he could pull her to safety. The strike missed the man, but it snapped one of the cords and sent the man swinging wildly around the plinth in a wide circle. Chaz bellowed again, this time beating his chest savagely. Snow White screamed and fainted dramatically; somehow in her fear she still managed to fall into a delicate and sultry pile.

Stanley had drawn himself up near Cyrus by now and was watching the scene play out above. It seemed so surreal, almost like a movie. In fact...

"Does this...I mean all of this," he spread his arms to indicate the entire scene to Cyrus, "seem a little familiar to you somehow?" Chaz was still swatting at the man on the broken trapeze, sending him into even wider and more erratic circles around the tower.

Cyrus gave Stanley a long look. "Does a giant ape abducting a bearded woman, climbing a tower and causing a standoff with flying acrobats seem 'familiar' to me?"

"Well," Stanley said sheepishly, "maybe not the acrobats part. Or the bearded part."

Cyrus narrowed his eyes at Stanley. "Son, have you been drinking at my circus? You do realize that this is a family show, right?"

"No, I just—never mind." Stanley worked his way over to Mother Hinkle, who was just putting the finishing touches on the knot that tied a now completely docile Leo to his cage. She patted the tiger on the head and gazed up toward where Goliath was just reaching the top of the ladder.

"That dang fool! What does he think he's goin' to do from up there? Out-ape him? Ha! I'll see about this."

Stanley started to follow her when Leo nudged him to the ground hoping to play, unintentionally pinning his pants to the ground with a long claw in the process.

"I'll just be here then, if you need me." He muttered to himself on the ground beside Leo as the tiger rolled over for a belly rub.

"YOU! You big dirty ape, you overgrown monkey! You get down here and take a bit a' what's comin' to ya! You leave that poor girl alone, you poo-throwin' fleabag!"

Mother Hinkle, in all her massive fury, gave the ape a tongue lashing like he'd never heard. It wasn't as if he had any idea of what she was saying; it was more the way in which she said it. Chaz looked down at the base of the podium and instantly fell in love all over again. So many choices! He looked down at the frail and unconscious Snow White in his arms and heaved a discontented and dismissive grunt. He dropped her without interest into Goliath's outstretched arms just as he reached the peak of the plinth, and performed a dismount that would have turned Olympic gold medalists green with envy. Mother Hinkle didn't even flinch when, from fifteen feet above, he hit the ground mere inches from her.

"I reckon' you think you're a show off, huh? You think you've got somethin' you can show *me*?" Mother Hinkle pressed her nose to his. Even with him drawn up to his full height she was still eye to eye with the ape. Chaz found himself having second thoughts about his romantic instincts and turned to the first of his masculine instincts when challenged. He bluffed. But only a half-hearted bluff.

"Uuhhnnkkh?"

"Is that all you got? You oughtta be ashamed of yourself! Running around here all gruntin' and grabbin' young ladies." Chaz took a few uncertain steps backwards. Goliath laid Snow White safely upon the platform and slid silently back down the ladder. Chaz grunted at her again, this time with such a lack of fortitude that it may have been the animal kingdom's equivalent of "Yes, Dear."

"Don't you even think about trying to suck up now. I'm so sick of your type! You think that just because you're big and strong you can push everyone around and treat women like possessions? You got another think comin'!" She jabbed her finger into his furry chest, driving him back the two feet needed to walk right into the cage Goliath had noiselessly wheeled up behind him.

Chaz almost seemed relieved when Mother Hinkle slammed it shut. He sat down to sulk in the corner and ate the banana he found waiting for him, but only after tearing off the glasses and smashing them beneath his hairy foot. In the span of just a few minutes he had already learned two very human axioms; sometimes ignorance truly is bliss, and hell hath no fury like a woman scorned. Well, like a woman, period.

Mother Hinkle paused, her heart still pounding, and looked at the ape in the cage one last time before turning her eyes back to Goliath. She opened her mouth to say something, but disappointment closed it again. She merely shook her head at him and stalked out of the tent to find what was left of her ruined fields, and her heart finished breaking when she saw the shambles that represented her living. Tents and carts looked as though they'd been tossed by a tornado, the animals that had yet eluded capture were digging and clawing, and people were still running as far away as they could get. Those who'd driven had left long muddy tire tracks trying to escape the throng of traffic in any direction they could. The chaos had spread to nearly every inch of her farm.

She reached down to free her foot from something that had snagged it on the ground, and pulled up a crushed and trodden young potato. Pieces of it fell away in her hands, unleashing hot tears from her eyes.

As she stood there, Goliath watched her shoulders heave with sobs. He didn't see the dirt smeared across her face and dress. He didn't see the tears in her dress, nor did he notice that her makeup was streaming away in rivulets down her cheeks. Right at that moment, as the red sunset was streaking through the settling dust, she was the most beautiful thing he'd ever seen. Guilt burned through him as he watched one of the battered silver ribbons finally detach itself from her sleeve and float, defeated, to the ground.

He reached out and laid his hand on her shoulder.

"Miranda—" he began.

She shrugged his hand off and stepped out of reach, not bothering to turn around.

"Don't. Just don't. You hear me? This was all I had, everything, right here." She shook the remains of the potato in her hand.

"Please, Miranda, I didn't—"

"You didn't nothin'! I knew better." She sighed and repeated herself more quietly. "I knew better, but I fell for it anyway. Because I wanted to. But I've learnt my lesson now."

With a glacial pace, she finally turned to face him. "Just get off my property, you hear? All of you get off, and don't you dare come back."

He watched her walk away. What did size and strength matter when he knew none of it would make her return? Somewhere in the back of his mind he was aware of Cyrus calling for him, but the inner Lynus finally won a round. He ignored Cyrus and went to see if his tent was still standing.

"Where is he? Damn it, will someone please tell me where that big oaf went?" Cyrus yelled. He was currently trying to help the trainer dislodge a very complacent and snoring Leo off Stanley's lap. Trying to help in his case, of course, meant he was standing and barking orders while very nearly actually touching the tiger.

"Hello! Has anyone forgotten anything down there? Like *me*?" A huffy voice added to the confusion. Snow White had apparently regained consciousness and realized that she'd been left alone on the platform. She'd be really annoyed later that everyone continued to ignore her.

Stanley barely noticed her calling. There was a ladder up there anyway. She'd find it eventually. Besides, he had other things on his mind. He was pretty certain he couldn't feel his left foot at all, unless cold and numb was what a foot was supposed to feel like.

Then there was suddenly the silence. This was not the same as the silence that occurred during a lull in conversation, or the silence that happened suddenly when driving under an overpass in a rain storm. This was the silence that followed disbelief. It was the silence that asked the question, "Was that another gunshot I just heard?"

The animals, their energy spent in their initial panic, this time barely responded to the same sound that had instigated the stampede. With the exception of Leo, all they cared about was that they were exhausted and happy to be back in their cages. While Leo hadn't noticed a gunshot, he *had* noticed that his nice comfy pillow had suddenly flipped him over and taken off in the direction of the sound, limping slightly.

It was in that second that the silence was broken by human screams and the words that Stanley was dreading.

"Help! He's been shot!"

He ran faster, ignoring the needle-like pains in his foot that signaled the return of circulation, and dodged past the people running away from the point of the shot. The sound had come from somewhere behind the carousel. In all of the confusion no one had thought to turn off the ride and it was still turning, pumping out its frenzied music. Without any riders, the horses, lions, and other various animals of reality and mythology alike appeared slightly malevolent and eerie. When he arrived there was already a crowd gathered that was in various stages of panic, helpful suggestions, and full-out gawking. Most people had run from the sound of the shot, but those who remained were a mix of the truly concerned and the morbidly curious. Stanley pushed through both sorts and found himself out of breath on the ground next to the victim.

"Mr. Gregory!" Stanley exclaimed.

Monty was beginning to stir, and then Stanley realized that he wasn't truly lying on the ground so much as simply floating motionlessly just above the earth. When Stanley touched him he drifted a few inches to the side. There was a smoking hole in the center of his costume, but Monty seemed otherwise unharmed with the exception of having fainted dead away, to use a pun, at the experience of having a confused bullet pass clear through him. He'd had to learn to make physical contact with the outside world in every way. He'd had to learn to walk, to touch, and to even just hold whiskey in his mouth. One thing that he hadn't done yet was learn how to be shot.

Stanley recovered his breath. He was relieved that no one had actually been killed, but this was still technically a shooting and attempted murder, depending on how you looked at it.

He looked at the base of the carousel behind where Monty was lying. It was a simple cinder block wall with a sturdy but light-weight layer of sheet metal over it, painted in gaudy colors and swirls. Right about chest level there was a deep dent, but the metal wasn't punctured. His eyes narrowed. The bullet must have sailed right through Monty and ricocheted from there to somewhere else. No one else seemed to be hurt, at least. He'd worry about where the bullet went later.

Monty groaned and his eyes finally opened, slowly at first, then he sat up like a bolt.

"He killed me!" He screamed. There was an uncomfortable silence from the crowd.

"Um, I don't think you can get any deader," said a crowd member hesitantly.

"No, you idiot! I mean he killed me the first time! That was the man who actually killed me!"

"Who was it? Where did he go?" Stanley grimaced at the pain in his leg as he jumped to his feet.

"I don't know and I don't know," Monty moaned. "I didn't know his name. He bought me a drink and that's the last I remember. I barely saw him just now, but I remember those eyes! I don't know where he went, but I think he took her."

Stanley was about to ask him what he meant by "her," but by this point Allen had arrived on the scene with his trusty camera on his shoulder and nearly knocked Stanley over trying to get a close-up of the hole in Monty's costume. Then Stanley noticed what was missing.

"Wait, where's Dana?"

Chapter Six

Fifteen minutes before...

The terrifying pounding of hooves, nearby growls, and animals sniffing at his hiding place below the truck had finally calmed and was replaced by the sound of the carnies restoring order to the circus. However, Erwin was no more confident as he stepped out of the safety of the vehicle and approached the news lady. For one thing, she was pretty, and he wasn't used to talking to pretty girls. Actually, he wasn't used to talking to girls at all. When he tried to talk to any of them except for his mom they usually just rolled their eyes and walked away. She wasn't quite alone, but he doubted he'd have another chance.

He'd only promised the Stranger he'd give her a message. Just one simple message. That wasn't so bad, right?

"Allen, look at the bear! Can you get that on camera?" Dana was directing Allen to film different parts of the carnage. Currently the bear was rolling around as if in pain at the end of a tether of other exhausted animals. What she'd thought at first was growling turned out to be the braying cries of a much-abused stomach full of sugar.

"Miss Perki?" Erwin tapped her on the arm lightly, realizing too late that there was a bit of gum goo still adhering to his hand. It drew away with a sticky string connecting his hand to her forearm.

"What...? Eww." She tried to shake the remnants off her arm.

"What do you want, Erwin?" She asked testily. He was already shy, but she watched him shrink even further into himself than he already was when she snapped at him. He was a pitiful mess of wrinkled clothes, food stains, and dirt from head to toe, and his hurt eyes filled her with delayed childhood guilt. Her demeanor and her voice softened with pity, "What can I do for you?"

He stared at his feet. "I j-just have a message to give you. From someone, not me."

"Yes?" She prompted.

"He says he knows what happened to the policeman and he'll tell, but he'll only talk to you 'cuz he knows you from TV and says you're nice."

"You're kidding! Where is he?" Her voice took on a manic edge. "Allen, get the camera! We've got a story!"

"He said he wanted to talk to you alone first, ma'am. He said alone or he'd go to someone else." The excitement was starting to come back for him and his chest swelled with as much pride as his scrawny rib cage would allow. He was just like a spy in a movie!

"Go ahead, Dana. It's not worth risking losing an interview like that. I'll keep getting footage around here. Just call me when you need me."

She paused; something didn't feel right. Her gut was telling her this was somehow dangerous and incautious, but if she could get the exclusive on breaking this story.... This was how field reporters became lead anchors. That thought was all she needed to make her decision.

"All right, I'll do it. Where is he?"

Erwin pointed across the ruined midway to where the carousel was still turning, oblivious to anything around it. She tried to find a non-sticky place to pat Erwin and settled for a "thanks" and a thumbs up before heading directly to the carousel, her notebook in hand.

Glad she'd worn flats today, she moved as quickly as she could through the piles of debris, animal waste, and collapsing tents that made the midway look like an apocalyptic movie set, right down to the abandoned clown horn half buried in the mud. She didn't see anyone as she approached the carousel, and even the destruction here wasn't as bad as she entered the little courtyard in front of the ride. Her stomach knotted as she realized the reason why; the carousel was almost completely isolated from the rest of the midway. Her nerves rattled a little louder, in part because she finally noticed the eeriness of the macabre collection of animals on the carousel itself. She wished she knew who'd decided that all carousels should be made up of nightmarish looking beasts so she could slap them right in the face. Even the horses seemed to be snarling and would have looked more fitting underneath a scythe-wielding skeleton in black robes than your average five year-old.

The rusty and graffiti-stained operator's box rested at the very back of the ride, and out of the corner of her eye she saw a hand beckon to her urgently before it was zipped back inside the booth. *Oh well,* she thought. At least it was out of the way of the clean-up efforts, and her interview could be safe from other eavesdropping reporters.

As she approached the booth she realized her heart was in her throat. All mammals have an inborn ability to sense danger. What humans possess in addition to this is an ability to sense that danger, and then reinterpret the sensations associated with that instinct and reassign their causes to something completely different and preferable. Dana was currently assigning the knot in her stomach to excitement over her impending fame for breaking the story of the decade.

"Hello?" She called to the mysterious stranger in the booth. Despite her excitement she was having difficulty convincing her feet to move closer. When he didn't respond, she forcibly picked her feet up and took another step, and ended up staring down the barrel of a hand gun.

"Stay right there," commanded the owner of the gun, his face still concealed within the shadows of the booth.

• • •

At the same moment another figure had, quite literally, drifted toward her from the opposite direction. Monty had spotted her approaching the carousel after he fled the main circus tent. He'd never been happier to see a familiar face and was wishing like mad that he could still take his nerve pills.

"Dana! I'm so glad to see...oh!" As he rounded the corner he saw her frozen in place, staring at the gun just inches from her nose. He rose another few inches off the ground in surprise and hovered there.

"No, you aren't even alive! *You can't be here!*" The gunman said, stepping out of the shadows and staring wide-eyed at Monty. His hand shook as he turned the gun from Dana toward Monty. The hammer cocked and released before either of them could scream.

• • •

"I thought she'd be here already," Allen was telling Stanley. "She came over here to get an exclusive from someone who claimed to know what happened to that Jostlem cop. Haven't you seen her?" As he spoke his camera dropped farther from his shoulder. Allen knew that she'd been in the general area of the gunshot, but hadn't for a moment thought that she might have been in the way of the shooter. Getting into trouble wasn't Dana's style.

Stanley stood up and surveyed the scene, letting one of the carnies deal with getting Monty up and his feet to stay on the ground. He might not have been able to do much in the face of a stampede, but he would damned well find a missing reporter in his town.

"You, you, and you." He pointed at random to three of the crowd of gawkers that he recognized as Merit citizens. "Get some people together with you and search every last inch of this circus in case she's still here. She may be a witness to a shooting at best.

At worst...well, you know. I want you to report back to me in an hour at the police station. Is that clear?"

The townspeople nodded. Two of them were smart enough to recognize that Stanley's normally easy-going tone had been replaced by angry authoritarian basses and was not to be questioned. One of them, however, was not.

"Does this mean we get to be deputies? Do we get one of them badges, too? Spelled right, I mean," he sniggered.

Stanley turned and smiled at the man. Sometimes a smile was the worst thing you could do to someone.

"Gregg?"

Gregg, quickly learning to distinguish between a time for jest and a time for shutting the hell up, responded more meekly this time. "Yes, Sheriff?"

"You just find that woman. If you don't find her, you can have my badge. But you won't like where I'll put it."

Monty was woefully staring at the hole in his costume when Stanley turned his attention back to him. Other reporters had come back down from their hiding spots and were trying to push through the crowd to get to Monty and Stanley, but they underestimated the staying power of the curiosity of the citizens of Merit. This was by far the most interesting day that the people of Merit had ever seen; therefore, they were as unmovable as a wall. The reporters tried shouting their questions over the heads and shoulders of the townspeople, but Stanley didn't spare them a glance. *Hyenas*, he thought. *Hyenas act like that. They show up not in time to stop the fight, not to help the wounded heal, but just in time to fight over the spoils.*

"Mr. Gregory, I need you to tell me everything that you remember. Where did he come from, what does he look like, *anything*. Right now I feel like I'm chasing a ghost. No offense."

"It's all right, I get it. Look, all I know is that he has brown hair, and he kind of looked like Sir Robert Anton Balding, Jr. in the movie

Which Way is Up? Remember that one? Especially the scene where he discovered his twin brother hadn't really been pushed out of the blimp over the volcano." There were knowing nods of approval from the crowd. This movie had been a popular one at Merit's single-screen theater the previous summer.

"Anyway, he was in the booth with the gun on her and flipped out when he saw me. He turned the gun on me and that's really all I remember."

Stanley gave Monty a look. "Out of a blimp, really? Oh, never mind." He pointed at Allen, who'd been unusually quiet the last few minutes. "You. What happened before she left the truck?"

"That kid...you know, the one with the snot nose and the goo all over him all the time?" Stanley mentally inserted *Erwin* while Allen was talking. "He said he had a message for her. Some guy said he knew what happened to the cop and he would only talk to her. If anyone else came he wouldn't talk to her."

"And you let her go? When does it ever turn out okay when someone says 'come alone or else'? Where is Erwin now?"

"Who?"

Stanley sighed in exasperation. "The gooey kid!"

"Oh, um, I think he left. I haven't seen him since."

"Stanley!"

Oh God, not now. He cringed angrily. For the first time in his career, Stanley was rising to the moment. He felt strong, confident, and capable of finally saving this town. He was getting things done. The last thing he needed now was Isabelle. Actually, he suddenly realized for the first time, she was usually the last thing he needed anytime. Much to his chagrin, the townspeople made a hole for her to pass through. Her reputation for retaliation preceded her. There wasn't a soul left in Merit between the ages of coherency that hadn't been burned by her temper at some point.

"Why didn't you come find me? I waited for you and you never came! I could've been killed!"

He turned and faced her.

"Not right now, Izzy, I'm working. There's been a shooting and Da...I mean, someone is still missing."

"Really? Who was shot? Was it anyone—?"

"I was!" Monty wailed, causing Isabelle to notice him for the first time. "And he's already killed me once!"

Isabelle was silent for a moment, a miracle which was only compounded by the fact that she had been interrupted and was not actually erupting in fury. In fact, she looked rather entranced.

"Aren't you Montana Gregory, the actor?" There was a tinge of wonder in her voice.

Recognizing the recently unfamiliar tones of awe, Monty straightened his back, sucked in his gut, and attempted the most dashing smile he could while wearing a toga made of someone's bed sheet with a big hole in front. He also tried to drop his voice almost an octave. Somewhere, a cow was almost certainly pricking up her ears in interest.

"Why, yes. I am he."

"I can't believe it! Here, in this backwards hick town?" She exclaimed, uncaring that she wasn't winning any friends among the observers. "Do you think I could get an autograph, Mr. Gregory?"

"I'd be delighted! Say, you haven't heard any particular rumors about me, have you? Because if you have, they are completely unfounded, I assure you."

"Good grief." Stanley walked away, leaving Monty and Isabelle behind. There wasn't a place that was "away" enough as far as he was concerned. But at least they could keep each other occupied and keep Isabelle out of his hair for a while.

"Bertie! Where have you been?" Stanley had never been so relieved to see Bertie's large frame, even in a full run. Bertie had entered and won the Merit talent competition the prior year for his ability to jump rope while bouncing a basketball with his stomach, so Bertie in full gallop was something to see. Stanley opened his mouth to shout at him for disappearing, but closed it again when he saw the look of concern on Bertie's face.

"It's the kids, Stanley! They wouldn't stop fighting," he panted. "One of them got hurt. The ringmaster was trying to stop them when I got there, but it's been like trying to stop...something...I don't know, like something that can't be stopped! You should probably come talk to the parents before things get worse."

When they reached the main tent again they found Cyrus indeed surrounded by the kids, but the scene was different from what he expected. They were all just watching, looking guilty. There were soft cries from a child on the ground, and one of the mothers was fussing over him while stopping intermittently to chastise the children for the fight.

"Ow! Stop it!" Brewer was holding his arm to his chest with tears streaming down his face.

"Just hold still and quit trying to move your arm, son. I think it's broken."

Cyrus saw Stanley's approach and looked up pleadingly. "He tried to climb the tower to get the drop on the other kids and fell off the ladder. I didn't see him climbing!" Cyrus was struggling with some rather new feelings. His concern for other people had usually been limited to where their concerns overlapped his. This time, however, was different. Somehow he was feeling responsible for this and guilt, shame, and remorse were not sentiments that he felt at all at home with.

"I didn't even see him," he repeated to himself.

"I think we should let them be, Bertie. The parents can take care of them now."

"Wait, Sheriff!" Jordan's mother—the crime show addict—grabbed Stanley's arm. "You aren't just going to let them get away with this, are you? This is tantamount to criminal negligence. A *child* is hurt!"

Cyrus's eyes went wide at the mention of the word 'criminal,' but was surprised when Stanley was the one who came to his sort-of rescue.

"Belinda, what did I tell you when all of you asked me about those permission slips?"

Belinda's look of rage began shifting back into guilt. "That it was a bad idea."

"Well, I was wrong. It was a *stupidly* bad idea. And you signed them anyway. If anyone is responsible for your children's safety, it's *you*. You don't get to just sign away that responsibility."

Stanley led Bertie away from the subdued scene and was stopped cold at the door. The tent behind was every bit as much a shambles as the rest of the circus and the fields. Props, chairs, instruments from the orchestra pit, and everything else that had been in use at the time of the stampede was strewn about the three rings and nearly cluttered the entrance. But what was especially cluttering the entrance was the crowd of reporters who'd followed Stanley from the scene of the shooting, rightly assuming that where Stanley was would be the story. Currently, they were barely being kept at bay by both Joes, Big and Little.

"Was one of the children injured in gang-related activities?"

"For the record, Sheriff, was this attack racially motivated?"

And simply because there was always one who wrote for *that* sort of paper: "Is there any truth to the rumors that the actor who was to star in tonight's show is not only dead, but *gay*?"

Stanley was amazed. They had just survived a stampede of large and exotic animals, seen the attempted re-murder of a ghost, and learned that a fellow reporter had just been potentially kidnapped by the man who quite possibly had something to do with the suspected murder of an officer in Jostlem. With all of these potentially paper-selling headlines, they had *still* reverted to the original storyline about racism that hadn't even been true to begin with. He'd never been so ashamed of the human race.

"Is there a back door...er, flap to this thing?" Stanley asked.

"You bet," the nearest Joe answered. "Just follow the yellow stone path behind the third ring and you'll be out like a shot."

Stanley was quiet, his brain forming the question but thinking better of it. Unfortunately, Bertie had no such filter. What was fortunate, however, was that he was slower on the uptake and didn't think of the question until they were out of earshot of the dwarf.

"Yellow stone path? Is that anything like a yellow brick road?"

"Just keep walking, Bertie."

The sun was setting as they emerged from the tent. It was, ironically, the most beautiful sunset he'd seen all year. Stanley looked around to make sure no one was in sight or earshot.

Then he threw a tantrum.

"What the heck?" He sighed. This was no time for "hecks." "What the *hell*? I *knew* something was going to happen tonight, I just knew it! Jesus!" He kicked the back of a hay bale. "Now I've had someone shot, I've got a friend—well, a reporter—missing, who *might* have seen the shooter, who turns out to be Mr. Gregory's killer, who might turn out to be the cop killer as well, and I don't know where to start! We have to find her. I've got three citizens forming search parties, but I should be the one to lead them. We just have to find her," he repeated grimly. "Bertie, I need you to get a copy of the movie *Which Way is Up* as soon as you can."

"Why?" Bertie was caught by surprise at this last request.

"Long story. Apparently our murderer stars in it."

"You're kidding! The murderer is Sir Robert Anton Balding, Jr.?"

Stanley looked long and hard at Bertie. Bertie was not a stupid man. Sometimes, however, he would play that way when he thought Stanley was in need of a confidence boost. It might have been more effective if Stanley hadn't caught on to this ruse years ago.

"No, Bertie, he just looks like him. Apparently everyone knows this movie but me. What else? I know I'm missing something here."

Thoughts were pouring fast through Stanley's mind. There were still pieces of the puzzle everywhere, but he felt like he was at least getting some of the edges to match.

Bertie waited patiently and let Stanley keep talking to himself when a sound on the periphery caught his attention.

"Do you hear that?"

• • •

Not far from where Bertie and Stanley stood Cud had been having the experience of a lifetime. Terriers were natural hunters and quite a bit of Cud's ancestry was, at least in parts, terrier mixtures of various blends. Presented with the pursuit opportunities of the last several minutes, he had been over-stimulated from chasing exotic and large animals that could also, as he learned, chase him as well. He had also been stimulated by an incident involving a circus poodle who, after closer investigation and against all visible evidence, had turned out to be male.

• • •

Stanley stopped his train of thought and followed Bertie to the opposite side of the tent, where definite sounds of a quiet struggle were escalating. It was beginning to sound like a rather wet struggle. What they found stumbling around in a circle was a reporter fighting with a small mangy dog.

"Stanley," Bertie whispered nervously. "That's Barbara Chase-Howard from the Jostlem Evening News! She's the biggest reporter on TV!"

Of course it is, he thought. *What could be more fitting?* "Cud, get over here right now!"

Relief had found its way to Cud through the benevolence of scent–the heavenly scent of what was undeniably bitch. Little did he know that the delightful aroma teasing his sensitive canine nose was due to the fact that Barbara's bichon frise had slept in her lap all the way from Jostlem to Merit. It was a tragedy that Dana wasn't there to appreciate the irony.

"Cud! Get off her leg!"

"Get this thing off me! I mean it, if you don't get this mongrel away from me right now I'll sue!"

Cud was especially unhappy when Stanley snatched him by his blue rhinestone-covered collar and pulled him away from Barbara's now soggy leg.

But Stanley and Bertie hadn't been the only ones attracted by the sounds of Cud's romantic overtures. A number of cameras had appeared with their owners in tow to capture Barbara's struggle. *Also like hyenas*, Stanley thought. A member of their pack was injured and they didn't stop to help. They smelled the blood in the air and began to drool.

"That mutt shouldn't be allowed to simply wander around attacking people! He should be put down! I'll be having a conversation about this with the mayor, you better believe. Don't be surprised if you see this on the 11:00 news!"

She turned toward the crowd of reporters who were also hoping to see it on the 11:00 news. Due to the competitive nature of televised newscasting, most of these were hopefuls and sworn nemeses, but all would have been anxious to see Barbara Chase-Howard taken down a peg even if they hadn't also smelled promotion opportunity.

"All of you, you wannabes! Just get away from me!"

Stanley's shock meter was past overworked. It was so far past, in fact, that all it was now registering were items to file for later consideration. The most passionate response he could muster when Barbara stormed away from him and the following crowd was a shrug as he continued to pat the panting and thoroughly satisfied Cud on the head.

"What's he doing here, Stanley? I didn't know you brought him to the circus with you."

"I didn't. I left him locked up at the office. He must have gotten out somehow." Stanley's eyes widened as he realized the implications. "Or someone let him out. Bertie, I think we better get to the station."

• • •

Dana awoke to the sound of a terrifyingly loud heartbeat. Its cadence filled the small room as she struggled to sit up. Her mouth was gagged by something that tasted sweaty, and a quick test confirmed that she was hogtied on a hard floor.
The heartbeat stopped.

"Pfefoah?" She ventured through her makeshift muzzle.

That was her first mistake.

• • •

Comparatively speaking, the walk, or run, to the sheriff's office had been a walk in the park. Traveling via rodeo bull would have been a paragon of Zen after the madness at the circus. Stanley's main goal en route to the station was to beat the setting sun, and it had been a close match. It wasn't that he couldn't turn on the lights once he arrived, but there was something comforting about the daylight, although all that remained of the day were just a few raggedy threads of sun left streaming through the branches of Old John's Christmas tree farm. Things always looked more manageable in sunlight than they did in moonlight. Even as he stood staring at the broken lock and split frame of the back door of the station he was clinging to the fact that it was, at least, not yet as dark as night.

Someone had kicked the door open. But who? Why? Where were they now? All of the requisite questions poured into Stanley's head, but he stopped short of voicing them. The only answer to any of them could only be the traditional "there's only one way to find out," and he just wasn't ready to get to that part yet. There was always the hope in these situations that the perpetrator was miles away already, but there was also the seed of doubt that had kept so many smart hunter-gatherer descendants alive rather than blindly walking into familiar caves in which lurking carnivores lay in wait.

Millennia of evolution spoke through Stanley. "Be careful, Bertie. Watch the door while I check the windows to see if anyone is still in there."

Cud, however, was obviously not one of these evolution-worthy descendants. He barked excitedly and pushed past both Stanley and Bertie as he ran up the steps and through the slightly ajar door, happily seeking his food bowl in the office.

"Oh, crap. Now we have to go in, don't we? So much for laying low and scoping the place out first."

Stanley had never heard Bertie whine like that before. He looked at the bigger man and realized that Bertie was staring at him expectantly, not to mention hopefully.

"It'll be all right, Bertie. I want you to wait out here for my signal and make sure no one tries to come out of there that isn't me. If you see anything odd, just yell."

Bertie nodded at his boss and suppressed a smile when he saw Stanley square his shoulders back and head bravely into the station. He released the smile when Stanley was through the door and out of sight.

Sometimes that boy just needed a little kick in the pants to be the man he wanted to be. It was just a shame Stanley's father wasn't around to see him now. The former sheriff would have been so proud of him.

• • •

The heartbeat resumed, faster now, and she realized that it was actually the limping footsteps of someone in the room with her. Her second mistake, as the steps neared her head, was trying to sit up and face her captor. This, for anyone who's never been hogtied, can make you feel like a broken rocking horse.

"Nnppht!" She grunted as her face hit the floor.

"Quit moving around! You're making too much noise," the limper said to her as he grabbed her restraints. He cut her feet loose from her hands but left them tied together. He picked her up roughly and set her down on a stack of empty sacks on the floor. She recognized him as the man from the circus as her memory finally started coming back into focus.

He wasn't what she would expect of a psychotic kidnapping murderer. To be fair, she'd have been hard put to tell you what she'd actually expect one to look like, but a list of likely descriptions certainly wouldn't have been "he looked like he could have been someone's grandfather." He wasn't old, but gaining on late middle age despite appearing in supreme physical shape. His eyes looked young and alert in contrast to his lined but tortured face.

What had he hit her with? Her head was pounding and her ears rang like an echo of a terminally ill school bell. She remembered the gun in her face suddenly, then hearing the shot... *That's right!*

"Uugh hhhod Nonny!"

"This isn't going to work, is it? This is going to sound cliché, but if I take off your gag, will you promise you won't scream?" He was speaking calmly. People who spoke calmly, especially while holding a gun, were people to be feared. She nodded. "Good. Because this part isn't so cliché. If you lied to me and you are planning to scream, I'll gag and tie you back up and drop you in the river. If you're lucky."

She held still while he cut the tape from her mouth and pulled out what appeared to be a balled up sock hat. She spat compulsively for a moment before repeating herself.

"You shot Monty!"

His fists clenched.

"Don't say that name!" She flinched as his cool demeanor shifted into rage. The gun in his hand, however, was still pointed at her and glinting sinisterly in the weak light of the lantern in the corner. "Don't you dare even think that name. He's the one who won't die. I didn't kill him!"

"Just because he's a ghost doesn't mean you can get away with shooting him!" For a moment, however, she found herself wondering, why not? No. There had to be a principle to the thing. Shooting people was still wrong, even if the people concerned were more mist and ectoplasm than flesh and blood.

"Shut up!" His face flushed and he stalked away to the other side of the small room and sat down against the wall. She took a chance to look around finally. The floor and walls were solid wood and very old. Not the variety of old wood that seemed likely to crumble if you leaned against it, but the sort that became as hard as steel with age. The roof was tin from the looks of it. This was a shed of some sort, she was certain. The air was musty and tasted of a metallic filth with a tinge of mold. Still, that was an improvement upon the lingering taste of the hat in her mouth. She was suddenly hoping that her captor hadn't found it discarded there and decided out of some inherent sense of cruelty to make use of it.

The wall across from her was covered in old cables and tools that she didn't recognize. Most of the shed, actually, was filled with things she didn't recognize now that she got a good look at it. There were things in there that might have been pulleys or levers, but *lots* of things that could make good weapons if she could just get her hands free. She worked her hands furtively behind her back while she continued examining the room, and her eyes fell on her captor.

The floor where he'd stood in front of her and where he was sitting now was glistening and wet.

• • •

Stanley surveyed what he was calling, for lack of a better word, his troops. Gregg Potter, Bucky Temple, and Jarhead Graff had rounded up a few of their friends and had searched the circus per Stanley's instructions. Even Allen and Albert Stiller were now a part of the little army. Allen had uncharacteristically abandoned his camera for the search and looked guilty as hell. *Rightfully* so, thought Stanley. Albert, however, was sporting a black eye that gave Stanley the feeling he was going to have to talk with Mrs. Stiller once things had settled down.

The search of the circus had turned up very little. The search of the ransacked police station had turned up more than Stanley wanted, however. The padlock to the gun cabinet had been cut and all three of the guns that belonged to the Merit Sheriff's Office had been stolen, along with several maps, flashlights, and the survival gear that Stanley had just taken from the mine that morning. Bertie was particularly miffed that his stash of hummus and pita bread was also missing. The damage was minor, but it seemed strangely evenly spread. Stanley had no doubt that it was the same man from the mine that morning. Had that really been just that morning? He rubbed his jaw reflexively.

Next to him on his desk was a picture he'd found shattered in its frame. He'd carefully rescued the photo from the shards while he waited for his back-up to arrive, and now his fingers kept wandering absently over to it. His eyes wandered down to find the image under his fingertips and he sighed. He'd had that photo for a very long time.

He could hear Bertie on the phone with Charlie Fountain arranging for all three Fountain men to meet them at the mine with lanterns and flash lights while Stanley addressed the assembled troops.

"It looks like between us we've got four guns, a baseball bat, a hatchet, tire irons, assorted hammers, and...you can't be serious! A rolling pin, Albert? Does she know you have this?" Stanley looked up at Albert's nervous and bruised face and reconsidered. In the Stiller house, this innocent looking cooking tool with a cheery little rooster print on the handles was practically a siege weapon. He suddenly had an appreciation for the nerve of the little man who picked it back up carefully as though it might go off in his hand.

"Never mind, but you might want to leave it here for good. All right, that's it for weapons. How many flashlights do we have?" There were rustles as the men laid various implements on the table next to their haphazard collection of weapons. There were four small lanterns, various flashlights, the light from Allen's camera, and now a Mighty Rocket Avengers light-up saber was rolled out of a sack. Everyone looked to Gregg, the sack holder.

"It's my kid's, okay? It's really freakin' bright, though. I just thought we could use it," he said sheepishly. He picked it up and flicked the switch. Sure enough, the toy saber glowed like a hand-held quasar on steroids.

"Wow," Stanley said as he shielded his eyes along with the rest of the troops. "Put it away for now, but bring it. I think you'd better stay behind us with that thing so you don't blind us."

"They're on the way, Stanley. Charlie and both his boys are going to meet us at the mine in twenty minutes with supplies." Bertie replaced the phone in its slightly broken cradle. It made a sad "ding, ding" as it sagged into place. "Do you really think he'll take her there?"

"I don't know, Bertie. But we know they left the circus and there isn't anywhere else in this town to hide that someone wouldn't stumble across him in short order. He's familiar with the mine so he might feel safe there," he finished doubtfully.

He looked at the jumpy faces and had a moment of panic. *What am I doing? I'm taking regular townspeople into a dark mine to search for an armed murderer. What's worse, I'm taking armed and scared townspeople into a dark mine where they may not be able to tell friend from foe.* He said hastily, "Bertie and I will take the guns. No buts," he cut off the first of the arguments. "If someone shoots anyone by mistake it had better be someone with a badge. Let's take the bat, tire irons, and the crow bars we have out back. Are you all sure you want to do this?"

"We ain't chicken, Sheriff. And this is our town, too. Any one o' us or our kids coulda been the ones to get hurt or taken today." Albert paused in his speech to re-arm himself with the hated rolling pin. He hefted it in his hand and smacked it into his palm. "We gotta show the crim'nal folk that if they wanna pass through here they'll wanna do it in a right damn hurry."

"He's right, Sheriff. Ain't one of us gonna back out on you now. Just lead the way and we'll be right behind you." Jarhead hoisted the baseball bat into the air in a show of camaraderie.

"Er, maybe not right behind me, please? Like a few feet past arm's reach?" He looked at the bat waving in the air and noticed something else below it all over Jarhead's sleeve.

"What happened to your arm? Your arm is bleeding!"

Jarhead looked unconcerned. "Ain't mine. I accident'ly lean't into a bunch of it back at the circus when we was lookin' for that reporter."

It should be mentioned here that Jarhead didn't earn his nickname for being a member of the honorable fighting force known fondly by that name for their iconic haircut. He'd earned it for having an IQ roughly equivalent to a jar of stale pickles with not quite enough pickling spice.

"Jarhead, I want you to tell me where you found that blood. Be specific." Stanley kicked himself for not having found where the ricocheted bullet had gone. What if she had gotten in the way of it?

"It was in that box with all them controls for the carousel ride. The floor was covered in it. I found it when I dropped my flashlight in there." He looked as though he were concentrating very hard. "I reckon that's all I know, pacifically."

Stanley blinked slowly.

"Bertie?"

"Yes, Stanley?"

"Stay here in case someone calls. The rest of you, it's time to move and I mean move now."

• • •

When Stanley and the troops were gone Bertie picked up the photo Stanley had left on the desk. That photo had been on the wall for the past eight years; a sad square of slightly brighter paint marked its place. Still, as with everything that remained in place for a long time, Bertie had largely forgotten about it and was now looking at it with fresh eyes.

The likeness was amazing.

It was of a boy in his father's arms, wearing his father's police hat, and his father's exact smile. When he thought about it, Stanley still had that smile.

He was the mirror image today of his father in the photograph.

• • •

Why would the floor be wet? It hadn't rained this evening and there was no rain in the forecast for the next week, much to Dana's dismay. She'd been hoping for rain just to take the pollen count down a notch.

She studied her captor. His back was to her now, but she could just make out a hint of shininess on his pants leg. It was soaked around his left calf, the very one that he was favoring so much. He was hurt! What she saw on the floor and his leg must be blood. She decided to keep quiet about it. She'd never been held captive by a gun-wielding mad man before, but she had a good idea that it would serve her well to not let on that she knew he was vulnerable. At least, not until he'd put that gun down and she'd gotten her hands loose. Not to mention wrapped around any one of the several sharp ended tools she'd spied around the walls.

Okay, so now what? She racked her brains. He seemed to be trying to come to some sort of a decision, and if that was the case she thought it might be in her best interest to keep him from making it just in case it happened to be the wrong decision for her. She thought distantly about the movies she'd seen that involved women in her situation. She sighed. Sooner or later she was going to have to ask The Question anyway. It was simply a matter of narrative necessity. Besides, weren't all mad men in the movies dying to answer it?

"So, what do you want with me? Why me?"

But her captor apparently wasn't following the same narrative. He ignored her while he talked to himself. Was he praying? *Oh no,* she thought. The words on the negative side of her list already read: Madman, gun, murdered once today already, tied up in shed. She now added "possible religious fanatic" to that list. The only thing on her positive list was that dark spreading pool of blood around his foot. He continued muttering fervently. He turned periodically as if trying to see something he thought was there. He waved violently at the air to his right. Voices *and* hallucinations? *Time to distract him for real,* she decided.

"Please, don't do this to me! What did I ever do to you?" She tried to whine pitifully and attempted a few sobs. This was no academy award-winning act, but she doubted he could tell the difference in his state.

"I told you not to yell!" The gun hand snaked back toward her and choked a couple of real sobs out of her in surprise. She was pretty sure there were even actual tears in her eyes. She decided to run with it and contrived to look like a helpless little girl, something that couldn't possibly be a threat to him.

"I'm sorry! I didn't mean to yell. I'm just scared. You're right, you didn't kill him, did you? He was already dead when you shot him so you couldn't have possibly killed him. If you just let me go—"

"SHUT UP! Shut up, shut up! Leave me alone!" It seemed to Dana that only half of what he said was directed to her. He seemed to be pleading with something to his left side and swatting the air as though a gnat were buzzing in his ear. His gun hand was unsteady, the barrel weaving a line that kept her too often in its sights, and his eyes bulged like an excited Chihuahua. Whatever internal struggle he'd been dealing with was definitely boiling to the surface, but he still seemed to be winning the battle. Within a few moments he regained nearly complete control of himself.

He moved toward her and shoved the gun into her face again, the only sign of his turmoil now in his still trembling hand. He stared at her, daring her to move.

"He was supposed to just die, don't you get it? Just die, just like all the others always did. Instead he's still here, haunting me. Haunting me! *Why won't he die?*" He said. Panic was beginning to edge back into his voice, yet even that was somehow less terrifying to Dana than when his words had been cold and merciless. "He might be haunting me, but I can damned well get rid of you!" He cocked the gun.

Dana squeezed her eyes tightly shut. *Oh god,* she thought, *I'm going to die in a shed in a hick town with the taste of sweaty armpit in my mouth, and I'm not even going to get a tiny byline on the story about my own death.*

She waited for the shot. And kept waiting.

"No, she won't come back!" He yelled at something unseen.

She heard a roar from her captor before everything went black.

Chapter Seven

The sun rose that morning with a troubled mind. It stalked hotly across the sleepy town as it peeked over the horizon and stifled the early morning sounds of Merit as though a blanket had been laid across her streets. Late in the night, or early in the morning, a rain cloud had stolen into the valley and now the brooding sun was busy burning the remnants of the unpredicted spring shower from the ground, making the air sticky, hot, and heavy. Cyrus rose from bed equally troubled and the humidity was making his job even more unbearable. He dabbed sweat from his brow as he surveyed his broken kingdom.

In the night, the dust had settled before being swept into a murky glaze by the rain, and now, as he carefully supervised the breaking-down of his Myriad of Marvels, the destruction had a muted and gray look to it. The faces of his staff were as drawn as his own as the carnies performed their well-practiced routines of packing and preparing for travel. Even Cyrus, who was normally barking orders at people who were already in the process of doing exactly what he was asking, simply watched. They were scheduled to be here for three more days, but he couldn't bear being here a day longer. At this point he was just hoping to get out of town before people began thinking of the word 'refund,' or possibly 'lawsuit.'

The stampede was going to cost him a lot of money, for one. In addition to that, his star performer had been shot and a woman had been kidnapped from his midway, and no carnie ever wanted to be in the middle of a police investigation. Everyone was feeling the tension, but it was really beginning to mess with Cyrus's head. He needed to get out of here to a place where he could clear his mind and try to wash his hands of some of these thoughts. None of this was his fault, so why was he feeling so involved, and worse, *guilty?*

He noticed that his employees were watching him expectantly and realized that he hadn't said a word to them all morning. The nearest nervous-looking acrobat was practically on the verge of tears. It was time he made an effort.

"You there!" He barked in his tone of Authority. The acrobat looked up hopefully. "Make sure you, you...do that, that thing you're doing... Just make sure you do it right! We don't need to be spending time re-doing things that weren't done right the first time around."

As typical ringmaster orders went this one was rather limp, but it seemed to cheer the acrobat immensely. It marked a return to something familiar after the confusion of the previous night, even if that something familiar was being yelled at by a cantankerous and blustering boss who would make even the Dalai Lama need a cigarette. If Cyrus were the type of boss to allow cigarette breaks, that is.

Cyrus moved on, more frustrated with himself than ever. He needed someone to talk to. There was only one person in his employ that he considered an equal and someone to discuss matters with, and he headed in the direction of Goliath's tent. Goliath always had the answers, or at least some archaic but soothing proverb that would make Cyrus feel better by distracting him from his problems while he tried to figure out what the hell Goliath was talking about.

When he arrived, there was a commotion at the entrance of Goliath's tent that promptly turned into awkward silence as realization spread that the boss was now in earshot.

"Cleansby's gonna flip his...pancake." The last to catch on finished lamely when he spotted the stony gaze of his boss. Cyrus was lord and master of the unreadable blank stare.

"And why would I flip this pancake of mine?" Cyrus asked coolly.

Various members of the crowd began to suddenly remember very urgent matters which they had just been passing through on their way to accomplish. The pancake flipper and the two nearest him remained locked under Cyrus's withering stare. One of them, Little Joe, managed to point to a note that had been taped to the flap of Goliath's tent.

"It's empty inside," he said. "He took his trunk and everything." Little Joe backed away from the note, leaving a wide berth between himself and his boss, flinching slightly in anticipation of an explosion.

Instead, and to the worry of those still watching, Cyrus was very calm. It was the sort of calm that occurred when someone threw a firecracker that didn't go off and then suddenly wondered as they reached for it if maybe it was just biding its time. He took the note in his hands and sighed. *Poetic to the end*, he thought.

"David didn't need a slingshot," he read aloud. " 'Twas beauty killed the beast."

It was signed "Lynus."

• • •

The sun had reached its steamy fingers into the Merit Sheriff's Office by now as well. The brightness hurt Stanley's eyes as he looked up from his maps of the town and squinted angrily at the window as though scolding the new day for dawning. As the light crept across the desk it also woke Bertie, who rose from his napping position against the phone with a near-perfect indentation of a number pad on his cheek and a sticky note on his chin for effect.

He stretched and lumbered over to the coffee pot, anxious to erase the taste of moldy carpet from his mouth.

Stanley barely noticed this. He barely noticed when Cud whined and begged for food, using his sweetest puppy eyes and most endearing ear perks, until the hungry dog dragged his heavy ceramic bowl over and dropped it on Stanley's toe. He'd also barely noticed when the townspeople had filed out one-by-one, murmuring of a need to get back to their families, after the long night's search of the mine, the woods around it, every empty house or building in town, and even the circus grounds again had been fruitless. Dana was nowhere to be found. It was as if she hadn't even existed.

The only civilian member of the search party who remained was Allen. He was currently curled up in the corner of the jail cell on the cot with his arms around his camera. He was snoring and on occasion mumbled things such as "and we're out" and "three... two...one." Once he'd shouted "Please don't make me wear the plaid skirt, Mommy," and would have been very glad to know that Stanley was too absorbed in what he was doing to notice.

The office was still a wreck, but during the long night Bertie had put together the essential elements for operation, beginning with the coffee pot and, in a sentimental gesture, had finished by removing the broken glass and re-hanging the photo of Stanley and his father.

After clearing his eyes and starting the coffee pot, Bertie took an appraising look at Stanley. *He's aged ten years overnight*, he thought.

"Stanley." He put his hand on Stanley's shoulder and pulled him away from the desk and to the chair. "You've got to quit staring at that before you go cross-eyed. That map isn't going to grow a new street to search just by you willing it."

"That's the problem, Bertie. It's a small town. *Tiny*. Short of walking door to door, I don't know what else to do. This just isn't a place you can disappear! Especially dragging a possibly injured woman with you. They couldn't have escaped by vehicle because it was a complete bottleneck getting through the gate at Mother Hinkle's. That means they have to still be here somewhere and it has to be on that map. And transporting someone out of town doesn't make sense, either. You can't just check into a hotel with a kidnapped woman. I'm missing something." Stanley began to realize just how exhausted he was as his body sank into the plush chair as though his muscles were made of lead.

"Sometimes you just have to step back from it for a little while. You need to close your eyes for a spell and rest. It's not going to get any clearer if you're sleepwalking."

"There's no time to rest! She could be—" Stanley blinked slowly and hazily tried to rise from his seat, but Bertie, in an uncharacteristically speedy move, had pushed him back down with a blanket.

"Thirty minutes, that's all. I'll wake you up, and then you can get back to searching your maps. There are lots of places to look between here and the river, and I'm sure you'll find what's missing."

"Between here and the river," Stanley mumbled. "But what if she's not between here and the river?"

He fell asleep.

• • •

"Doesn't anybody *work* in this town?"

Isabelle growled as she slammed the phone down in its receiver. She'd tried her father's attorney's office five times this morning already. She looked at the clock irritably: 7:13 a.m. She huffed with the exasperation of someone who'd never had to perform a day's work in their lives and couldn't understand why the engine of industry did not answer to her every twenty-four-hour whim. Things such as business hours and administrative overhead were mystifying notions to her. From her point of view all businesses were there to serve her needs. She had a need now, therefore, the business should be open to serve her now. From her point of view, this was actually a logical conclusion.

She returned to her frantic pacing while the cloud that was her hair bobbed up and down in a rhythm just slightly behind her own beat. Her tempo this morning would have given a salsa band tendonitis.

She looked sternly at the clock again; this did not help. It was 7:15 a.m.

She grabbed the phone and dialed once more, and was even more infuriated when nobody answered, yet again.

She cut her pacing short at lap number 97 and yanked open the wide island drawer that contained her favorite stress relievers. The metal shimmered as her collection of prized knives appeared, arranged in the drawer like the teeth of a giant predator with immaculate dental hygiene. There was something soothing to her about the way they caught the light, like the glow of a precious metal. She let her finger run across the smooth ebony handles and felt a bit of her anxiety melt away.

"All right, time to think." She did a mental about-face, which was a disturbing ability all by itself, and closed the drawer with one last longing glance.

Isabelle inspected her kitchen with purpose. At last she rummaged through a junk drawer and removed an innocent looking unmarked key. She took this key to the garage and used it to open the deep freeze, which Stanley had always assumed held the remnants of her brief attempt at canning. She never did figure out that an entire uncooked apple shouldn't be sealed in a jar, core, peel, and all.

Among the frost-laden containers filled with now unrecognizable fruits, vegetables, and legumes was a package wrapped in wax paper and sealed in plastic. She hovered over it thoughtfully. This package contained her secret stash of oysters and clams, which she'd had to order from Jostlem since the only butcher in town knew about Stanley's allergy.

"Oh, foo!"

She cursed incongruently for someone with homicidal tendencies. She'd heard about the epinephrine on hand at the hospital, too.

Slamming the lid shut she went back in the house and tossed the key back to its inconspicuous home. Her next stop was at the cabinet under the sink. Had anyone inventoried the contents of the cleaning cabinet in the Grace house they would have discovered a treasure trove of chemicals and compounds that would have made an alchemist green with envy. Or possibly green and bubbly had he not read the labels carefully before use.

The possibilities were infinite. However, most of those possibilities included quite a mess and quite a lot of explaining that even what would be her tremendous inheritance may not have been able to silence. It was one thing to accidentally be underneath a collapsing shelf covered with sharp or heavy objects, or maybe to mistakenly ingest an item to which you were deathly allergic, but quite another to accidentally drink a bottle of ammonia-based pipe cleaner.

No, that definitely wouldn't work. She sat down and thought hard, occasionally rifling through a cabinet here, a drawer there.

The phone rang when the clock read 8:05 a.m. and interrupted her study of the car manual about the necessity of well-maintained brake lines, with more interest in what happens if those brake lines *aren't* well-maintained, of course. An enterprising young clerk had listened to one of her many phone messages and found the courage to return her call, despite the stories he'd heard around the office. When he actually spoke to her he discovered that the stories were wrong. She didn't have the temper of a kangaroo with gout. That was far, far too mild of a description.

After ten minutes of being threatened, harangued, denigrated, belittled, and screamed at, the clerk had decided that being in the way of her temper was much more like being charged by a rhinoceros with a chronic migraine, personality disorder, and who was having a bad-horn day on top of that. If he'd been able to see her hairdo, he might have understood the irony in his last thought. There simply shouldn't be that much pent-up hostility in one person. Small terrorist-filled countries were mere white dwarfs when compared with the supernova of her rage.

After that conversation he went home to bed and pulled the blanket over his head to cry. Isabelle, however, was smiling. She'd gotten what she wanted. Most of all, she couldn't believe her luck.

This was going to be far easier than she ever would have thought.

• • •

Not all of the citizens of Merit who'd risen early that morning were hard at work. There were a few stealing quietly from their houses, bleary eyed and yawning, trying to be as silent as mice. They were afraid of waking their parents.

The Crackers and the Brothers, née the Upper and Lower Jelly River Gangs, were having a terrible week. It began with the fight for which they'd been grounded, but that was no big deal, really. They were used to being grounded. Then it had just turned *weird*. Now the whole town hated them, their own parents were crying and wondering where they went wrong, and Brewer was at home with a broken arm. Things had gone too far.

Word went out to meet after dawn. It was time for another truce.

This was accomplished by a means of communication system that would have made Rube Goldberg weep with ecstasy. The recipe for this fantastic system consisted of equal helpings of imagination and free time, a desire for secrecy, and an almost encyclopedic knowledge of the contents of the junk yard. Using a telephone would have meant waking up parents, and this was simply not an acceptable risk. When Tyler sent out word it began with a loud whisper into the funnel attached to the long garden hose that stretched between his bedroom window and Beazer's next door after a brief trip winding around the tree. Beazer whispered back before hastily scrawling a message onto a piece of paper and sealing it into one half of a plastic ball, then replaced the other half. He peered out of his doorway for any sign of his parents and tiptoed down the stairs and out the door, where he grabbed his bicycle pump and horn from the shed. Behind the shed he moved a small bench that hid the mouth of a small black tube that opened just above the ground and unscrewed the cap. He pulled the plastic ball out of his pocket and dropped it into the tube and replaced the cap. There was a small hole in the cap into which he inserted the nozzle for his bicycle pump.

Beazer rolled up his sleeves and began pumping air into the small opening as fast as he could. After several experiments last summer they'd discovered that roughly twenty seconds of pumping would push the ball with its secret message all the way through the patched segments of tube that had been buried underground—beginning behind the shed and running under the fence, across the drainage ditch, and around Jordan's mother's tomato garden—and reappeared snaking in through the crawl space, and was carefully hidden behind the air grate that led to Jordan's room in her family's farm house. When Beazer was confident that the ball would have dropped into place in the grate he stopped pumping and uncovered the tube again long enough to honk his bicycle horn three short times in the end. It was quiet by the time it reached Jordan's ears, but loud enough to wake her.

Jordan jumped out of bed and retrieved the message from the grate. She nodded to herself, stuffed the paper back into the ball, and dressed as quietly as a mouse. She raised her window and dropped into the flower bed, startling her grey and white cat away from the mouse it was hunting, and ran behind the house. After a quick look around to be sure no one was watching, she placed the ball in a basket made from the back of a toy dump truck and hauled on the string to lift it high into the oak tree above her. As it reached the top of its trek a stick tipped the basket and dumped the ball into a wire basket hanging from a cord attached to a pulley. Jordan pulled on another rope that connected to the pulley and began to speed the basket with its secret contents across the rope that stretched between the massive oak in Jordan's yard to a cabinet handle they had screwed into the top of Bub's window frame upstairs in his house next door. When it reached the pulley and stopped, she yanked on the cord three times to make the lightweight basket bang against the window, and waited for it to open.

Bub had already been awake when the tap-tap-tap came. He put his book down on one of the many book shelves that lined his room and pulled the ball inside. He read its contents and yanked once on the cord to signal that he would be there.

"And so it goes," he said quietly to himself, quoting his favorite book. He retrieved his homemade rope ladder from underneath the bed. He wasn't worried about hurrying; Tyler would still have to get the Lowers on the way. The summons had been to the place where they only met when both gangs needed to hash out business under a flag of peace. He looked at the note in spiky handwriting one last time before putting it in the trash.

"Hall of War ASAP. Get the Others."

• • •

As the spring day ticked from early dawn to genuine morning the sun was getting a full dress rehearsal for the heat it would smother the town with come August. Even the cocks were trying their best to avoid the moment when they would absolutely have to come out of the shade and admit to the town that yes, the day had begun. The air smelled terrible and could probably be chalked up to the fact that the early sun was already baking the piles of dung that had been left behind on the fields from yesterday's stampede. By noon the smell would be unbearable and the former potato field would be awash with ecstatic flies wallowing in the stench. On the upside, this stench did mean that next year's crops would be lush, indeed.

The scattered piles were also making an already difficult walk even harder for a man who was unaccustomed to wearing dress shoes. Unaccustomed to wearing real clothes at all, for that matter.

Goliath was sweating heavily under his tight collar and walking stiffly in pants that would not be forgiving of any sudden movements or steps more than around eleven inches apart. This led to a shuffling that made it nearly impossible to keep from stepping in something undesirable. The suit he wore had been made by a highly-skilled tailor several years ago in a city where they'd made a rare prolonged stop for more than two weeks. Unfortunately, in the past few years since he'd been measured for it, his neckline had grown at least another inch to match other parts of him that were becoming ever more muscular from the highly-physical performances he gave at the circus. Wrestling with bears and towing trucks by brute strength would either keep a man at his strongest or put him in a wheel chair.

He stopped in the field and stared with hope at the vision waiting in front of him. Mad Mother Hinkle, with her back to him, was hanging her laundry out to dry on the clothesline. Her hair was wrapped loosely in a bandana and she was balancing the clothes basket on her expansive hip. Suddenly she slipped the bandana out of her hair and shook out what turned out to be an amazing length of strong brown hair. She used the bandana to mop the sweat from her face and cursed the heat loudly.

Goliath sighed dreamily. He steeled his nerve.

"Miranda?"

She froze in mid-hanging. Slowly, she removed the clothes pin from her mouth and clipped it to the sheet.

"I thought I told you to get off my property," she said without turning around.

"You did, and they are. The circus is packing up even now. But I'm not going with them."

"Oh? Branchin' out on your own, are you?" She sniffed disinterestedly and tossed a few feet of hair over her shoulder.

"Maybe. I guess that all depends on you, Miranda," he said to the back of her head.

She was thoughtful for a moment. When she was certain she had her expression under control she turned to face him. He was holding a suitcase in one hand and a bouquet of daisies in the other. *He looks positively dashing*, she thought. "Dashing" was a word she'd read in the romance novels she secretly ordered from Jostlem. She'd never known exactly what that meant, but she was pretty sure the giant, dark, and handsome man in front of her must be it.

But dashing or not, he was still the same man who'd used his wiles to get her to trust him before letting her fields get ruined. So instead of answering him, she crossed her arms and waited.

"I'm definitely not going back to the circus. I've made up my mind and left a resignation of sorts. That part of my life is over. But I don't want my new start to be on my own."

Despite herself she raised a curious eyebrow. Seeing an opening, he pushed forward.

"Give me one chance, that's all I'm asking. I've spent my entire life hiding from who I really am by being Goliath the Circus Freak instead of trying to just be Lynus Minor. Then I met you, and suddenly I feel like every day I spent being Goliath was a day wasted in cowardice. I've missed out on so much already in this life, but I'm not willing to risk missing out on *you*, Miranda. I promise you, if you give me that chance I'll do everything in my power to make this up to you." He gestured around at the trampled fields. "Even if it means strapping a plow to my back and replanting the fields myself. If not, I'll go away and won't bother you again. But I have to tell you that I'm willing to beg for that chance, Miranda. Please?"

The colossus suddenly looked so fragile and vulnerable that even Mother Hinkle's well-guarded heart warmed. Doors began to open after the emotional equivalent of a struggle with a very large ring of keys. Blood rushed to her cheeks and she felt like one of the damsels in her romance novels, albeit a somewhat senior damsel wearing a size 22-XXL pair of overalls.

"Stop. You had me at hello," she replied breathily.

Goliath looked confused. "But I don't I think I said—"

"Just shut up an' kiss me before I change my mind."

• • •

Dana opened her eyes, a simple feat which she had never before been so pleased to be able to accomplish. Judging by the horrible taste in her mouth, rumbling from her stomach, and awful headache, she was pretty sure that she wasn't dead. Not to mention the pressure on her bladder. She'd heard it firsthand that ghosts never had to pee like a racehorse.

She took a look around herself and was at first relieved that she was alone. Then an even more disturbing thought crept into her mind: psychotic killer that he was, at least she had the hope of pleading with him when he was there. What if he'd just left her there to die? She didn't know where she was or even how far from civilization she was. She could die of thirst in, what was it she'd read, three days? The way her body was hurting she began to wonder if she could die of muscle cramps from being tied up overnight.

She stretched her legs as much as the ropes allowed. At least last night he'd cut her legs loose from her hands, and though they were still bound together she at least had a tiny bit more freedom than she had before. Her hands were still tied behind her back, however, and her first attempt at standing ended with her slamming down on her knees then further down onto her shoulder when she couldn't find her balance. She was learning just how much the human body relied on the arms as counterweights.

She rolled onto her back and scooted back up on the sacks so she was at least closer to a sitting position. Her neck sent furious messages of pain to her brain as she turned it to see if anything behind the sacks could be useful. Nothing but a bare wall to her left, but to her right side was a pipe that ran all the way from the floor to the ceiling. It was perfect! She scooted her way over to it and leaned her back against it with her hands grasping it as high as they could. It was time to see if those gymnastics classes she'd taken in college were going to finally pay off.

She stretched her body one last time. *This is going to hurt,* she thought. She placed her feet flat down on the floor a short way from her body and, grasping the pole firmly behind her, pressed her body up, up, and out until she was in a very painful bridge position. She inched her hands up the pole and hopped her feet in closer to her body until, centimeter by centimeter, she was standing upright and waiting for the complaints to stop coming from various muscles that had previously been in non-pensioned retirement.

Dana had gone from lying prostrate on the floor to now standing on her own two feet. This was a tremendous improvement in her situation, ignoring the fact that her upright position had the life expectancy of a spinning top. As soon as she let go of the pole she wobbled as gravity tried to reclaim its hold on her. Steadying herself again, she took a few small test hops toward the door, constantly leaning against the wall. After a few near misses she got into a hip-swaying rhythm of twist-scoot, twist-scoot that she was grateful no one could see.

She finally made it to the door and turned her back to grab at the handle, but even on the tip of her toes she could only get high enough to get two fingers on it. She cursed; even if she were able to get it open she'd still be helpless, but the prospect of an open door was so much better than being locked in that disgusting place any longer. She kept working at the knob with the fingers that could reach it until both her toes and fingers were numb, but then the door was thrown open, sending her sprawling painfully down to the floor. Light flashed behind her eyes as her forehead hit the ground, and for a long moment she was certain she was still falling. The ground underneath her rolled like a ship at sea and even her captor's voice sounded distant when he spoke to her. Saliva welled in her mouth along with bile.

"Awake, I see. I hope you didn't think I'd left you," he said. "Here, I brought you some company."

She rolled over on her elbow, taking shallow breaths to slow the nausea that was flooding her in waves, but even that breath caught in her throat when she saw what the man was carrying in both arms.

"No! Let them go! Please! You monster!"

He dropped them both, a little boy and a little girl, unconscious on the floor beside her.

• • •

Tyler was deep in thought on his way to the Hall of War when he was tackled to the ground. A hand shoved over his mouth when he tried to cry out and another pair of hands held his arms down. He was still fighting to roll over and throw a punch when his attacker hissed his name.

"Tyler, it's us! Stop fightin', dummy!"

He recognized Carrie's voice and stopped moving, but when he sat up and realized he'd been tackled by a *girl*, an angry flush settled over his cheeks. Even Spike was hiding a grin, albeit poorly. Bub rounded a tree with Crow; at least neither of them had seen it happen and Tyler hoped the dirty look he was giving Spike would keep him from opening his big mouth about it.

"So what's going on? Why are you—?" He flinched when Carrie clapped her hand over his mouth to quiet him.

"Shhh! We're tryin' to tell you! He got Jordan and Beazer!"

"What do you mean? *Who* got Jordan and Beazer?" Tyler whispered when she finally let go of his mouth.

"Some man, I don't know. He's in the Hall of War and he took 'em in there with him. They got here first and we weren't far behind, but he didn't see us. He hit 'em and knocked 'em out!"

"We've been hiding out here waitin' for you guys forever. He hasn't come back out yet." Spike kept his eyes on the door of the Hall of War while they all crouched behind the bushes.

"We've gotta go get help!" Tyler insisted.

"No, we can't," Bub answered. "We're not supposed to be here and if anything happens to them they'll just blame us." He paused for effect. "It's up to us to save them."

"How are we s'posed to do that?"

"There's five of us, only one of him. We can take 'im!" Carrie punched the air bravely.

"We can't just rush in there or he'll get all of us. Didn't you see his gun? Let me think for a minute."

Bub stared at the shed in silence. Though he wasn't a leader, both gangs knew it was by his own choice. He was usually quiet, but he was *smart*. When he did say something, everyone knew it was going to be important and everyone, no matter which gang they were in, listened to him.

Suddenly, while Bub was working on the battle plan, the shed door burst open and the man ran out. He flailed his arms at the air and spun in circles screaming, "Shut up, shut up, you stupid ghost! Leave me alone! Go away!"

The man dropped to his knees and clasped his hands to his ears. Finally, he looked up and around himself cautiously as if trying to sense if a presence had departed. Slowly, he got up from the ground and went back to the shed, watching behind him all the while.

"Is he crazy?" Carrie asked with a hint of awe. She'd never seen a real live crazy person before.

Bub watched the scene thoughtfully. *So… the stranger is afraid of ghosts, is he?* He grinned.

"I think I have an idea. Gather as many small rocks as you can and I'll run back to the tree house for a few things. Stay out of sight until I get back, but keep an eye on things. We're going to have some fun."

• • •

Jordan was the first to wake. The man, mad or not, had still felt a pang of guilt at hitting a little girl and held back when he'd hit her with the butt of the gun. Beazer hadn't been so lucky. There was a small trickle of blood blooming from his hairline that had Dana very concerned. Both children were bound with duct tape at their hands and feet and, after Dana's near-escape attempt, the man tied all three of them to the same pipe that Dana had used to hoist herself to her feet.

Dana nudged Jordan to get her attention when she saw the first signs of panic.

"Shh! Just stay calm and we'll be all right, sweetie. Okay? Don't be scared."

"What happened?" Jordan asked with tears brimming in her eyes.

"We just have to stay here with this man for a while," she dropped her voice so he wouldn't hear, "until someone comes and rescues us. So just sit tight and everything will be just fine." She ignored the vicious growl from her stomach. "What's your name, honey?" She looked up to see him pacing at the other end of the shed. He looked like he hadn't slept all night. His mouth was moving constantly.

"Jordan, ma'am. This is Beazer." Jordan looked at her unconscious friend and her lower lip began to tremble. She whispered to Dana, "What happened to the others?"

"Others? Were you supposed to meet more friends here?" She barely moved her lips and watched him for signs that he was aware of their conversation.

"We were all supposed to meet here this morning. This is our secret club house. We thought nobody else knew about it!"

"I hope for our sake you're wrong about that part," she said. She gave Jordan a weak smile of encouragement and then cringed when she looked back up and caught the eyes of the madman.

He was glaring at them again, whatever silent argument he'd been having finished, and he'd come to a decision. He lifted the gun.

"They found me once," he said, gesturing at the children with the gun. Jordan tried to stifle a squeal in her throat as she buried her face against Dana's shoulder. "That means more will come, too. I have to do this now so I can leave."

"Wait!" Dana cried. *Think fast, think fast. What did he say last night before he knocked me back out?* Two and a half knocks to the head were muddying her thoughts, but something was nagging at her memory as her instincts outraced her mind in an effort for survival.

He said that I couldn't come back. He meant like Monty.

"He told me the secret!" She screamed at him.

The man paused and held his breath. "What do you mean?"

"I mean Monty told me the secret of how to come back! And I told these children. If you do anything to us I swear to God we'll haunt you forever just like he is!" *That's it,* she thought. *That's been his button all along. Why didn't I see it? Probably the brain swelling.* She sighed.

• • •

*Yes...*the man heard whispered in his ear. He swatted at the sound with his gun hand.

"No! They can't, they can't do it. Just shut up!"

"We will, dammit!" Jordan cried out, getting into the spirit of things. She felt a brief thrill that no one was scolding her for language at the moment.

They'll follow you... The whisper was relentless now. For years it had been there; there would be a breath, a chill, a hint of a word or a touch, but weak enough that he could live his life and pretend it wasn't there. Now it wouldn't go away at all. *Forever...it said.*

"Get away from me!" The man cried and ran out the door.

Beazer was awake now, his first conscious sight a man with a gun who looked ready to use it. He was scared to death and was working up to a cry.

"Quick!" Dana leaned in toward both children, stretching her restraints to the max. "I don't think we'll have much time. You're Beazer, right?"

The boy was wide-eyed and silent so Jordan filled in. "Yes, ma'am. He's one of us. It's okay, Beaz, don't cry," she continued bravely.

"Beazer, I'm Dana. We're in a scary spot here, but everything will be fine. Just keep playing along, kids. He won't hurt us if he thinks we'll be like Mr. Monty."

"Will we really be ghosts? Like, floating above the ground and not having to sleep and stuff?" He finally found his voice to ask.

"I really hope we don't have to find out."

"Oh."

Dana wasn't sure, but she thought the boy sounded disappointed. "We're just pretending now. It's like a game, right? Whatever you do, don't act scared."

"I'm not scared!" Beazer said defiantly and sniffed at a tear that had run down to his nose. Jordan rolled her eyes and winked at Dana conspiratorially.

"It's just a game," Dana repeated to herself. *I only hope he'll be playing along, too,* she thought.

When the man walked back into the shed he seemed to have gotten a grip on himself. The open door let a blast of hot humid air into the already stifling room; it was slowly becoming a furnace in there. He sat down in the corner and stared at his feet for several minutes.

"Please, we need water. It's so hot in here! At least for the children. You don't want us dying of thirst, do you?"

He shuddered, but ignored her. She decided not to press. All she'd really wanted to do was test the waters, anyway. It seemed like they had him docile for a while. It was time to let it go at that. Surely someone would be looking for the children. If other kids were coming, they had to have seen or heard something. And then they'd have run straight for help. Right?

• • •

"All right guys, are you ready?" Bub called down quietly from the tree. The heads of Carrie, Spike, Crow, and Tyler nodded in unison from their posts hiding behind various trees. Bub slid further out on the branch until he was just almost over the shed. He had several handfuls of pebbles in his pockets, a make-shift fishing rod, a slightly stained bed sheet, and the remnants of what had been a feather pillow in its former life, and was now mostly just a cloth sack with dirty feathers in it. Among the down had been added various duck, pigeon, robin, and chicken feathers.

Bub waved a thumbs-up at Tyler. "Okay, go!" He whispered.

• • •

Plink! Plink, plink!

It sounded like rain hitting the tin roof of the shed. Outside of the window was still sunny and cloudless. Dana and the children looked at each other. Had they heard that? The man hadn't budged in the near twenty minutes they'd sat in silence.

"Whoo-ohooo-hooo!" They heard in a ghostly cry from outside the shed.

"That's Tyler, I know it is!" Jordan whispered as silently as she dared. That was the same ghost voice he'd used last fall when they did *The Legend of Sleepy Hollow* at school.

Smart kids, Dana thought. *No wonder they've caused so much trouble.* "Pretend like you didn't hear anything and act normal!" She hissed back, trying to act nonchalant.

This resulted in Beazer trying to whistle and Jordan attempting to hum along.

"Okay, don't act so hard!" Dana amended. The kids got quiet.

Their captor, however, did not.

"Did one of you just—?" he faltered.

A picture of innocence, Dana replied, "Just what?"

"Did you hear that?"

As if scripted, another terrifying sounding howl pealed from the forest around them. Dana and the kids didn't flinch.

"Who did that?" The man yelled. He buried his head between his hands.

*Ghosts...*the whisper spat into his ear. *We're all back...*

This was a man who had killed often and without compassion for very large sums of money. Now, for the first time in at least thirty years he was remembering his Catholic upbringing and all of the demons the nuns had frightened him with in school. He could still count the number of terrified faces of all ages looking up at him and begging for their lives. He'd taken them all without regard and without pity. They were just jobs. There had to have been dozens. *Dozens.*

He screamed.

• • •

Phones were terrible, evil things. They had no soul, no mercy, and no compassion. They didn't care that the baby had just fallen asleep after a terrible bout with colic, or that the lady of the house had a headache, or that someone had just gotten to the best part of the book they were enjoying. They would shriek at someone mercilessly until they finally answered their demands and informed the bothersome caller that no, they didn't take the paper, and no, they didn't want a subscription even if it came with a lovely frog-shaped alarm clock just for signing up.

This time Stanley was the victim. The station had three phones, and each of them rang in a slightly different pitch of shrill and in slightly different time so that the effect on one waking up was tantamount to teeth-drilling. He cringed until he heard Bertie answer.

Any second now, he thought, *Bertie's going to come tell me I need to get the phone. I know he is. That's just what's going to happen. And then I'll have to wake up and remember that everything has been going to hell in a hand basket while I slept.*

"Um, Stanley? Are you awake?"

"Aha!"

"What?" Bertie looked puzzled.

"Nothing, nothing. There's a phone call, right? And I need to come take it, right?"

"Ri–ight," Bertie faltered. "It's Jostlem PD. Captain Green, actually," he continued tentatively. Stanley sighed heavily.

In the last twenty-two years since his father's death Stanley had spoken to his father's former deputy only three times. The first time at his father's funeral, the second time at his grandmother's funeral, and the third at his mother's. Both men seemed to connect ill-bodings with their brief encounters and, despite the close relationship Jeremiah Green had with Stanley's family when his father was alive, he maintained a respectful distance.

Stanley knew that if Captain Green was calling him personally that it wasn't going to come with good news. Not even with bad news. This was going to be Grade-A Terrible News.

"Jeremiah?" Stanley asked after he shuffled over to the phone, clinging to the blanket still wrapped around him. He was hoping for the remote possibility that there was another Captain Green that he didn't know about.

"Stanley. It's good to hear your voice, son."

Stanley thawed a bit. "Yours, too. I mean it." He found he really did mean it. A warmth from childhood was welling up in Stanley. In happier days this was the man he'd called "Uncle Jerry." "I've got a feeling that you didn't call just to catch up, though."

"Do we ever get to do that?" The man asked remorsefully. "I'm afraid your instincts were right. I got a call this morning from our guys about that uniform you sent up to us yesterday."

"It did belong to the missing cop, didn't it." It was more a statement than a question.

Captain Green hesitated. "Yes, it did, but there's something more troubling than that."

"More troubling than a police uniform covered in blood?"

"It wasn't his blood."

• • •

While Jordan buried her face against Dana's shoulder trying not to laugh, Dana and Beazer pretended to sleep, completely unbothered by the apparent infestation of ghosts in the woods. This was easy for Beazer who still had a terrible headache from being struck. Dana, however, was using the time to focus. She was busily composing a story that would get that Barbara Chase-Howard booted back to a weather girl while Dana took over as anchor.

On the opposite end of the shed was the sound of crying.

• • •

"Give it another howl, Tyler!" Bub hissed while he hoisted another small handful of pebbles at the roof. Carrie ran from the cover of her tree and aimed another three nearly rotten potatoes at the windowless backside from her slingshot. In quick succession, three nearly rotten potatoes pounding on a wall sounded quite like three ominous knocks from beyond the grave. They smelled like it, too. And no one was faster at reloading the sling shot than Carrie.

Crow was giving his best animal snarls and low growls. He was doing very well if what he was going for was a dyspeptic schnauzer.

Now it was Spike's turn. Spike was what could be termed an "early bloomer" in that, after several months of embarrassing cracks and sudden body hair in strange places, his voice had turned into a rather deep bass for a not quite eleven-year-old.

He cleared his throat and brought the rolled up poster of Miss July to his mouth like an amplifier.

"I AM THE GHOST...." Spike intoned heavily and deeply, his voice reverberating eerily through the woods. "WHO HAS AWO-KENED ME?"

Bub cringed, but concluded that it probably wasn't necessary for ghosts to have perfect grammar.

After Spike finished his lines, Bub ducked back behind the tree and cast the fishing line out with the sheet hooked to the end of it. He swiped it back and forth across the window quickly, just enough to make a frightening shadow, and yanked it back into the tree before sending a flurry of feathers falling from the pillow stash.

He'd been right. This *was* fun.

• • •

"Pigs blood," Stanley said.

He looked up from the phone he'd just replaced and stared at Bertie. "He said it was pig's blood on the uniform. We're not looking for the man who killed the cop, Bertie. We're looking for the cop." Captain Green was on his way with a few of his officers. It would still take more than an hour for them to get there.

What he'd learned from the captain scraped the rest of the

flesh from Stanley's already raw nerves.

"We think it was a matter of him wanting people to think he was dead, at least long enough that he could disappear with his money," Captain Green had said. "That's why the tears in the uniform didn't really correspond to the blood patterns. It was torn, or cut, and the blood added later."

This man, this Officer Walter Heeding, was on the run. He'd been suspected and even investigated for possibly taking bribes and of coercing confessions out of suspects, but now evidence for far worse crimes was turning up. Money trails, reluctant confessions, and other sources all pointed to a man planning to disappear with his ill-gotten gains into retirement. He'd probably only planned to lie low outside Merit until the search passed him over, but no one could have expected the chaos started by Erwin's article. Stanley was still digesting the worst of what Captain Green told him. It was believed that he'd even secretly been a hit man for the Byazi clan in Jostlem since the mob heydays when the city was first going through its growing pains. Around the same time the mob had ordered the hit on his father, in fact.

Stanley felt sick.

"I should tell you," he'd said, "that if this is the man we're looking for, then he's also responsible for the recent murder of the actor Montana Gregory."

"How do you know this?" The captain sounded shocked.

"Mr. Gregory told me. It's a long story," he'd added before the obvious question could come up.

"A dirty cop?" Bertie asked incredulously. This was not the kind of thing that happened around there.

"Not just a dirty cop. A murderer." Captain Green wouldn't have come out and said it, but Stanley knew what they were thinking. This man may have had something to do with his father's murder. And now he had Dana, too.

His fists clenched.

He was still lost in thought by the phone a moment later but was vaguely aware that the door to the station had opened and the room was now filling with people who were trying to get his attention.

"Yes?" He turned toward them with his eyes half closed. Bertie was busy trying to calm a woman who was crying. *It's the parents,* he realized. *All of them.*

"What's going on?" He asked, alert enough to realize that no one would look him in the eye. "Wait," he said without looking down. "Bertie, did you give me the blanket with the bunnies on it?"

"It was the first one I could find, Stanley," he answered rather sheepishly.

Stanley tugged it from his shoulders and handed it to Jordan's mother with as much dignity as he could muster. The kids had left a few things behind after their brief tenure in the cell earlier that week, and he was wishing that he'd taken more care to return them quickly.

"I'm sorry about that. Now tell me, what's wrong?"

Every face was lined with worry. The week had taken a heavy toll on the parents.

"They're gone, Sheriff. Every last one of 'em." Tyler's mother sniffed into a tissue, her body shaking expansively with the effort. "We woke up and they weren't in their beds. We all called each other and nobody saw or heard anything. They just up an' disappeared!"

"Do you think they ran away?" Jordan's mother clutched her daughter's bunny blanket for comfort and tried to ignore the fact that it now smelled like aftershave.

"They would have left a note, wouldn't they?" Beazer's mother asked hopefully.

They all looked to Stanley expectantly. He sighed. This was getting worse by the second.

"I'm sure they're just hiding somewhere and will come out by lunch time when they get hungry," he supplied lamely. "For right now I need you to go home and keep your eyes out for them and call us if you hear from any of them. We'll call all of you if we see them first," he added when he saw the first sign of dissent from Spike's father.

Please go, he thought. *I need you out of my way so I can think, and maybe panic a little in private.*

"Really, I mean it. They might even be back there right now waiting for breakfast." He tried to smile and sound cheery.

After a few more empty reassurances he was able to usher them out the door.

"What do we do now?" Bertie asked. He was pale and drawn like Stanley had never seen him before. "They could be out there anywhere and this murderer—"

"I know," Stanley interrupted sharply. He regretted his tone when he saw Bertie flinch with the rebuke.

"I know," he repeated more gently. "Now we just find them. We find them before he does. Let's take another look at that map now that I'm rested."

• • •

If ever a word were invented that described perfectly the act it named, it was the word "trudge." It was a heavy, ponderous, and even a gloomy sounding word and it perfectly conveyed the sentiment of the action. Currently Monty was doing just that. He was trudging along the street on a path between Porter's and the sheriff's office. Porter had been kind enough to let him stay at the bar overnight, rightly judging that no one would try to rob a bar with a ghost in it, and appreciated the security since there had been some strange people in town of late. It wasn't like Monty needed to sleep anyway. He just sat and watched TV all night and wished he could eat the bowl of peanuts on the bar.

His heart was heavy as he paced, and he found himself meandering down side roads that didn't lead directly to the station. He had a responsibility to complete that he was in no hurry to get to.

Maybe another side street wouldn't hurt....

The hell with this, he finally decided, and headed back to the bar.

• • •

"What about the football field? They could be in one of the field houses."

"No," said Stanley thoughtfully. "That's too close to the school. If they really did run away they would have never gone anywhere near the school."

A yawning, stumbling Allen was finally making his way from the cot in the cell. Stanley had almost forgotten that he was even there. Cud wandered out behind him fresh from his own nap and looked toward his recently emptied bowl.

"What'd I miss, guys?" He scratched himself inappropriately. Cud followed his cue.

"Only everything. Coffee's on the desk." Stanley went back to his map and scolded himself. It wasn't Allen's fault that Dana had been taken. *She's a grown woman and can make her own decisions,* he told himself. *So why am I so mad at him?*

"What about the circus? Do you think it's worth going back there to look?"

"They'd have been rounded up there already. The Ringmaster sent a messenger by while you were asleep. They're pulling up camp and getting out of town as quick as they can."

And before too many questions are likely to be asked, Stanley thought bitterly.

The room darkened. Two large shadows filled up the doorway.

"Uh-oh," Bertie said quietly. The room seemed to shrink considerably after Mother Hinkle and Goliath made their way in through the small doorway.

Not for the first time today, Stanley cringed. He just knew this was going to be about the potato patch. Of all times...

Then he noticed she was smiling. He tried hard to think if he'd ever seen her smile before. Suddenly he realized that she must have been at least striking if not pretty when she was younger. He'd never noticed it before.

"Stanley, my boy, we need your help. You're the sheriff and the justice of the peace around here and that makes you the only one who can help us right now."

He stared blankly at the two smiling behemoths. His subconscious was working up to a suspicion that his mind wasn't yet ready to handle.

"We're getting married!" Goliath filled in the blank, causing Stanley's subconscious to send a smug "I told you so!" to his brain.

Stanley's mouth slowly caught up. "But what about Pastor Blevins? I'm sure he'd be a much better..." He stopped mid-sentence when he saw the dark storm clouds cross Mother Hinkle's face.

"Boy, you know I won't be havin' with that nonsense. I wouldn't trust that snake oil salesman to get his collar on straight, let alone perform our nuptials!"

"I've never...I mean, I don't even know how I would do it!"

"Don't be silly. Anybody can do it. You just tell me to take him and him to take me and we'll kiss and be out of here and off to our honeymoon." She giggled.

There were two words in that sentence that Stanley knew would give him minor nightmares for the rest of his life. Not that there was anything wrong with the words in principle, but the idea of Mother Hinkle kissing and going on a honeymoon was treacherous food for an active imagination.

Focus! His subconscious shouted at him. It was being very vocal today. He shook the images from his mind.

"All right, I'll be glad to, to…marry you." He formed the word with some difficulty. "But we're still in the middle of an emergency right now."

"Can we help?" Goliath offered, looking guilty. In his happiness he'd almost put the tragic events from the evening completely out of his mind.

Stanley, still furious with the circus, was about to say "no" on principle, but then he looked the beast up and down. Goliath was a one-man army.

"Definitely." *We could even use you to knock down doors in a pinch*, he added to himself. "You know about the missing reporter, right? Well, things have gotten worse. We're not just looking for Dana now," he said heavily and stopped, unsure of how much to say next.

"The children have gone missing now, too," Bertie finished for him.

Good answer, Stanley thought. *No sense in burdening them with the whole truth about a deranged contract killer just yet.*

"That's horrible! Did they run away?"

"We don't know yet. They have to be around here somewhere, though. I know the key is on here and I'm just not seeing it." Stanley gestured at the map in frustration. "We can run all over town knocking on doors and traipsing through the woods all day, but if we don't know where to look we'll be wasting our time and miss them somewhere."

Allen walked over to check out the small and unimpressive map of Merit while he stirred his coffee. He pointed to a large open area.

"Is this where the circus was set up?"

"Yes, and this is where we are now," Stanley answered and pointed out the location of the sheriff's office on the map.

Allen peered more closely at the map. "Where is the Forest of Dred?"

"What?" A distant bell was ringing madly for Stanley's attention.

"The Forest of Dred. It was on the map on the wall back in the cell but I don't see it on here. It sounded pretty interesting."

Stanley smacked his own forehead.

"Of course!" He cried. The bell was no longer distant. The map in front of him was made by conventional adults marking points of interest that another conventional adult might need to find. What he *needed* was a map that was made by imaginative children that marked points of interest that another ten-year-old would want to find. Thankfully, they just so happened to have one like that and, even more thankfully, they hadn't washed it off the wall yet.

The phone, being true to its intrinsically evil nature, began to ring again.

"Bertie, will you get that? Allen, come with me!" He grabbed the map off the table and ran to the cell. Cud, alarmed by the sudden motion, ran along behind barking excitedly and nipping at Stanley's ankles.

He stood in front of the purple map and looked from landmark to landmark. It was right there all along.

Allen caught up with him, still wiping the coffee away that he'd sloshed on his shirt when Stanley startled him.

"We have to check out every place we find here that isn't on the town map. Somewhere on here is where they'll be!"

His mind was racing. There was the Bottomless Pit, the Sea of Deth, the Scorpion Dessert—*probably the sandbox at the park*, he thought—among other things. Where to start?

"The Golden Cassle?" Allen asked dubiously. He had also noticed that the children were in need of extra spelling lessons.

"I think that's probably Mrs. Patterson's house." Senile old Mrs. Patterson loved tulips and painted her house, tin roof, and shutters all in bright spring yellow. It was difficult for the neighbors to look out of their windows facing her house without sunglasses.

"I think I can help." Bertie rounded into the cell with Goliath and Mother Hinkle looking anxious behind him. "That was Bub's mother. She found a note in his trash that said they were to meet at the Hall of War. Right here." He pointed at a purple square on the map.

"That's the opposite side of the town from where the murd…I mean, kidnapper was hiding to begin with." Stanley's stomach knotted. What would they find when they got there? He looked at Bertie, who nodded in understanding.

"I'll get the car."

• • •

"So, Jordan, tell me," Dana fumbled for something to say to keep the children distracted from the theatrics going on outside the shed. "What grade are you in?"

"No! Stopitstopitstopistopitstopit…" burbled from the man now cowering with his back against the door and his eyes glued to the windows, where shadows crisscrossed back and forth. He'd opened the door twice and sworn there was nothing out there. Except the whisper…

"We're both in the fourth grade, Miss Dana. What grade…I mean, how old are you?"

Oh, for the tact of the young.

"Old enough," Dana replied somewhat bitterly.

For crying out loud, she thought. *This has been going on for over half an hour now. I thought he'd have cracked by now. Maybe we're just making him think he's crazy. Think now… would you rather believe you were crazy or truly believe that you were being stalked by ghosts?*

"Kids," she whispered, "follow my lead, but take it easy, okay?" They nodded at her.

"Hey, did you guys just hear something?" She said it just loudly enough to catch their captor's attention. He looked away from the window where the sheet had just flipped a shadow across and looked right at her. She pretended not to notice.

"I think maybe I did. Yeah," Jordan answered. "Did you hear something, Beaz?"

"Was it like a moan, or something?"

"Oh, just like a moan. Like someone in terrible pain. Like someone very *angry*," Dana hit the last word hard for emphasis.

"What did you hear? There's nothing out there!" The man jumped up from the door just in time for three more loud knocks to come from somewhere outside. He growled deep in his throat, his eyes trying so hard to watch both windows at once that they seemed in danger of splitting apart.

"I definitely heard that!" Beazer piped in. "Yeah, someone's *really* mad!"

"I think it's kind of scary," Dana added, trying to make her voice sound frightened. "I think it sounds like...like a ghost!"

And then the noises failed her. Silence came from the forest. It was the silence after a din that left you feeling that your ears were roaring with the quiet. The man waited, listening, and jumped when the sound of an angry mockingbird filtered into the room. Then he looked triumphant.

"You see? See? They're gone! They can't hurt me! *You* can't hurt me!"

He started to raise the gun toward them when the fires of childhood imagination intervened.

"No." Jordan suddenly looked twice her age. She'd be quite the actress one day. "I think it's like the calm before the storm." She paused for effect. "I think it means they're coming! They're going to get us all!" Dana and Beazer gasped for effect and huddled closely together as though terrified.

If a mental collapse made a noise it would sound exactly like the complicated string of consonants that tried to escape his mouth at once. The gun fell, clattering on the floor as he yanked open the door and ran out screaming...

And ran right into a broad and somewhat mushy wall. His eyes swiveled up to the furious face of Mother Hinkle, and to the right where he saw the face of another ghost.

*Gotcha...*breathed the whisper.

"You!" He pointed at Stanley and screamed. "You leave me alone! You're dead! I killed you!"

"Get your hands off my future wife!"

For the first time in his life, Lynus Minor, née Goliath the Strong Man, balled up his fist and struck a man down. Officer Walter Heeding fell in a tear-stained pile at their feet.

"What did he mean by saying he killed you, Stanley?" Allen, standing nearby with the baseball bat in hand, was just now relaxing his pose. Stanley stared at his father's killer and tried to swallow the thousands of competing emotions welling in his heart. He was glad suddenly that he wasn't the one holding the bat.

"I think I know," Bertie answered, watching Stanley carefully. "Stanley, I think you should come over by Goliath now—"

"Lynus."

"I'm sorry, Lynus...and let me take care of the suspect. Okay?"

Stanley slowly looked away from his father's killer.

"I'm okay, Bertie." He turned to the trees around the clearing. "Kids, come on out now! You're all going to be safe now." Little heads began popping around bushes and Stanley counted five. Brewer was still in the hospital, so that left two missing.

His feet, naturally faster at subtraction than his brain, were already moving in a dead run toward the shed. Before he even reached the door he heard Dana calling his name.

Stanley had always hated his name. He'd also never been so pleased to hear it.

• • •

Unique among the creatures of the world, an individual human being is capable of terrifyingly profound depths of emotion that shape not only themselves, but the world around them. The raw power of strong human emotion pulls on the heart as the moon pulls the ocean, creating a tide of feeling that can only be sustained at one extreme for so long before rebounding back to the opposite state. It was for this reason that the only possible appropriate ending for a week which had encompassed fear, hate, loss, anger, and near death was quite a rowdy party.

The wedding had lasted approximately seventy-three seconds. That was about ten seconds for Stanley to fumble through a Bible to find something appropriate to say, ten seconds for Mother Hinkle to tell him what she'd do to him if he didn't get on with it, twenty seconds for the "Do yous," and thirty-three seconds for what was to be a kiss that Merit would never forget.

Especially the sound.

Now most of the town was at the sheriff's office to partake in the impromptu wedding reception and breathe a sigh of relief for quieter days to come. Excitement, they were learning, was better when it happened to other people. The Upper and Lower Jelly River gangs were oppressively hugged by their parents until they escaped into the back yard to play together. They announced formally at the start of the reception that they were now one gang—The Jelly River Gang—and anyone who had anything to say about it or about who they could be friends with from now on could go to you-know-where.

Even Erwin came to the party, albeit at full protest. His mother dropped him off by the punch bowl as per her usual routine and retreated to the bathroom to double and triple check her make-up. Weddings were excellent places to meet men, she'd heard.

Erwin made it a full five minutes before the first cup of punch spilled down his shirt. Tyler saw it happen and for once squashed the urge to laugh. Erwin stood with his back to the crowd and his head hung in shame as he furiously tried to wring the punch out of his shirt while tears ran down his cheeks. A few minutes later, Tyler was standing next to him with a Mighty Rocket Avengers tee shirt in his hand.

"Here, this was in my mom's car. It's mostly red, so if you spill more punch on it nobody would even know."

Erwin didn't know what to say. "But I—"

"Don't worry about it. When you change just come outside. We're playin' Hide and Seek with Sheriff Stanley's dog. He's really good at seeking. Not so good at hiding, though. You can smell him a mile away." Tyler walked away with a smile. Erwin was different, sure. But Tyler was coming to learn that being different could actually be pretty cool.

Mother Hinkle and Goliath were smiling for pictures and being toasted by all of the citizens of Merit. Some were even already trying to test out the new name of Mad Mother Minor, albeit far out of earshot of both Mr. and Mrs. Goliath, as he would forever be known when the speaker thought they were speaking in private. Goliath was one of those people who could only ever be Sir to his face. Actually, it turned out that he would be a Sir just about anywhere he went, and not just because of his size.

Goliath had been with the circus his entire adult life and had earned an assistant manager's pay for most of it. The circus also paid for all of his food, clothes, and lodging, so everything Goliath had earned was put directly into CDs or other investments, and he was a very shrewd investor. Now he and his blushing bride were the wealthiest citizens of Merit, next to the Youngbloods.

Everyone was happy. Almost.

Dana had been searching for Stanley since she finally got the doctor to let her go. She was a little dehydrated and had taken a few nasty knocks to the head, but she'd been a reporter in human interest stories far too long to let that keep her down. Covering ceramic kitten collections that made the Guinness Book of Records with a straight face tended to toughen one up. With the number of similar stories she'd done, she should have been bullet proof by now.

She and Allen were being called back to Jostlem, where she had a pretty good feeling she was about to get a promotion. But she wasn't leaving without seeing Stanley. When she finally found him, he was in the back of the station near the cell. He wasn't alone.

Captain Green had arrived just before the wedding and Bertie filled him in on what he'd missed. Now Stanley and his Uncle Jerry were sitting together in silence with two largely untouched glasses of wine.

They were watching the man in the cell.

He seemed unaware of either of them. He also seemed unaware of who or where he was. There were even two wet drool stains on his shirt.

She hesitated, deciding that what she wanted to say could wait a few minutes. Jostlem could wait another hour, too. She went back to the party to congratulate the happy couple and filled her wine glass.

The two men were oblivious to everything outside of their small corner of the station. The noise of the party reached the cell easily, but there was a wall between their ears and the outside world. Finally, Stanley found the words to speak.

"I'm supposed to feel better now, aren't I?"

Captain Green responded carefully. "How do you mean?"

"I mean, that's the man that killed my father. Right there. I arrested him today and now he's in my cell and I doubt he'll ever be sane again. I don't know what happened to him, but I should be glad, right? In the end it all works out because the killer is coming to justice. I know the story. But I can't make it fit with how I feel."

"I think it only works like that in books and movies, Stanley. Your dad..." he faltered. "Peter was my best friend in the world. I used to dream about catching this bastard and seeing him behind bars." He took a drink of his neglected wine. "But now I just want him to go away where I never have to see him again or think about what he took from us."

Another watcher slinked, or more probably floated, into the hallway and was watching the scene with his mouth open. Monty had finally worked up the nerve to come and face Stanley, but his resolve evaporated the moment he saw what was with him. Standing unseen by any living eyes next to the sheriff was a reflection of the man himself. A shimmer almost, but it was unmistakable that the ghost was a relation. He'd heard the stories around town. It had to be his father.

Monty started to say something but the shimmer looked up at him and shook his head. It put its finger to his mouth in the old familiar gesture. *Our secret...it* said.

There was a sudden moan from the cell. Stanley and Captain Green sighed almost in unison.

"I miss him, Jerry."

"Me, too, Stan. We've still got each other, though." Captain Green put his hand on Stanley's shoulder.

Stanley fought back the tears. "Yeah," he said. "Yeah, we do."

The shimmer smiled then and nodded at something over his shoulder. Monty saw a faint glow coming from behind Stanley's father. It grew larger and brighter until it threatened to fill up the entire room.

That strange tugging sensation was back again, too. He opened his eyes enough to see Stanley's father disappearing into the blinding light as he waved to the son who couldn't see him. The ghost seemed so content, right up until the moment he was gone. The light lingered there after the man was gone, however, and it seemed to be edging frighteningly closer to Monty.

"No! I don't have to go! I still have unfinished business! Unfinished business!" He whimpered at the light with his arm over his eyes.

"Mr. Gregory?"

Monty opened his eyes and realized that not only was the light gone, but both men were staring at him curiously.

"So, this is the ghost that Bertie told me about? The one *he* killed?" The captain gestured reluctantly at the man in the cell.

"The very same."

"Then I do at least have good news for you, Mr. Gregory," the captain continued. "We have someone you know in our office in Jostlem. One of my detectives called me down here to let me know that it turns out that your agent, one Mr. Gary Taylor, had taken out a large insurance policy on you as being a valuable intellectual property."

"Me? An intellectual?"

"That's not... quite the same thing. More emphasis on the property part. It turns out that he'd convinced an insurance agent to insure against his losses in the event that something happened to you. It was a sneaky way to get life insurance on you, basically. He didn't even wait until the ink was dry to hire this man to kill you."

Monty was stunned. He'd never thought Gary liked him, but this was a bit much.

"He confessed?" He asked. Gary had always been one to see a lie through to the end.

"He was rather anxious to, I heard. I'm sure it's harder to live with a guilty conscience when you have to spend every day wondering if the guy you had killed is going to figure out that it was you who did it."

I ought to fire him as soon as I get back to Jostlem, Monty thought. Then he remembered himself.

"That's actually not why I came here. Sheriff, can I speak to you for a moment outside?"

Stanley and the captain exchanged a look.

"Go ahead, Stan. I'm going to have my guys load him on up and get him out of here. I'd like to come back for a visit this weekend, though, if that's okay with you."

Stanley nodded. "I'd like that, Jerry. I'll be back in a bit."

Feeling better, though still exhausted and now confused, Stanley followed Monty out to the back patio where the kids were taking turns signing Brewer's cast and giving tummy scratches to a blissfully happy Cud.

"I've come to confess, Sheriff. It's only the right thing to do."

"What are you talking about?"

Monty stretched his dramatic abilities to the breaking point. "In every man's life—"

"Or afterlife?"

"Or afterlife," Monty conceded, irritated at the interruption. "He may hope just once to find something so rare and so perfect, not to mention *innocent*," he emphasized, "purely innocent, as true love. I believe I have found that true love, Sheriff, and I need your forgiveness."

"For what?" Stanley was beyond confused.

"I'm in love with Isabelle," Monty finished with a flourish.

Stanley nearly choked on his own tongue.

"What? What would you go and do that for? Are we talking about the same Isabelle? Red hair, scary temper, big knives?"

"Yes! I mean…no! Isabelle is the queen of my heart!"

Stanley looked thoughtful for a moment. "But how do you…you know? Is it even possible to…?"

"Sheriff! I'm insulted! Our love is purely innocent and beyond physical. I wouldn't have sullied the beauty of falling in love by being a 'back door man.' We talked and talked for hours last night and discovered that we're practically soul mates!"

Stanley bit his tongue to keep from laughing.

Monty had expected anger, a fight, *anything* other than bewildered amusement. "Sheriff, are you sure you don't want to hit me, or challenge me to a fight of some sort? You might feel better. Actually, I might feel better."

Stanley gave up on not laughing. "Oh, I think I feel better already, Mr. Gregory." He smiled.

"Monty!"

A screech that was only too familiar to Stanley pealed from the back door of the station.

"I told you not to come down here! I *said* I would take care of it!" She hissed.

"I'm so sorry, sweetness! I just had to. It was the gentlemanly thing to do!"

"If I want a gentleman I'll let you know!" She turned her withering look to Stanley and tugged a nervous looking man by the arm down the stairs toward both of them.

"Now Stanley, I think it's time we had a talk. This is Mr. Baker from Daddy's law firm, and he's going to record everything just to make sure we remember it right later, okay?"

"Okay," he responded, not really sure that it was.

"Stanley, you're not happy, are you? I mean, with us? Not deep down happy at all, are you?"

"God no! It's been awful, quite frankly." He couldn't believe the words were coming out of his mouth. Maybe his ability to sugar coat—not to mention tolerate close proximity to evil—had been undone by the exhaustion.

"So, would you say that you think you'd like to divorce me? All legally and officially?"

He glanced at the clerk, who seemed to be screaming for help with his eyes.

"Yes," he answered slowly. "I think I would say that, in fact."

"Great!" She squealed. She practically knocked a folder out of Mr. Baker's hands and grabbed a pen from somewhere in the cumulus region of her hairdo.

"Then if you'll just sign here it can be official! And here, and here." She gestured at three documents the clerk was struggling to support and smiled broadly.

No, Stanley thought as he took the pen out of her hand. *Not quite smiling. More like sneering.* Had her smile always looked like that? *Probably,* he decided.

"Stanley, stop!"

Dana came running down the steps with Rupert Youngblood drunkenly in tow behind her.

"Don't sign anything. She's trying to trick you!" Dana pulled the pen from Stanley's hand. She'd found Rupert at the party where he was planning to stop Isabelle, but had been sidetracked by an unending supply of wine. When he told Dana about the call he'd gotten from his lawyer that morning she nearly spat her own wine in her hurry to get him to Stanley.

"I'm afraid the young lady is right, lad," Rupert said. Isabelle was glaring daggers at Dana behind her father's back. "She browbeat one of the newer clerks at the firm this morning into telling her that the only way the inheritance reverts back to her other than your death is if you divorce her. She can't file because then she gets nothing. She just wants the money back. Do you understand this? If you divorce her she gets *everything*."

"Is that true?" Monty asked her with a mixture of greed and guilt in his eyes.

"Yes!" Dana answered for her. "Don't do it, Stanley. It's not worth it. There are other ways!"

Stanley looked at all of them. This was nothing. He'd already fried bigger fish today.

"Let me get this straight. If I go ahead and sign these papers I lose money that was never even really mine, but I'm free of her for good?" He rolled his eyes. "Give me that pen back!"

He signed the papers there, there, and there, and handed the pen back to Izzy, who was suddenly fuming that he hadn't put up a fight to keep her. The feeling of victory fizzled in the knowledge that Stanley, this ridiculous pipsqueak, was actually that anxious to divorce *her*. She snatched the papers back, casting a last scornful glance at Dana.

"Well! I hope you're both happy. You and your little dog, too!" She jerked Monty's arm. "Come, Montana. It's time to go."

Isabelle was the master of the haughty exit. This time, however, it was ruined by Monty looking over his shoulder and calling back, "Bye, Dana. Hope I'll see you around!" It was followed by a thump and a cry as Isabelle hit him in the back of his head with her heavy designer purse.

Rupert beamed at Stanley. "Baker, go on inside. There's wine, whiskey, and beer in there. Go ahead and take the rest of the afternoon off. You've earned it."

They watched the clerk run inside, keeping a healthy distance behind Isabelle and her new beau.

Rupert looked thoughtful. "If he weren't already dead, I'd say the man had a death wish."

Stanley reflected on the past several years of matrimonial discord. "At least he won't *technically* live to regret it." Stanley scratched his head and looked up at the man. "You seem like you've got something to say, Rupert." After years of losing to him at cards Stanley had learned to recognize when his former father-in-law had a trump up his sleeve.

Rupert grinned wider. "Let's just say she's in for quite a surprise."

"You mean other than that she's running off with a washed-up celebrity ghost who's possibly gay?"

"One that she'll hate even more. She's *poor*, Stanley!"

"What do you mean?"

Rupert hiccupped. "I'm flat broke! I've got three mortgages on the house, the rubber plant belongs to the banks, and I'm going to have to sell the mine back to the county."

"I don't understand. What about everything your father built and saved?"

"Let's just say I'm not always so good at cheating at cards, son. Now I'm going to go get another glass of whiskey. If I'm going to have to learn how to be a cheap drunk I may as well start now. Ha! A toast to the barren empire my vulture of a daughter will inherit!"

He raised his empty glass to the air. "Besides, I get the idea that you may have something to talk to this lovely young lady about." He winked at Dana and went back into the station, where the sounds of the party were far from dimming.

Stanley and Dana stood in awkward silence for a moment before Stanley noticed something was missing.

"Do you realize you've finally quit sneezing?"

She looked surprised for a moment. "You know, I don't think I even noticed. I guess I'm getting used to this town and all of its pollen just in time to leave," she said sadly.

"I guess you're going back to Jostlem now?" He asked awkwardly.

"My boss wants to meet with me as soon as possible. I have a feeling it'll be good news."

"No more human interest stories for you, eh?"

Glancing at where the children were playing nearby, teaching Erwin how to play tag, she smiled. "I think I've got room for one more. This time a story about brave, brilliant children who held on to each other and their friendship when the adults became too focused on the reasons they couldn't be friends to realize that those reasons didn't really exist. Not here, anyway. The only thing this exposé exposed was a horrible flaw in the system. There's still a story to tell in Merit, and this time I'll make sure we get it right."

"So if there's still more to the story, does that mean you'll need to come back for more... research?

She looked at her feet. "Possibly. Know anyone who'd be willing to be interviewed, Sherriff Stanley with two R's?"

He was staring at her when she looked up.

"Jostlem is only an hour away from here, you know. It's really not that far at all." He wasn't sure, but he thought his eyes might just be smoldering. That, or they were twitching with exhaustion.

"Look, he's finally going to kiss her!"

The whisper and giggle of Jordan, a sound Dana had spent the morning getting familiar with, carried over from the yard. She took him by the arm and walked with him around to the other side of the station, away from their young audience.

"You know, I think the story can wait another few minutes." She leaned into him. "Don't you?"

"Actually…" he leaned even closer, "I think the story is only just starting to get good."

The End

Ashley Chappell writes satire and young adult epic fantasy featuring expansive world-building and universes filled with magic, mayhem, and monsters. Ms. Chappell currently resides in Huntsville, Alabama. When not writing or reading one of her well-worn Terry Pratchett or Neil Gaiman novels, she can be found sailing or working alongside her husband building their off-grid, semi-underground dream home in the foothills of the Appalachians.

www.ingramcontent.com/pod-product-compliance
Lightning Source LLC
Chambersburg PA
CBHW071152180726
48291CB00007B/2421